I WOUND THROUGH THE ROOMS, SHINING THE FLASHLIGHT IN corners to be certain I hadn't missed anything. I moved past beds and tables and chairs, my eyes slowly adjusting to the dark. I was looking in one of the fake shower stalls when I heard it: a faint coughing. It was coming from my right, a few rooms away. "Here," a voice called weakly. "Eve? I'm here."

I covered my mouth, too shaken to reply. Instead I ran, weaving through the rooms, my heart light. Caleb was alive. He was here. He had survived.

As I got closer I spotted three candles on the floor. A man's silhouette was visible on the bed. I started toward him, but when I reached the bedroom, he wasn't alone. There were more of them—three men altogether.

"Hello, Eve," the man on the bed offered. "We've been waiting for you."

ANNA CAREY

HARPER

An Imprint of HarperCollins*Publishers*

Once

alloyentertainment

Produced by Alloy Entertainment
151 West 26th Street, New York, NY 10001

Library of Congress Cataloging-in-Publication Data

Carey, Anna.
    Once / by Anna Carey. — 1st ed.
        p.   cm.
    Sequel to: Eve.
    Summary: "In the second book of this dystopian adventure, Eve will come face to face with the king who has been ruthlessly hunting her—and learn shocking truth about who she really is"— Provided by publisher.
    ISBN 978-0-06-204855-4
    [1. Kings, queens, rulers, etc.—Fiction.   2. Identity—Fiction.   3. Love—Fiction.   4. Science fiction.]   I. Title.
PZ7.C21On   2012   2012004294
[Fic]—dc23   CIP
                                                                              AC

Design by Liz Dresner

13 14 15 16 17   LP/RRDH   10 9 8 7 6 5 4 3 2 1
❖
First paperback edition, 2013

For my family (from Baltimore to New York)

one

I STARTED OVER THE ROCKS, CLUTCHING A KNIFE IN ONE hand. The beach was strewn with sun-battered boats, long since wrecked on shore. The ship before me had washed in just this morning. It stood twenty feet tall, nearly twice as large as the others. I climbed up its side, feeling the cool wind coming in off the water. The sky was still thick with fog.

As I wandered over the boat's peeling deck, I felt Caleb beside me, his hand resting on the small of my back. He pointed at the sky, showing me the pelicans plummeting into the sea or the way the fog rolled over the mountains, covering everything with a layer of white. Sometimes I found myself speaking to him, muttering sweet, muted words only I could hear.

It had been nearly three months since I'd last seen him. I'd been living in Califia, the all-female settlement founded more than ten years before as a haven for women and girls in the wild. We had come from all over, crossing the Golden Gate Bridge into Marin County. Some had been widowed after the plague and no longer felt safe living alone. Some had escaped violent gangs who'd held them hostage. Others, like me, were escapees from the government Schools.

Growing up in that walled-in compound, I'd spent every day looking over the lake at the windowless building on the other side—the trade school where we would have gone after graduation. But the night before the ceremony, I found out my friends and I weren't going to learn skills to contribute to The New America. With the population decimated by the plague, they didn't need artists or teachers—they needed children, and we were destined to provide them. I barely escaped, only to discover my true fate was so much worse. As valedictorian of the School, I had been promised to the King as his future wife, to bring his heirs into the world. He would always be searching for me, wouldn't stop until I was locked inside the walls of the City of Sand.

I climbed a ladder to the boat's top cabin. Two chairs sat in front of a broken windshield and a metal steering wheel so rusted it no longer moved. Waterlogged papers were piled up in corners. I sorted through the cabinets underneath the controls, looking for cans of food, salvageable clothing, any tools or utensils I could bring back to town. I tucked a metal compass in my knapsack, along with some frayed plastic rope.

Down on the deck, I approached the main cabin, covering my nose with my shirt. I slid open the cracked glass door. Inside, the curtains were drawn. A corpse wrapped in a blanket lay on a couch, sunken into its moldy cushions. I moved quickly, careful to breathe through my mouth, and ran my flashlight over the cabinets, finding an unmarked can of food and some damp books. I was checking the damage to the books when the boat shifted slightly beneath my feet. Someone was shuffling around in the sleeping cabin below. I drew my knife and pressed myself against the wall beside the cabin door, listening to the footsteps.

The stairs below creaked. I gripped the knife. I could hear breathing on the other side of the door. Light streamed in between the curtains, a sliver of sun moving across the cabin wall. In an instant the door flew open.

A figure rushed in. I grabbed his collar, sending him hurtling onto the floor. I jumped on top of him, my knees pressing his shoulders to the ground, the knife blade resting against the side of his neck.

"It's me, it's me!" Quinn's dark eyes peered up at me. Her arms were pinned to the floor.

I sat back, feeling my heartbeat slow. "What are you doing here?"

"Same thing as you," she said.

In the struggle, I'd let my shirt fall away from my mouth and nose, and the room's putrid stink was choking me. I helped Quinn up as fast as I could. She brushed off her clothes as we stumbled outside, the stinging, salty air a relief.

"Look what I found." She held up a pair of purple sneakers, their laces knotted together. The circular emblem on the ankles read CONVERSE ALL STAR. "I'm not trading these. Going to keep them for myself."

"I don't blame you." I offered her a small smile. The canvas was miraculously intact, in great shape compared to most of the items I'd found. Califia used a barter system, and beyond that we all contributed in different ways—scavenging, cooking, growing crops, hunting, repairing the crumbling houses and storefronts. I had a post in the bookshop, restoring old novels and encyclopedias, lending extra copies, and offering reading tutorials for anyone interested.

A tiny cut had appeared on Quinn's neck. She rubbed at it, smearing blood between her fingers. "I'm so sorry," I said. "Maeve's always warning me about Strays." Maeve was one of the Founding Mothers, a term given to the eight women who had first settled in Marin. She had taken me in, letting me share a bedroom with her seven-year-old daughter, Lilac. During my first days in Califia, Maeve and I had gone out every morning to explore. She'd shown me which areas were safe and how to defend myself should I come across a Stray.

"I've been through worse," Quinn said, letting out a low laugh. She climbed down the side of the boat to the beach. She was shorter than most of the women in Califia, with curly black hair and tiny features crowded in the center of her heart-shaped face. She lived in a houseboat on the bay with two other women, and they spent most of their days hunting in the thick woods around the settlement, bringing back deer and wild boar.

She helped me cross the rocky beach, her dark eyes studying my face. "How are you holding up?"

I watched the waves hit the sand, the water white and

relentless. "Much better. Each day it's easier." I tried to sound buoyant, happy, but it was only partially true. When I'd first arrived in Califia, Caleb had been by my side, his leg wounded from an encounter with the King's troops. But he wasn't allowed in. No men were—it was a rule. Caleb had known all along, and had brought me here not so we could be together, but because he thought it was the only place I'd be safe. I'd waited all this time to hear word of him, but he hadn't sent a message to me through the Trail, the secret network that connected escapees and rebels. He hadn't left word with the guards at the gate.

"You've only been here a few months. It takes time to forget." Quinn rested her hand on my shoulder, leading me toward the edge of the beach, where the back wheel of her bike stuck out of the dune grass.

Those first weeks I'd been in Califia, I was hardly present. I'd sit with the women at dinner, pushing soft white fish around my plate, only half listening to the conversations going on around me. Quinn was the one who'd first drawn me out. We'd spend afternoons in a restored restaurant near the bay, drinking beer the women brewed in plastic pails. She told me about her School, about how she'd escaped by crawling out a broken window and stalking the gate, waiting for the supply trucks to make their weekly delivery. I told her about the months I'd spent on the run. The other women knew the broad strokes of my story—an encoded message detailing the murders in Sedona had already come through the radio used by the Trail. The women knew the King was after me, and they had seen the injured boy I'd helped across the bridge. But in the quiet of the restaurant I'd told Quinn everything about Caleb and Arden and Pip.

"That's what I'm worried about," I said. Already the past was receding, the details of what had happened growing hazier each day I was in Califia. It was getting harder to remember Pip's laugh or the green of Caleb's eyes.

"I know how you feel about him," Quinn said, working at a knot in her black hair. Her caramel skin was flawless except for the small dry patch along her nose, red and peeling from the sun. "But things will get easier. You just need time."

I stepped onto a piece of driftwood, feeling satisfied when it snapped in half. We were the lucky ones—I knew that. Every time I peered down the table at meals, I thought about all we'd escaped from, how many girls were still stuck in the Schools and how many more were under the King's control in the City of Sand. But knowing I was safe didn't stop the nightmares: Caleb, alone in some room, blood in a dry, black pool around his legs. The images were so vivid they woke me, my heart knocking in my chest, the sheets damp with sweat. "I just want to know if he's alive," I managed.

"You might never know," Quinn said, shrugging. "I left people behind. A friend of mine was caught while we were escaping. I used to think about her, obsess about what I could've done. Could we have gone out a different exit? What if I was the one trailing behind? Memories can ruin you if you let them."

That was my cue from Quinn: *Enough.* I'd already stopped talking about it with everyone else. Instead, I carried the thoughts like stones, holding them to feel their weight. *No more thinking about the past*, Maeve had told me one day. *Everyone here has something to forget.*

We walked along the edge of the beach, our feet swallowed by the sand. Gulls circled above. My bike was hidden on the other side of the hill. I pulled it from beneath a prickly shrub and started toward Quinn. She sat on hers, one foot resting on a pedal, tying back her curly hair with a piece of twine. She was wearing a loose turquoise T-shirt, I ♥ NY printed on it in block letters. It rode up in the front, exposing the top of the pink scars that crisscrossed her abdomen. She'd told me how she'd escaped, but she wouldn't talk about the three years she'd spent inside the School, or the children she'd had there. I let my eyes linger on the swollen lines, thinking of Ruby and Pip.

We started up the road, pedaling in silence, the only sound the wind rustling the trees. Parts of the mountain had crumbled onto the pavement, leaving piles of rocks and branches that threatened to burst our tires. I concentrated on maneuvering through them.

Somewhere far off, a shout split the air.

I glanced over my shoulder, trying to figure out where it had come from. The beach was empty and the tide was coming in, the rocks and sand caught in the endless churning of the waves. Quinn moved off the road, finding cover behind the thick trees, and gestured for me to follow. We huddled together in the overgrowth, our knives out, until a figure finally appeared on the road.

Harriet slowly came into view, her face twisted and strange as she rode toward us on her bike. She was one of the gardeners who distributed fresh herbs and vegetables to Califia's restaurants. She always smelled of mint. "Harriet—what's wrong?" Quinn called, immediately lowering her knife.

Harriet hopped off her bike and walked toward us, her hair a wild mess from the wind. She leaned forward and rested her hands on her knees as she struggled to catch her breath. "There's been movement in the city. Someone's on the other side of the bridge."

Quinn turned to me. Since I'd arrived, guards had stood at the entrance to Califia, scanning the ruined city of San Francisco, looking for signs of the King's troops. But no lights had been spotted. No Jeeps, no men.

Until now.

Quinn grabbed her bike from the underbrush and started up the road, pulling me along. "They've found you," she said. "There's not much time."

two

HARRIET PEDALED AROUND THE BEND. "THIS IS WHY WE HAVE A plan," Quinn said, speeding alongside me so I could hear her. She glanced sideways, a few matted black curls blown in her eyes. "You're going to be fine."

"I don't feel fine," I said, turning so she couldn't see my face. My chest was tight, each breath short and painful. I'd been discovered. The King was close, and coming closer still.

Quinn leaned into a sharp turn. The edge of the pavement, a crumbling cliff fifty feet high, was only a few feet away. I held tight to the handlebars, now slippery with sweat, as we climbed the road to the bridge. It was rumored that the regime knew about the community of women nestled in the hills of Sausalito. They believed it to be a small group of female Strays, not a hidden depository for the Trail. The last time they had come through to check on the settlement was nearly five years ago, and the women had scattered into the hills, hiding out for the night. The soldiers had passed their houses and apartments, not noticing the shelters camouflaged by blankets of overgrown ivy.

The bridge came into view ahead. The towering red structure had been the site of a huge fire. It was piled with burned cars, debris from fallen beams and cables, and the skeletons of those who'd been trapped there while trying to escape the city. I held onto Quinn's words: *This is why we have a plan.* If troops were spotted, Quinn and I would leave Sausalito, not stopping until we were deep in the labyrinth of Muir Woods, where an underground bunker had been built years ago. I would stay there, relying on stockpiled supplies, while the soldiers swept through Califia. The rest of the women would move west, up toward Stinson Beach, where they'd wait out the invasion in an abandoned motel. They'd be in enough danger if the settlement were discovered . . . much more if the soldiers found out they'd been hiding me from the King.

"There's movement on the other side," Isis called out from Califia's entrance, hidden behind a patch of dense shrubs. She was leaning over the stone ledge, her black hair tied back with a bandanna, a pair of binoculars in her hand. We let the bikes fall and gathered around her. Maeve was perched over the trapdoor behind the ledge, doling out extra rifles and ammunition.

Maeve pressed a gun into Harriet's hands, then handed another to Quinn. "Line up against the wall." All the women followed her lead. She was one of the youngest Founding Mothers, and the most vocal about what was expected of everyone in the settlement. Tall, with ropy muscles and braided blond hair, Maeve looked exactly the same as she did the day I'd first met her, standing outside Califia's entrance. She was the one who'd turned Caleb away. I'd accepted the room in her house, the food and clothing she'd given me, the post she'd found for me at the bookstore, knowing it was her way of saying what couldn't be spoken: *I'm sorry, but I had to.*

I took a rifle and joined the rest of the women, feeling the cold weight of the gun in my hands. I remembered what Caleb had said, back when I was staying at his camp: *Killing a New American soldier is an offense punishable by death.* I thought of the two soldiers I'd shot in self-defense. We'd left their bodies on the road beside their government Jeep. I'd held the third soldier at gunpoint, forcing him to drive us toward Califia, his hands trembling on the wheel. Caleb had slumped against the backseat, his leg bleeding where he'd been stabbed. The soldier had been younger than me—I let him go when we were right outside San Francisco. "Maeve, do we need the guns? We shouldn't use—"

"If they discover the escapees they'll drag them all back to their Schools, where the girls will spend the next years pregnant and on so many drugs they won't even remember their names. That's not an option." She walked along the row of women, pressing each of their shoulders forward to adjust their aim.

I looked down the barrel, out across the bridge and the gray ocean, trying not to dwell on Maeve's omissions. She didn't mention what would happen to me. Instead, the statement had the slight tone of an accusation—as if I had personally invited the soldiers here.

We kept our eyes ahead. I listened to the sound of Harriet's breathing as the figures made their way over the bridge. From such a distance I could only see two dark shapes, one smaller than the other, moving between the burned cars. After a moment, Isis set down the binoculars.

"There's a dog with him," she said. "A Rottweiler."

Maeve took the binoculars. "Keep your aim, and if there's any aggression, don't hesitate to shoot." The two figures moved closer. The man was hunched over, his black shirt camouflaging him against the charred pavement.

"He isn't wearing a uniform." Quinn eased her grip on her gun.

Maeve kept the binoculars to her face. "That doesn't mean anything. We've seen them out of uniform before." I studied the figure, looking for any resemblance to Caleb.

When he was less than two hundred yards away he stopped to rest beside a car. He squinted at the hillside, searching for signs of life. We crouched further down behind the ledge, but the man didn't look away. "He sees us," Harriet hissed, her cheek pressed against the stone. The man reached into his knapsack and pulled something out.

"Is it a weapon?" Isis asked.

"I can't tell," Maeve replied. Isis moved her finger, resting it lightly on the trigger.

The man stalked forward, a new resolve in him, and Quinn aimed her gun. "Stop!" she yelled out to him, keeping low so he couldn't see her behind the ledge. "Do not go any further!" But the man was running now. The dog was right beside him, its thick black body heaving with the effort.

Maeve inched forward, whispering in Quinn's ear. "Don't let him get off the bridge. No matter what."

Her eyes betrayed no feeling. The day I came across the bridge with Caleb, we were unbearably tired, the past weeks weighing us down, making every step difficult. His pant leg was soaked through with blood, the fabric stiff and wrinkled where it had dried. Maeve had stood at the entrance to Califia, an arrow aimed at my chest, the same hard expression on her face. No matter what threat this man posed, at that instant he was only guilty of trespassing—nothing more. I took the binoculars from Maeve's hands.

The man was quickly approaching the end of the bridge. "Do not go any further!" Quinn yelled again. "Stop!" I steadied the binoculars, trying to catch a glimpse of him. Then, for only an instant, he looked up. His face was like a corpse's, with sunken eyes and hollowed cheeks. His lips were gray and chapped from days without water, and his hair was cropped close to the skull. But I felt the pull of recognition.

I looked at Quinn's gun, and then at the figure racing

toward the end of the bridge, moving steadily around overturned cars and piles of charred debris. "Don't shoot!" I yelled.

I started down the hill, the thick brush scratching my legs. I ignored Maeve's shouts behind me. Instead, I tucked the rifle under my arm, my eyes on the figure as I moved closer. "Arden," I whispered, my throat choked. She had stopped, one arm resting on the hood of a truck, her back hunched from the effort of breathing. She looked at me and smiled, tears spilling down her cheeks. "You're here."

The dog lunged at me but Arden held it back, whispering something in its ear to calm it. I ran toward them, not stopping until we were together. I wrapped my arms around her frail body, enveloping her. Her head was shaved, she was twenty pounds lighter, and her shoulder was bleeding—but she was alive.

"You made it," I said, squeezing her tighter.

"Yes," she managed, her tears soaking my shirt. "I made it."

three

THAT EVENING, I TOOK ARDEN TO MAEVE'S HOUSE. THE narrow two-story home was connected to six more, the whole row of them nestled into the side of the hill. Residences in Califia were easier to conceal if they were spread out, so of the six, hers was the only one that was occupied. The walls were patched in places, the floors a mosaic of mismatched tiles. Arden and I were in the small bedroom upstairs, our skin rosy in the lantern light. Maeve slept in the next room, Lilac beside her.

Arden stripped off her long black shirt and stood before the dresser in her tank top, pressing a wet towel to her face and neck. "When I arrived and you weren't here, I thought the worst," I said, leaning against the bunk bed where I slept. The room's flowered wallpaper was peeling in places, a few strips held up with tacks. "I thought the soldiers had found you. That you were being held somewhere, tortured, or . . ." I trailed off, not wanting to go on.

Arden worked at her skin with the towel, clearing away patches of dirt on her arms. In the lantern light I could see each of her vertebrae, tiny pebbles trapped beneath her skin. I remembered her face the last day I had seen her, when we were hiding behind the shack. Her cheeks were full, her eyes alert. Now she was so thin her shoulder blades jutted out of her back. Fresh scabs dotted her scalp.

"They never caught me," she said, not turning around. She watched herself in the cracked mirror, her reflection split in half. "The day I left you by Marjorie and Otis's house, the soldiers chased me through the woods. I got a lead on them when I reached the outskirts of town but there wasn't anywhere to hide. I found this metal door in the street, a sewer, and went underground. I just followed the tunnels, moving through the sludge, and kept waiting for them to track me there. But they never did."

The giant dog lay at her feet, its chin resting on the

floor. I kept my eyes on it, remembering all those warnings we'd heard at School about people being mauled by the packs of wild dogs roaming the woods. "Where'd you find him?" I asked, nodding at the animal, whose head was nearly as big as mine.

"*She* found me," Arden laughed, setting down the towel. "I was roasting a squirrel. I guess she'd been separated from her pack and was hungry. So I gave her some food. And then she started following me." She kneeled down, taking the dog's head in her hands. "Don't judge Heddy by her appearance—she's really sweet. Aren't you, girl?"

Arden looked up at me, smiling, and I noticed the thick red scar that snaked down her collarbone and over her right breast. It was still bleeding in places. Just the sight of it made me wince. "You're hurt," I said, standing to get a closer look. "What happened? Who did this to you?" I grabbed her shoulder and turned her toward the light.

Arden swatted me away. She fished the towel from the washbasin and covered her neck. "I don't want to talk about it. I'm here now and I'm not missing an arm or an eye. Let's just leave it at that."

"Let's not leave it at that," I said, but Arden was already climbing into the bottom bunk. She threw herself down next to Lilac's old dolls. Most of them were naked, their hair matted from years of neglect. "Arden," I said again, pleading. "What happened?" The dog followed me to the ladder and whimpered, trying to get up on the mattress.

Arden sighed. "You don't want to know." She pressed the wet towel to her chest, willing me away, but I didn't move.

"Tell me."

She turned to me, her eyes glassy in the lantern light. "I got lost," she said, her voice soft. "That's why it took me so long to get here. I went north out of Sedona and then I found Heddy. We'd been together a week when it got so hot I could barely walk during the day. Heddy kept darting under the bushes, trying to avoid the sun. Finally I decided we'd just wait out the heat wave. Find a place to rest." She moved the wet towel over her cracked lips, sloughing off the dead skin. "We took our supplies into this underground parking lot. As we went down each ramp it got cooler, more bearable, but darker, too. I was trying to get this car door open when I heard a man's voice. He was yelling, but nothing he said made any sense."

I lay down beside her, curling myself into a ball. Her

mouth twisted into a half smile, and she looked up at the bottom of the other mattress, its springs straining against the fabric. "It was so dark, but I could smell him. It was foul. He grabbed me and pushed me over the hood of a car. He was choking me, and I felt the blade on my neck. Then, before I could even process it, he was on the ground and Heddy was on top of him. She kept going until he was quiet." I looked down at the dog, whose face was crusted with dirt. Patches of hair on her neck were missing, the exposed skin pocked and scabbed. "I've never heard silence like that."

"I hate that I wasn't there," I said. "I'm so sorry, Arden."

Arden pulled the towel away from her neck. "I didn't even realize he'd gotten me until after we were above ground, in the light. Heddy and I were both covered in blood." The dog jumped onto the bed and lay at our feet, the mattress sagging under her weight. She rested her chin beside Arden's foot. "I would've died if it hadn't been for her."

Arden ran her hand over her head. Soft black fuzz was growing in, but I could still see the skin of her skull. "That's why I did this. I thought it would be safer to travel as a man. Only a few other Strays spotted me after that, and they all left me alone. A single man in the wild doesn't draw as much attention as a woman."

"I hope that's the case," I said, my thoughts drifting back to Caleb. My gaze settled on the window. Maeve's house was up the road from the water. I could just make out the moon's reflection on the surface of the bay. "Caleb found me after I left you. He tracked me down, and we came here together."

"They wouldn't let him stay, would they?" Arden asked. She pulled the crocheted blanket over herself, her fingers peeking out from the colorful wool squares. "They thought it was too dangerous?"

"His leg was wounded. He could barely walk," I said. I twisted a fistful of blanket in my hands, not wanting to revisit that moment at the end of the bridge.

Arden shifted so her body was pressed against the wall. She tucked her toes underneath Heddy, who was still curled up at the foot of the bed, the sound of her breath filling the small room. "He'll find his way back to the dugout," she offered. "He's been living in the wild for years. He'll be okay."

I ducked under the covers, careful not to upset the dog. "Right, I know," I said softly, pressing my cheek against the musty pillow. But the thoughts took hold again. I kept imagining Caleb in an abandoned house, his leg badly infected.

Arden closed her eyes. Her face relaxed, her features softening. She fell asleep easily, her grip on the blanket loosening a little with each passing minute. I inched closer to her, letting my head rest on her shoulder. I lay like that for a while, listening to her breaths, each one a faint reminder that I was no longer alone.

four

I WAS IN THE FIELD AGAIN, MY FACE PRESSED INTO THE EARTH. I'd just escaped from Fletcher's truck. He was coming through the trees, the thin branches snapping under his weight, his breath heavy and choked with phlegm. Wildflowers were crushed under me. Their delicate blooms released a sickening scent as I stared at my hands, my fingers orange from the pollen. Then he saw me. He raised his gun. I tried to run, tried to get away, but it was too late. He pulled the trigger, the blast echoing through the field.

I shot up in bed. My skin was covered in a thin layer of sweat. It took me a moment to realize I was in Califia, in Maeve's house, in the tiny room with the flowered wallpaper. I'd heard something downstairs—a door banging shut. I looked around. The candle had gone out. Cold air rushed through a crack in the window. I rubbed at my eyes, waiting for them to adjust to the dark.

Someone was in the downstairs foyer. Heddy raised her massive head, listening as closely as I was. "Quiet down," I heard Maeve say. She was in the living room, or the kitchen, maybe, speaking to whoever had just come inside. "She's upstairs."

Heddy let out a low growl, and Arden started awake beside me. "What is it?" she asked, sitting up, her back rigid. Her eyes darted around the room. "Who's there?"

I brought my finger to my lips to silence her, then pointed to the door. It was open just a crack. I crept toward it, signaling for her to follow. The voices had quieted down, but I could still hear Maeve's urgent whispers, and another woman's tense, hurried replies.

The hallway was dark. The staircase was surrounded by a fragile wooden banister, its posts missing in places. Arden shut Heddy inside the bedroom, and we crawled along the floor until we reached the stairs. Lying on our stomachs, we peered over the ledge. An eerie light glowed in the living room. "He knows she's here—he was the one who brought her. And now this new girl shows up," Isis said, her low, raspy voice giving her away. "Who else is out there looking for her? This isn't how we've operated in the past, we can't just—"

"Since when do we have a policy of throwing women out into the wild?" I recognized Quinn's turquoise shirt. She was leaning against the doorframe, her back to us, gesturing with her hands as she spoke.

Isis raised her voice. "This is different. All the women are talking—all of them are concerned. We're practically begging the King to track her here. Maybe today wasn't the day, but it's only a matter of time."

I turned toward Arden, letting my cheek rest on the cold floor. Most of the women had been welcoming since I'd arrived, but there was always the worry, just beneath the surface, that I could upset the balance of Califia. That all those years of building their city, clearing out the old storefronts and houses and reclaiming them, all those years of hiding behind a layer of ivy and moss, the days spent in darkness every time movement was detected inside the city—all of it would be gone in a moment if the King ever discovered me.

"She's no more of a threat than we were," Quinn said.

"We were all property of the King. When I showed up no one argued that I should be thrown out because troops might storm Califia. When Greta was rescued from that gang, no one cared about the raids that might happen. Those men could've killed us all."

"Please," Isis hissed. "You know this is different." I leaned farther forward, but I still couldn't see her through the doorway. "They've been looking for her for months now. You've heard the alerts on the radio. It doesn't seem like they'll be stopping anytime soon."

Her words raised the fine hairs on my arms. Isis had lived in a houseboat for the last two years. She was one of the other Founding Mothers, and had survived in San Francisco after the plague by seeking refuge in an abandoned warehouse before finding her way across the bridge. I'd sat in her kitchen, eaten meals at her table, talked with her about the antique jewelry one of the women had recovered or her friend who was training to cut hair. I felt stupid now for having trusted her.

"I'm not throwing her out," Quinn said. "Tell her, Maeve. Tell her we won't."

I could hear Maeve pacing back and forth, the floor creaking underneath her feet. Even in my darkest moments, when I imagined what might've happened to Caleb, when I wondered about Pip, or Ruby, or the fate of my other friends, I never considered that I'd be forced out of Califia, that I'd be sent back into the wild, alone.

After a long pause, Maeve finally let out a breath. "We're not throwing anyone out," she said. Arden squeezed my fingers so hard it hurt. In the faint light, her face looked even thinner, her cheeks hollow and gray. "Besides, it would be silly not to use this to our advantage. If the King discovers her here, he discovers all of us. And we'll need her as a bargaining chip."

My chest tightened. "If that's how you rationalize letting her stay, fine," Quinn tried again. "But he won't track her here. She's no more of a risk than anyone else."

"I hope you're right," Maeve said. "But if he does, we won't be martyred on her behalf. You'll take her to the bunker and stay there until we're ready to release her to the troops. This could be our chance at independence from the regime."

I felt sick, remembering how I had thanked Maeve endlessly after I'd arrived—when she set a plate of food in front of me, when she found clothes for me at the store, when she heated rainwater for my baths. *It's nothing*, she'd said, waving me off. *We're happy to have you.*

A few more whispered words passed between them before Maeve strode out of the living room, Isis and Quinn following right behind. Arden and I slid back, trying to stay out of sight. "They're not going to find her here—they have no reason to," Quinn said, one last time.

"It's nearly four," Maeve said, holding up her hand. "There's nothing more to say. Why don't you two go home and get some rest?" She carefully opened the door and parted the thick curtain of ivy that hid the front entrance. As they left, I could hear Isis starting the argument again.

Maeve turned the lock and started up the stairs. All the breath left my body. Arden and I scurried along the wall like mice, desperate to get back to our room. We landed in bed just as Maeve reached the top step. I pulled the blanket up over us and lay my head down, closing my eyes, pretending to be asleep.

The door opened. The glow of a lantern warmed our faces. *She knows you were listening*, I thought, my mind sprinting ahead of me. *She knows and now she'll lock you in that bunker until she turns you over to the King.*

But the light was steady. She didn't move. I only felt the

heavy dog at my feet, her head lifting, probably offering Maeve the same sweet gaze she'd offered me.

"What are you looking at?" Maeve finally muttered. Then she closed the door behind her and started down the hall, leaving us there in the dark.

THE FOLLOWING DAY WAS OPPRESSIVELY BRIGHT. I'D GOTTEN
used to the gray skies of San Francisco, the fog that settled
on us every morning, rolling over the hills and out to sea.
Now, as Arden and I left Maeve's house, the sun burned
my skin. The reflection off the bay was blinding. Even the
birds seemed too cheerful, chattering away in the trees.

"Remember—we didn't hear anything," I whispered.
But Arden's lips were pressed into a thin line. She'd never
been good at pretending. Back at School she'd been in
a miserable mood in the weeks before her escape. She'd
separated herself from the rest of us, standing at the sink
in the corner as she brushed her teeth, not looking at us

as she hunched over the dining hall table during meals. I'd suspected she was planning something that night before graduation, but had assumed it was another of her stupid pranks. I never would've guessed the truth.

We wound down the narrow, vine-covered path until it emptied out to the waterfront. The skeletal remains of boats were piled up on the rocks, their windows smashed in, their paint peeling away. A few rested belly-up. Out across the bay, the rest of Marin was just a green mound, the trees growing between the houses, hiding them under their leaves.

Arden pulled the linen shirt around her thin frame, steeling herself against the wind blowing in off the water. "I could barely look at Maeve at breakfast," she said. Heddy walked beside us, her black fur shining in the sunlight. "Knowing she's planning to—"

"We can't talk about this here," I said, glancing at the row of shrouded storefronts. The front window of a café was covered with newspaper, but I could hear women cooking—pots clanking against one another, water sloshing around in the sink. "Wait until we're on the boat."

It was impossible to find privacy in the small city, which housed over two hundred women. A few of the shops and restaurants along the shore were in working order, while others remained hidden and unused in the dense brush. Every woman had carved out a place for herself, a purpose.

"Good morning, Eve!" Coral, one of the oldest Founding Mothers, called as she came down the path. She was carrying three chickens to slaughter, their bodies paralyzed as they hung upside down by their feet. Heddy barked at the birds, but Arden yanked her back. "Beautiful day, isn't it? Reminds me of life before." Coral glanced at the sky, the green, tangled hillside, the broken dock that stretched into the water.

"Lovely," I said quickly, trying my best to smile. I had taken an immediate liking to Coral when I'd arrived. She'd spent her whole life in Mill Valley with her husband. They lived as Strays for three years before he died. I loved the stories she told, of how she'd grown her own garden and cooked on an open fire in her backyard. She'd once lured a gang across town so they wouldn't discover the stockpile of goods in her storm cellar. But now even she seemed unfriendly. I wondered if she knew about the plan. I wondered if she'd always seen me as a way of negotiating Califia's independence.

The old woman passed. Up ahead, Maeve and Isis were coming along the path on a horse, towing a cartload of reclaimed clothes. Every month they traveled to a different town beyond Muir Woods and searched the houses to find goods to distribute or barter at the shops in Califia.

I glanced sideways at Arden, then at the rowboat tied to the dock. It was one of the few boats the women had restored, its insides coated with a thin layer of wax. "We better go now," I said. I could feel Maeve's eyes on us. She had dismounted and approached the shore as we started toward the dock.

I untied the boat, looking over my shoulder to address her. "Thought I'd take Arden and Heddy out on the bay today. Show them what Califia has to offer." I climbed in, trying to keep my movements calm and deliberate. I took an oar in each hand, thankful when the wood dipped into the water, the resistance steadying my shaking fingers. Arden lowered herself into the boat and called for Heddy to follow.

"What about the bookstore? There's work to do," Maeve said. She stepped over the slippery rocks and into the shallows, letting her hiking boots get wet.

I just kept rowing, my body relaxing with each yard I put between us. "Trina knows I'm not coming in. She said it's fine."

Maeve crossed her arms over her chest. She was the most muscular of the women, with a chiseled stomach and legs thick from running. "Be careful of the current! And sharks! One was spotted yesterday in the bay." I cringed at the mention of sharks, but it seemed unlikely, more like a desperate attempt to keep us tethered to the dock, in her sights. She stood there, feet planted in the water, until we were nearly a hundred yards out.

"Can we talk now?" Arden asked, when I set the oars back down. Heddy settled into the bottom of the boat, her paws outstretched, and Arden planted her feet on either side of the dog's shoulders.

Maeve had pulled binoculars from the cart and was peering through them, following the boat as it drifted with the current. I smiled, let my hair out of its bun, and waved. "She's still watching us," I said. "Stop scowling, Arden, will you?"

Arden threw her head back and laughed, a deep throaty laugh I'd never heard before. "Don't you see the irony in all of this?" she asked, smiling now, her expression strange, creepy even, because it didn't match her words. "We've traveled all this way to get here, to escape Headmistress Burns, all her lies. This feels oddly familiar."

I knew what she meant. I hadn't gone back to sleep the night before. Instead, I'd lain awake imagining what would happen if Maeve found out I knew her plans for me. She believed Califia was my final destination, that I would never leave—that I couldn't. If she thought I had any desire to run away, she might send word to the City of Sand to let them know she had me.

"When Caleb and I came here we thought it was the only place I'd be safe." I looked down at my hands, working at the calluses on my palm, thick from time spent reinforcing the low stone wall behind Maeve's house. "It seemed like my only choice then, but now . . ."

Over Arden's shoulder, I could still see Maeve on shore. She had dropped the binoculars and started back up the path, turning to check on us every few steps. I was trapped. Out on the bay, closed in on three sides by high rock walls, a hundred eyes were always watching me, wherever I went. Across the bay, San Francisco was just a tiny, overgrown mound of moss. "We have to get out of here."

Arden stroked Heddy's head, gazing beyond me. "We just need time. We'll figure something out—we always do." But for a long while neither of us spoke. The only sounds were the waves lapping at the sides of the boat and the gulls calling high above, their wings beating against the sky.

———+———

AN HOUR PASSED. THE BOAT DRIFTED WITH THE CURRENT. I was relieved when the conversation turned to lighter topics. "I hadn't named her yet," Arden said. She stroked the dog's head as she spoke. "I just didn't think we'd be sticking together very long, and I didn't want to get attached. But then she sat down in front of the fire and I stared at her. And it hit me. I knew just what I should call her." Arden pressed her palms against her face and pulled down, making her cheeks look like thick jowls. "Heddy—after Headmistress Burns."

I laughed, my first real laugh in weeks, remembering Headmistress's sagging face. "That's a little unfair to Heddy, don't you think?"

"She understands my sense of humor." Arden smiled. Her eyes seemed softer, her pale cheeks pink from the sun. "I used to hate dogs. But I wouldn't have survived without her. She saved me." Her voice went up a few octaves, as if she were talking to a child. "I love you, Heddy. I do." She held the dog's face in her hands and rubbed it, planting kisses on the soft fur of her forehead.

I'd never heard Arden speak that way. The entire time we were at School she'd built a reputation of hating everything—the figs they served with dinner, our math requirements, the board games stacked in the library archives. Arden had prided herself on being separate from everyone else, on relying on no one. She had, for the first twelve years that I'd known her, insisted she was not like the rest of us orphans at School—she had parents waiting for her in the City of Sand. It wasn't until we found each other in the wild, and Arden became ill, that she disclosed the truth. There were never any parents. Her grandfather, a bitter man who died when she was six, had raised her. Those words—*I love you*—took me by surprise. I had thought they simply weren't in her vocabulary.

I let the dog sniff my hand, ignoring my nerves as my fingers approached her mouth. Then I petted her head, stroking her muzzle and ears. I was about to run my hand along her back when something knocked against the underside of the boat. I gripped the sides and looked at Arden, the same thought in our minds: a shark. We were over a hundred yards out in the bay. Maeve was no longer watching us, and the water below was menacingly black.

"What do we do?" she asked, peering over the side. Heddy sniffed the bottom of the boat, growling.

I froze, my hands tightening on the gunwales. "Don't move," I said. But the boat rocked again. When I looked over the side, a dark mass was right below us.

"What the hell . . . ," Arden muttered, pointing into the water. Then she started laughing, her hand covering her mouth. "Is that a seal? Look—there's more!" Another appeared next to it, then another. Their slick, brown heads popped up from the surface then ducked quickly below.

I loosened my grip on the boat, laughing at myself, at the panicked thoughts of Maeve and Califia, of imagined sharks. "They're all around us." I leaned over the edge, letting my fingertips graze the water. There were nearly ten seals surrounding the boat, their friendly little faces peering up at us. A tiny one flipped over and swam on its back. A few yards away, a larger one with long white whiskers let out a yelping bark. Heddy barked in response, scaring them all below the surface.

"Don't mind her," Arden called, looking happier than I'd seen her since we'd escaped. "Heddy, you scared them." She wagged a finger at the big dog.

The seals took off into the bay. The tiny one looked back, as if apologizing for his friends' rude behavior. "Nice meeting you, too!" Arden called, raising her hand

in a wave. Heddy let out another loud bark, seeming satisfied with herself.

The seals kept going until they were just tiny black
dots on the surface of the bay. The sun didn't seem too
bright anymore. The birds were welcome visitors over-
head. Sitting in the boat with Arden, I forgot about Maeve
and whatever she was planning back on shore. I was with
my friend. We were out on the windblown water, alone
and free.

six

WHEN WE RETURNED TO THE DOCK, THE SUN WAS LOW IN THE sky. The restaurant that had become Califia's de facto dining hall was livelier than it had been in weeks. I parted a tangled curtain of vines and ivy, exposing the restored interior. A long bar jutted out from one wall. Wooden tables and benches were crowded together in the center of the room, covered with the remains of boiled Dungeness crab, sole, and abalone. A two-foot-tall statue of Sappho was perched on a shelf in the corner; it had earned the place the affectionate nickname "Sappho's Bust."

"Well, looky here!" Betty called from behind the bar, her big cheeks already red from a few beers. "It's Lady and the Tramp!" The women on the stools all laughed. One took a quick swig of bathtub ale, the homemade beer Betty brewed.

Arden glanced sideways at me, frowning. "I suppose I'm the tramp?"

I took in her shaved head, spotted with scabs, her thin face, her skin crisscrossed with tiny scratches, and her fingernails, still dirty despite two baths. "Yeah." I shrugged. "You're definitely the tramp."

The back doors were open, letting in the smell of the campfire burning behind the restaurant. Delia and Missy, two of the earliest escapees on the Trail, were flipping green coins into one another's drinks. It was a stupid game they liked to play after dinner, to the exclusion of everyone else. They stopped when Arden and I walked past, Delia nudging Missy hard in the side.

Some women sat along the tables in the back, chatting as they broke apart crab legs. I spotted Maeve and Isis in the corner. Maeve, her sleeves rolled up to the elbows, was opening an abalone shell for Lilac.

Betty set two mugs of beer on the bar. "Where's the dog?" she asked, checking the floor by Arden's feet for signs of Heddy.

"Left her behind." Arden took the mug and swigged

it. Then she stared at Betty, her brow furrowed in annoyance, until the woman left to attend to someone at the other end of the bar. Arden swallowed. Her whole body seized as she coughed, the beer nearly coming back up. "Since when do you drink?" she whispered, looking at the amber liquid.

I took a few sips, enjoying the sudden lightness in my head. "Nearly everyone does here," I said, wiping my mouth with the back of my hand.

I thought of those first days, when I would sit alone in Lilac's bedroom in the middle of the afternoon, having already completed my chores. Everything had seemed so foreign. The women chopped wood in the clearing above us, the sound following me through the house. The branches rapped on the windows, refusing to let me sleep. Quinn would come retrieve me, insisting I accompany her to the dining hall, where she would sit with me for hours. Sometimes we'd play cards. Betty would pour us her newest batch and I'd sip it slowly, telling Quinn about my journey to Califia.

When I looked up, Arden was still studying me. "Besides," I added. "It wasn't exactly easy to lose you and Caleb in the same month."

Regina, a heavyset widow who'd lived in Califia for

two years, teetered on the stool beside us. "Caleb is Eve's boyfriend," she whispered to Arden. "I used to have a husband, you know. They're not as bad as everyone here says they are." She raised her glass, signaling for another drink.

"Boyfriend?" Arden narrowed her eyes at me.

"I guess," I said, resting my hand on Regina's back to steady her. "Isn't that what he would be called?" At School we'd learned about "boyfriends" and "husbands," but only to be warned against them. In our Dangers of Boys and Men class, the Teachers told us stories of their own heartbreaks, of the men who had left them for other women or the husbands who'd leveraged their money and influence to keep their wives in domestic slavery. After seeing all that men were capable of in the wild—the gangs who slaughtered one another, the men who sold women they'd captured, the Strays who resorted to cannibalism in desperation—some of the women in Califia, especially the escapees from School, still believed that men were universally bad. Life after the plague seemed to prove that, over and over again. But there were also the few who still remembered husbands or past loves fondly. Many called Regina and me hopeless, to our faces and behind our backs. But when I awoke in the middle of the night, my hands searching the bed for where Caleb should've been, hopeless seemed too mild a term for how love made me feel.

Delia and Missy were arguing now, the packed tables quieting as their voices grew louder. Everyone's attention shifted to their side of the room. "Let it be! Enough!" Delia yelled. She gripped her drink, letting the green coin clink around the bottom of the glass.

"Just tell her," Missy urged. She turned around in her seat, waving frantically at me. "Eve! Hey, Eve—"

Delia reached over the table and gave Missy one good push, sending her tumbling backward onto the floor. "I told you to shut it," she said. Missy rubbed her head where it had met the hard wood. "Just shut your stupid mouth," Delia continued. She got up and started around the table, but Maeve pulled her back.

"All right now. Enough." Maeve glanced around the room. "Guess you two need to learn to slow down. Isis— get them to bed, will you?" Her eyes darted to me and Arden, as if gauging our reactions.

"Tell me what?" I asked, still stuck on Missy's words.

Isis laughed. "Missy's just drunk—right, Delia?" she urged. Delia wiped the sweat from her forehead, but didn't respond.

"Somebody saw him," Missy muttered, brushing the dirt off her pants. She was speaking so low I had to stoop down to hear. "Someone saw that boy Caleb. She knows," she repeated, pointing at Delia again.

Maeve stood and grabbed Missy's other arm, helping her up. "That's silly. This is just—"

"I didn't want to tell you," Delia started, cutting her off. Everyone in the hall was quiet. Even Betty had stopped talking, standing silently behind the bar with a stack of dirty dishes in her hands. "But when I was in the city the other day, scavenging for supplies, I ran into a Stray. I'd seen him around last week. He'd asked me where I'd come from, where I was heading—"

"You said nothing, right?" Maeve interrupted, her voice flat.

"Of course," Delia snapped. She was calmer now that she was in Isis's and Maeve's grip. She refused to look them in the eye. "He had tried to barter with me for my boots. And then the other day he pointed to the new ones he was wearing and laughed, saying he'd stolen them from a guy he found out on Route Eighty."

Every part of me was awake, alive, my fingers and toes pulsing with energy. "What did they look like . . . the boots?"

Delia wiped the corners of her mouth, where a thin coat of spittle had formed. "They were brown with green laces. Came up to about here." She pointed to the soft flesh above her ankle.

I let out a deep breath, determined to keep calm. They sounded like the boots Caleb had worn as he walked beside me, winding our way through the city streets. I couldn't be certain. "Was the boy alive?"

"He said he found him in that furniture warehouse on the side of the road, in that stretch right before San Francisco," she said, looking at one of the older women. "IKEA? He said that he was badly injured. His leg was infected from a stab wound."

I only saw Delia's lips moving, heard the words that were coming out of her mouth. I tried to process them one by one. "Where? Where is that?"

"Now listen." Maeve put up her hands. "This is probably just a rumor. There's nothing to prove that—"

"He could be dead by now," I said softly, the thought even more frightening now that I'd spoken it aloud.

Isis shook her head. "He was probably making it up. He's a Stray."

Regina was smiling. "She loves him. She can't just leave him out there."

A few of the women started to agree, but Maeve raised her hand to silence them. "No one is going to find Caleb," Maeve announced. "Because Caleb isn't even there. The Stray probably lied. They always do." Then she turned to me, her face full of concern. "Besides, we couldn't have you going back into the wild now, not with the King after you."

All I heard were the intentions lurking behind each word. *You will never leave here*, she seemed to say. *I won't let you.* She grabbed my arm and ushered me out, following close behind Isis, who was taking Delia. A few other women helped Missy into a chair, offering her their condolences for the knot forming on the back of her head.

Outside, the night was cold and damp. I slipped out of Maeve's grip. "You're right," I said meekly. "It has to be a lie. I guess I just wanted to believe it."

Maeve's face softened and she reached out to squeeze my shoulder. She held Lilac close to her side. "We hear these types of things all the time. Better not to entertain them."

I shook my head. "I won't then. I promise."

But as we walked back to her house I slowed my pace, letting her, Lilac, Delia, and Isis get a few steps ahead.

Arden ran up behind me. We were both smiling in the dark. She nodded toward the bridge, the idea already taking root. The question that had consumed us was answered. Finally, we knew what to do.

seven

"JUST A LITTLE FARTHER," ARDEN SAID. SHE CROUCHED BEHIND
a burned-out car, her breath short as she pulled Heddy to
her, gripping the dog's rope collar so she wouldn't move.
"We're almost there."

I peered through the binoculars, looking at the tiny,
nearly imperceptible lantern light that shone at the top of
the stone ledge. Isis was just outside the front entrance to
Califia, a black dot moving against the gray landscape.
"I can't tell if she's using her binoculars anymore," I said.
That night, long after Maeve and Lilac had gone to sleep,
we crept into the storage room, carefully collecting supplies and loading them into two backpacks. Then we'd

made our way across the bridge, darting from car to truck to car, zigzagging so as not to be seen. Now we'd nearly reached the end: Only a few yards separated us from the short tunnel leading into the city.

"Let's sprint it just in case," I said. Each step was unsteady, and my legs felt like they might give out beneath me.

Arden looked at Heddy, smoothing down her soft black ears. "You ready, girl?" she asked. "You have to run fast. Can you do that?" The dog stared at her with big amber eyes, as if she understood. Then Arden turned to me and nodded, signaling for me to go first.

I sprang up from our hiding place, pumping my legs as fast as I could, not looking back at Califia or the lantern or Isis's silhouette, pacing in front of the stone ledge. Arden followed close behind, jumping over deflated tires, charred bones, and overturned motor-cycles. The bag was heavy on my back. The jarred berries and meats inside clanked together as Arden darted ahead, the dog right beside her. I kept running, clutching the binoculars and sprinting toward the black mouth of the tunnel.

I didn't even see the battered cart. It was lying beneath a truck, its hooked handle reaching for my ankle as

I passed. It pulled me, pack and all, to the ground. I screamed as my knee met the pavement.

As Arden ran she turned back, her gaze scanning the mountains. "Get up, get up, get up," she urged, stepping over the last of the debris until she was safe, out of sight, in the entrance of the tunnel. She and Heddy watched me from there, her voice calling beyond the darkness.

I scrambled to my feet and grabbed the binoculars, which had been crushed beneath me in the fall. My backpack was dripping, and something thick and purple ran down my legs as I limped forward, trying to get out of Isis's line of sight. When I reached the tunnel, I collapsed against the wall.

"Has she spotted us?" Arden asked, holding the dog back to keep her from licking my face. "Where are the binoculars?"

"Right here." I held them up. The center had cracked, leaving the two scopes connected by only a narrow piece of plastic. I pressed them to my face, searching the hillside for signs of her, but both lenses were black. "I can't see anything," I said frantically, banging the binoculars against the palm of my hand, trying to fix them.

Isis was probably halfway down the dirt path by now, sprinting to the houses to wake up Maeve. It wouldn't be long before she came across the bridge to retrieve us. "Come on," I whispered to myself, shaking the silly contraption to get it to work.

But when I held them to my face again I still couldn't see anything. No Isis. No Quinn. No Maeve. There was only infinite black in front of me, and my eyes, bloodshot and frightened, reflected in the glass.

—■—

THE NARROW HOUSES OF SAN FRANCISCO WERE COVERED IN colorful, ornate carvings, their paint peeling off in sheets. Burned-out cars were piled at the bottom of each hill. There was shattered glass everywhere, making the pavement sparkle.

"We need to pick up the pace," Arden said. She and Heddy were a few yards ahead of me, wading through the litter on the sidewalk, crushed plastic bottles and foil wrappers coming up past her ankles. She glanced above us. The moon was disappearing, the giant black dome of the sky now streaked with light. "We have to get there before the sun rises."

"I'm coming," I said, looking over my shoulder at the store behind me. A car had smashed through its front window, shattering the glass. Vines and moss hung down over the opening. Inside, beyond some overturned shelves, something moved. I squinted into the darkness, trying to make sense of the shadow, but then it was bounding toward me.

Heddy barked as the deer sprinted out of the store. I watched it disappear down the road. We'd been traveling for four hours, maybe more, snaking our way through the city. We were almost at Route 80 and the bridge that would take us to Caleb. Soon the entrance ramp appeared, covered in moss. I kept waiting for Maeve or Quinn to show up, or for a Stray to jump out and force us to surrender our supplies. But neither happened. I was going to be with Caleb again. With each step I took, it seemed more certain, more real. From now on, it would be Caleb, me, Arden, and Heddy—our own little tribe—hiding out in the wild.

We made our way up the ramp onto 80, weaving through the cars that would be forever frozen in traffic. My steps were lighter as we passed the old construction site Caleb and I had seen the day we'd first arrived. "That's it!" I cried, as the road curved up, hugging the ocean. The giant building was just ahead, its blue plaster falling down in clumps. IK A was spelled out in yellow letters, with only a faint shadow where the E had once been.

All that separated me from Caleb was an empty parking lot and a concrete wall. I started running, ignoring the ache in my knee from where I had fallen, and Arden's voice calling out behind me. "You shouldn't go alone," she tried.

I had thought about this moment so many times. In those weeks after I arrived in Califia, I'd stare up at the sky, reminding myself that Caleb and I were both underneath it. That wherever he was, whatever he was doing (Hunting? Sleeping? Preparing dinner over a fire?), we would always share something. Sometimes I'd pick a specific building in the city and imagine him inside, reading a water-stained book as he rested there, waiting for his leg to heal. I was convinced we would return to one another—it was only the how and when that had yet to be decided.

When I reached the glass doors, they were locked, their metal handles threaded with a heavy chain. But two of the bottom panes had been kicked out, and I crawled through, careful not to cut myself on the shards of glass. Inside, the massive store was dark and silent. The morning light coming in through the doors cast a faint glow on the concrete floor. I felt for the flashlight in my pack and turned it on, making my way farther in.

The beam flitted around the room, settling on a crate of moldy pillows, then on an old bed frame and a dresser, a lamp and books sitting on top of it as though it were someone's home. A kitchen was nestled in one corner, the refrigerator and stove still in place, and a sitting room down the hall with a long blue sofa. I had passed stores before, seen their long, narrow interiors, but this felt like a giant maze, with each room spilling into the next.

I heard a rustling and jumped back, the beam of the flashlight hitting the floor just in time to reveal a rat scurrying by. In the dining room beyond, a few of the chairs were turned on their sides. I didn't want to risk calling out into the darkness. Instead I kept silent, walking as lightly as I could over litter and broken glass.

I wound through the rooms, shining the flashlight in corners to be certain I hadn't missed anything. I moved past beds and tables and chairs, my eyes slowly adjusting to the dark. I was looking in one of the fake shower stalls when I heard it: a faint coughing. It was coming from my right, a few rooms away. "Here," a voice called weakly. "Eve? I'm here."

I covered my mouth, too shaken to reply. Instead I ran, weaving through the rooms, my heart light. Caleb was alive. He was here. He had survived.

As I got closer I spotted three candles on the floor. A man's silhouette was visible on the bed. I started toward him, but when I reached the bedroom, he wasn't alone. There were more of them—three men altogether. One sat in an armchair in the corner, his skin ghostly pale. Another stood by the room's other entrance, blocking the path through. His face was scarred, and he wore dirt-caked pants and the same boots Missy had described in Califia. The others were in uniform, the New American crest pasted on their shirtsleeves.

"Hello, Eve," the man on the bed offered. "We've been waiting for you." He sat up slowly and studied me, his face half in shadow. The thin hairs on the back of my neck bristled. I knew him. I knew this man.

His eyes looked out from behind thick black lashes. He was young—no older than seventeen—but his face seemed more mature than it did when we'd encountered him at the base of the mountain that day. The day I had shot and killed the two soldiers. After he had stitched up Caleb's leg, I had released him. I had let him go free, only to find him here, now, in this strange place.

The soldier with the scarred face crossed his arms over his chest. "I was wondering how long it would take for you to get the message." He looked to the others.

"Word spreads quickly among Strays, doesn't it?"

My thoughts went immediately to Arden. She and Heddy were probably at the door, working their way inside the building. They had followed me here, on my stupid insistence. I had led Arden into danger once before. It couldn't happen again.

I needed to warn them.

The young soldier nodded to the other two and they rushed forward. The flashlight was heavy in my hand. I didn't think. As the pale one came at me, I swung, landing one blow across his cheekbone. He stumbled backward, into the other one, giving me just enough time to slip away. I took off through the maze, jumping over chairs and tables and broken lamps. I could hear them gaining on me, their steps close as I reached the entrance.

Arden was readying herself to climb through the broken glass door. Heddy started barking, growing more frantic as we neared. Boots pounded the concrete floor behind me. Heddy barked even louder. I kept running, aiming for the opening in the door. I didn't look back as I threw myself through it, screaming the only word I could manage.

"Run!"

eight

GLASS SLICED INTO MY BARE ARM. FOR A BRIEF MOMENT THE world was completely still. My body was halfway through the broken door. I saw the empty parking lot before me, weeds sprouting up through the cracks in the pavement. Heddy was snarling. Frantic, Arden grabbed me under the arms and pulled, trying to get me out. Then a hand was on my ankle, fingernails digging into my skin as one of the soldiers dragged me back into the warehouse.

Heddy bolted through the door beside me and sank her teeth into his leg. "It's on me," the young soldier screamed to the others. Heddy was growling, a low rumbling sound that filled the air as she shook her head back and forth, tearing through his pants and into his flesh. She knocked him down and he finally released me. I turned to see his head smash into the floor, his eyes squeezed shut in pain. "Shoot it!" he yelled.

Arden kept pulling, my blood soaking her sleeve, until I was out in the open air of the parking lot. It was nearly fifty yards to the road. Woods spread out behind the warehouse; the dense trees would provide cover. I got up and ran toward them but Arden was frozen, staring at the doors. Heddy was still inside. She had the soldier pinned down and was barking in his face. When the other two came out of the darkness she bared her teeth, as if guarding a fresh kill. "Heddy, come, come here," Arden urged, smacking her hand on her thigh. "Get over here!"

The soldier dressed as a Stray pulled a gun from his waist. He aimed at the dog but she lurched suddenly, biting into the young soldier's arm. "Just shoot it!" he yelled from the floor.

"We have to go," I said, pulling Arden away.

"Come, Heddy!" Arden tried again as she ran backward, away from the store. "Come—"

A shot sounded. Heddy let out a horrible whimper and staggered away, her side bleeding. The soldier helped the boy up, then shot the chain holding the doors closed until it broke. The three men walked out into the parking lot.

I grabbed Arden's hand, pulling her toward the woods behind the warehouse, but she dragged her feet, staring at the building. Heddy had started limping after the men, her hind leg completely paralyzed. "Arden, we have to go," I urged, yanking her in my wake. The men followed us, but Arden was barely moving, her neck craned backward at the suffering dog. "Come on," I pleaded.

But it was no use. Within seconds, they had caught up to us. "Lowell, get her," the young soldier said, pointing at Arden. The pale one grabbed Arden's elbow and yanked her arms behind her back. She kicked wildly but the other one grabbed her legs, tying a plastic restraint around her ankles. In one swift motion he tightened it and she stopped kicking, her legs twisted and trapped.

As they held her down, the young soldier came toward me. His steps were unhurried. His leg was raw where Heddy had bitten him, a bloodstain spreading over the thin green fabric of his uniform.

"I'm taking you in," he said calmly. His face was more angular than I remembered. His nose had a large red bump on its bridge, as if it had been broken recently. He grabbed my wrist but I pulled my fist downward, just as Maeve had shown me all those weeks before, when I'd first arrived in Califia. It slipped out from underneath his thumb. Then I leaned down, levering myself against the pavement, and landed my elbow into the soft nook of his crotch. He doubled over, his bloodshot eyes watering.

I ran at the two others. The one with the scar looked surprised right before I punched him, as hard as I could, in the neck. He made a wheezing noise and staggered back, releasing Arden's legs. The pale one dropped Arden on the ground and sprang on top of me, pressing me to the pavement. "You're lucky," he whispered in my ear. I could feel his breath, hot and wet, against my skin. "If you were anyone else I'd slit your throat." He took a plastic restraint from his pocket and looped it over my wrists, pulling it so tight the blood throbbed in my hands.

The young soldier slowly got up, gesturing for the scarred one to retrieve something from the woods. He staggered off, his hand still clutching his neck. I turned to Arden. She was curled on the ground, crying, her eyes locked on Heddy. "It's okay, girl," she whispered. Her cheeks were wet and splotchy. "I'm here, girl. I'm here." The dog's whines grew louder as she dragged herself forward. Blood was streaming down her limp hind leg.

The air filled with the grating, familiar sound of a Jeep's engine. The scarred soldier pulled the truck out of the woods into the empty lot, while the two others loaded us, one by one, into the back bed. "Enough," the pale soldier yelled at Arden, unable to stand her crying any longer. "I can't listen to this."

The scarred soldier spun the Jeep around and started back toward the highway. "We can't leave her like that!" Arden's voice was choked with sobs. "Can't you see she's suffering?"

I pulled at my restraints, wishing I could hold Arden and comfort her. The tears soaked her hair and shirt. But the men ignored her, their eyes on the ramp that led back to 80. She threw herself into the backs of their seats and screamed. "You can't do this, you can't leave her," she cried. "Kill her, please, please, kill her," she repeated, over and over again, until she was out of breath. Exhausted, she leaned her head against the seat. "What's wrong with you? Just put her out of her misery."

The young soldier put his hand on the driver's arm, signaling for him to stop. Heddy's painful cries filled the air. She licked at her side, as if trying to stop the blood.

The young soldier got out and walked across the parking lot toward her. He didn't flinch, just raised his gun. I turned away. I heard the blast, saw Arden's crumpled face, and felt the air go still and silent.

As we drove away, Arden buried her face in my neck, her body heaving with quiet sobs. "It's okay, Arden," I whispered in her ear, my head resting on hers. But the tears only came faster, her cries inconsolable as the Jeep moved east, into the rising sun.

nine

FIVE HOURS LATER, THE JEEP CAME TO A STOP OUTSIDE A WALL nearly thirty feet high, ivy snaking up its stone front. My skin was sweaty and sunburned, and my hands and feet had gone numb from the restraints. I squinted against the sun, awake and alert. Months on the run, so many near misses and escapes—none of it had mattered. I'd ended up here anyway. The City of Sand.

"Arden—wake up," I whispered, nudging her in the side. She had fallen asleep a few hours into the trip, her sobs giving way to exhaustion. Her face was red and streaked with tears, her eyes nearly swollen shut.

"This is Stark," the young soldier spoke into a handset

in the front seat. "Nine-five-two-one-eight-zero. We have her here." I cringed at how cocky he seemed now that he had me sitting, hands tied, in the back of the truck. He'd been in the front seat during the five-hour ride, talking the driver through each turn, answering the radio whenever it buzzed. The other two glanced at him before doing anything, as if seeking permission. An hour into the journey, Arden and I had loosened the plastic ties and tried to jump from the moving car, but the soldier in the backseat caught sight of us and tied our wrists to the Jeep's metal carriage.

The air filled with static. "Opening the gate now. You can pull inside," a voice replied through the handset.

I pulled at the rope threaded through my wrist restraints. "It's smaller than I thought it would be," Arden whispered, looking up at the wall. Her shirt hung loose around her chest, exposing the top of the thick pink scar. "All that talk about its grandeur. A bunch of crock."

Those twelve years I'd been at School it was always a point among the Teachers, and in all those radio addresses they broadcast in the main hall—the City of Sand was an extraordinary place, the center of The New America, a city in the middle of the desert, restored by the King. Pip and I had talked about our future inside its walls, of the massive luxury apartments overlooking elegant fountains, the train that passed on a track above the street, the shops filled with restored clothing and jewelry. We dreamed of the roller coasters and amusement parks, the zoos, and the towering Palace filled with restaurants and shops. This was nothing like the grand metropolis we'd envisioned. The wall was hardly higher than the one at School, and there were no glittering towers visible beyond it.

The metal gate clanked and shifted, opening slowly. The pale soldier, whose name was Lowell, got out of the Jeep and circled around to Arden, cutting the rope that tied her to the carriage. Stark cut me free as the gate pulled back, exposing a short brick building. His hand was on my arm, moving me from the Jeep's bed to the backseat.

"No," Arden muttered as we both realized where we were, her body turning to dead weight as she dropped to the ground. "I'm not going back." Lowell yanked her arm, trying to get her on her feet.

Standing on either side of the gate were Joby and Cleo, the two guards who had been fixtures at School for so many years. Their machine guns were aimed at the woods behind us. From the back, the brick building looked smaller than I remembered, with a row of low, barred windows. A grassy yard was beside it, surrounded by a chain-link fence, its top curved inward to prevent escape. A few of the girls were outside, dressed in identical blue paper robes, sitting at two wide stone tables.

The Jeep pulled forward. I ran toward Arden, throwing myself at Lowell. I rammed my shoulder into his side, but with my hands tied behind my back, it was practically useless. He quickly caught his balance, then began pulling Arden through the gate. Cleo grabbed her legs to keep her from kicking. "You can't do this," I yelled. Stark's hand closed around my arm as he escorted me back to the Jeep.

"This is where she belongs," he said coldly. I looked back at her over my shoulder. Arden struggled against the soldiers, her feet and hands still bound. Lowell covered her mouth as they entered the fenced-in area. He and Cleo passed her off to the two guards by the door as if she were a sack of rice.

"Just one minute," I pleaded, digging my heels into the earth, refusing to take even one more step. Stark turned to look at me, but his hand was still on my arm. "Can't you allow me that? You have her here—you did what you came to do. I'm going to the City of Sand. Now I want one minute, just one, to say good-bye." He stared at the high fences on either side of the dirt path, then at the building ahead, its stone facade nearly thirty feet high. The soldiers had pulled the Jeep sideways, blocking the gate. There was nowhere for me to go.

Stark finally released me. "You have one minute," he said. "Do what you need to." I started up the dirt path, my skin stinging where he had grabbed me. A woman came out of the building. She wore a paper mask over her mouth. She wheeled a metal bed to the entrance and Cleo strapped Arden down, exchanging the plastic restraints for thicker, sturdier leather ones.

My eyes met Arden's. When she saw me there, beyond the fence, her body relaxed. "I won't let them do this to you," I said. "I won't." She opened her mouth to respond, but Joby pulled her inside, the lock clicking behind them. She was gone.

"What about me?" a familiar voice asked.

I froze, knowing who it was before I turned my head. She stood just two yards away from me, her hands gripping the chain-link fence. I walked toward her, taking in her sweat-dampened black hair, the bruises around her wrists and ankles, the scratchy paper gown that came down to her knees. "Ruby," I said, looking down at her stomach, hidden behind the robe. She didn't look like she was pregnant—at least not yet. "You're okay."

The night I left, I had stood there in the doorway to our bedroom, listening to my friends' breathing, and wondered when I'd be able to return. In Califia, every time Maeve taught me something—how to use a knife, shoot an arrow, climb a rope—I'd imagined bringing the women of Califia with me back to School, Quinn or Isis beside me as we charged through the dim dormitory, waking the girls from sleep. I hadn't imagined things happening like this.

Ruby's eyes were half closed. As she clung to the fence her body swayed back and forth, her limbs loose. "What's wrong? What did they do to you?" I asked. My eyes darted around the small lawn. I noticed a few girls from my class, and a few more from the year above, sitting at the stone picnic tables. Maxine, a button-nosed girl who had gossiped incessantly, had her head down on the table. "Ruby?"

"Get away from the fence," a guard called from inside. The woman was short and thickset, her cheeks covered in pockmarks. "Stand back!" She pointed her gun at me but I ignored her, instead pressing my face against the fence so my nose nearly touched Ruby's.

"Where's Pip?" I whispered. Ruby didn't look at me,

her eyes fixed on my battered gray boots. "Ruby, answer me," I hissed more urgently. The guard inside the pen was coming toward us. Stark had climbed out of the Jeep. We didn't have much time.

Ruby looked up at the sky. The sun hit her chestnut eyes, illuminating the browns and golds hidden in their depths. *Say something,* I thought as Stark started toward me, Lowell right behind him. *Please just say something.*

"Back away from the fence, Eve! Enough," Stark called. Then, to the guard, "Lower your weapon!"

"Please," I urged.

She parted her lips to speak. "Where did all the birds go?" she asked, then rested her forehead on the fence.

Stark grabbed my elbow. He raised his hand to the guard, signaling for her to lower her weapon. "All right, enough. Back in the truck," he muttered, his fingers digging into the soft flesh of my arm.

As they loaded me back into the Jeep and tied me to the carriage once more, I kept my eyes on Ruby. She was still leaning against the fence, her mouth moving, as if she hadn't even noticed I'd gone.

Lowell started the engine and the Jeep's tires ground against the hard earth. The gate pulled back. I felt that familiar loneliness, the bottomless, empty feeling of having no one. The place that had stolen Pip and Ruby from me had taken Arden, too. I watched the stone wall disappear behind the trees as the gate shut, so much of my life still trapped inside.

ten

THE SUN SLIPPED BEHIND THE MOUNTAINS. THE WOODS WERE giving way to wide stretches of sand. I sat tied to the Jeep's metal insides, my body stiff and sore from so many hours in the truck. We were forced to drive on the bumpy, bare ground beside the asphalt to avoid the many motionless, scorched cars blocking the roadway. The Jeep passed under giant signs, their paper ripped and peeling, images faded in the sun. PALMS, one read. ONE RESORT. TOO MANY TEMPTATIONS. Another showed bottles of amber liquid, the glass beaded with sweat. The word BUDWEISER was barely legible.

We sped toward the City's walls. Massive towers rose

up from the desert, just as we'd been told at School. My thoughts were with Arden and Pip, strapped to those metal beds, and with Ruby and her unfocused stare. Ruby's question kept playing in my head—*What about me?* The guilt returned. I hadn't done enough. I had left that night, assuming there would be a chance to come back. More time. Now, with my hands bound, just outside the City of Sand, there was nothing I could do to help them.

As we approached the fifty-foot wall, Stark pulled a circular badge from his pocket and held it out for the guards to see. After a long pause, a gate opened in the wall's side, just big enough for the Jeep to pull through. We drove inside, then rolled to a stop in front of a barricade. Soldiers circled the Jeep, their rifles drawn. "State your names," someone yelled from the darkness. Stark held out his badge and recited his name and number. The other two men in the truck did the same. A soldier with sunburned skin studied the badge, while others checked the car, shining lights beneath the metal carriage, on the men's faces, and on the floor around their feet. The beam ran over my hands, still in their plastic restraints. "A prisoner?" one of the troops asked. He kept the flashlight on my wrists. "Do you have papers for her?"

"No papers necessary," Stark answered. "This is the girl."

The soldier studied me with beady eyes, smirking. "In that case, welcome home." He signaled for the troops to fall back. The metal barricade rose up. Stark pressed his foot on the pedal and we sped toward the glittering City.

We passed buildings lit from within, bright blue and green and white, just as my Teachers had described. I remembered sitting in the cafeteria at School, listening to the King's addresses over the radio, telling of the restoration. Luxury hotels were being turned into apartment buildings and offices. Water was supplied by a local reservoir called Lake Mead. The lights shone in the top floors of every tower, the pools glowed a perfect crystal blue, all of it powered by the great Hoover Dam.

The Jeep sped through a sprawling construction site on the outskirts of the City. Sand drifts were ten feet high in some places. Troops walked along the top of the wall, their guns pointed out into the night. We passed crumbling houses, piles of debris, and a massive pen filled with farm animals. The smell of waste stung my nostrils. Giant palm trees towered above us, their trunks withered and brown.

As we neared the center of the City, the land opened up. Gardens spread out on our left and a concrete lot on our right. Rusted airplanes sat in front of a decrepit building with a sign that read McCARRAN AIRPORT. We sped past wrecked neighborhoods and the shells of old cars, until buildings rose up around us, each one grander than the next. They were all different colors, buzzing with electric light.

"Impressive, right?" The soldier with the scar asked. He sat beside me in the backseat, twisting open his canteen.

I stared at the building in front of us: a giant gold pyramid. A green tower rose up on the right, its glassy surface reflecting the moon. Impressive wasn't the word. The polished structures were unlike anything I'd seen before. I'd only known the wild—broken roads, houses with their roofs caved in, black mold that spread over the School walls. People strolled on metal overpasses above the streets. At the end of the main road a tower shot up into the stars, a bright red needle against the night sky. *We've survived*, the City seemed to say, with every glittering skyscraper, every paved road or planted tree. *The world will go on.*

The Jeep was the only car on the street. It moved so quickly that people went by in a blur. I could tell they were mostly men from their broad shoulders and heavy builds. Tiny white dogs roamed the street, nearly a third the size of Heddy. "What are those?" I asked.

"Rat terriers," the scarred soldier said. "The King had them bred to deal with the rodent infestation."

Before I could respond, the Jeep was turning left, cutting up a long road that snaked toward a massive white building. Rows of government Jeeps sat out front. Soldiers were stationed along a strip of narrow trees, machine guns slung across their backs. I stared up at the expansive white structure. The main entrance was lined with sculptures—winged angels, horses, women with their heads cut off. After driving so many miles, we were here. The Palace.

The King was upstairs, waiting for me.

Stark took me from the Jeep, his hand clamping down on my arm. I could barely breathe as we entered the circular marble lobby. The King's face had haunted me for months. I thought of the photo I'd grown up with in School. His thin gray hair hung over his forehead. His skin was loose around his jowls and his beady eyes were always watching, following you wherever you went.

Soldiers milled about the lobby, some talking, others pacing in front of a fountain. Stark took me through a set of gold doors into a small mirrored elevator and punched a code into a keypad inside. The doors slid shut and then we were moving, up, up, my stomach rocking as the floors flew past—fifty gone, then fifty more.

"You're going to regret this," I said, straining against the plastic bands around my wrists. "I'll tell him what you did. How your men threw me onto the ground in that parking lot. How you threatened to kill me." I looked down at the gash in my arm, the crusted blood turned black.

Stark shook his head. "Whatever it takes," he said, his voice flat. "Those were my orders. Do whatever it takes to bring you here." Then he turned to me, his eyes blood-shot. He clutched the collar of my shirt and pulled me toward him so my face was just inches from his. "Those men you killed were like brothers to me. They served with me every day for three years. The King will never punish you for what you did, but I will make sure you never forget what happened that day."

The doors opened before us with a terrifying *bing!* Stark's nails dug into my arm as he led me to a room across the carpeted hall. "You'll wait for him here." Then he pulled a knife from his pocket and sliced the plastic restraints in two. My hands tingled from the sudden rush of blood to my fingers.

The door closed. I leaped up and grabbed the handle, knowing before I even tried it that it would be locked. A long mahogany table sat in the center of the room, surrounded by a few heavy chairs. A massive window looked out onto the City, a two-foot ledge just a few inches below. I went to the glass, wedging my fingers beneath the pane, straining against it. "Please open," I muttered under my breath, "please just open." I had to get out of that room. It didn't matter how.

"They're sealed shut," a low voice said. My spine stiffened. I turned. Standing in the doorway was a man of about sixty, with gray hair and thin, papery skin.

I stepped away from the window, my hands dropping to my sides. He wore a deep-blue suit and a silk tie, the New American crest embroidered on his lapel. He stalked forward, taking one slow lap around me, his eyes scanning my tangled auburn hair, the linen shirt soaked through with sweat, the scrapes around my wrists from where I'd been bound, and the wound on my arm. When he finally finished his survey, he stood before me, then reached out and stroked my cheek. "My beautiful girl," he said, running his thumb over my brow.

I smacked his hand away and staggered backward, trying to put as much space between us as possible. "Stay away from me," I said. "I don't care who you are."

He just stood there, staring. Then he took a step forward, and another, trying to get closer to me.

"I know why I'm here," I spat, circling the table, moving backward until I was pressed against the wall. "And I would rather die than bear your child. Do you hear me?" I raised my arm to strike him but he caught my wrist instead, his grip firm. His eyes were wet. He leaned down until his face was level with mine.

When he finally spoke, each word was slow and measured.

"You aren't here to bear my child." He let out a strange laugh. "You *are* my child." He pulled me toward him, cradling my head in his hand, and kissed my forehead. "My Genevieve."

eleven

WE STOOD LIKE THAT FOR A SECOND, HIS HAND ON THE BACK of my head, until I broke free. I couldn't speak. His words rushed in and corrupted everything—past and present— with their horrible implications.

I felt light-headed. What had my mother told me? What had she said? It was always the two of us, for as long as I remembered. There were no pictures of my father on the wall above the staircase, no stories told about him at bedtime. When I was finally old enough to realize I was different from the children I played with, the plague had swept through, taking their fathers as well. He was gone, that was all I needed to know, she'd said. And she loved me enough for both of them.

He produced a shiny piece of paper from the inside pocket of his suit jacket and held it out to me. A photograph. I took it, studying the picture of him, many years before, his face not yet touched by time. He looked happy, handsome even, with his arm around a young woman, her dark bangs falling in her eyes. He was gazing down at her as she stared into the camera, unsmiling. Her face held the confident expression of a woman who knows she is beautiful.

I held the picture to my chest. It was her. I remembered every line of my mother's face, the slight dimple in her chin, the way her black hair fell onto her forehead. She was always scrambling for a pin to hold it back. We had played dress up that day in my room, before the plague came. I could still hear the children outside, shouting and laughing, the sound of skateboards on the pavement. I wore my shoes with the pink bows. She took my other elephant barrette and put it in her hair, right above her ear. *Look, my sweet girl*, she said, kissing my hand, *now we are twins.*

"I met her two years before you were born," the King began. He led me to the table, pulling out a chair for me. I obliged, thankful when my body sunk into the cushion, my legs still shaking. "I was already the Governor then, and was doing a fund-raising event at the museum where she worked. She was a curator before it happened," he said. "But I'm sure you know that."

"I hardly know anything about her," I managed, staring at her eyes in the photo.

He stood behind me, his hands resting on the back of the chair, looking over my shoulder. "She was giving me a private tour of the gardens, pointing out these plants that smelled like garlic and kept the deer away." He sat down beside me, raking his fingers through his hair. "And there was something in the way she spoke that struck me, as if she were always laughing at some joke only she understood. I stayed two weeks there, and then we kept in touch after. I would come to see her whenever I wasn't in Sacramento. But eventually the distance was too much for us. We lost touch.

"Two years later, the plague came. It was gradual at first. There were news reports of the disease in China, in parts of Europe. For a long time we thought it had been contained abroad. American doctors were coming up with a vaccine. Then it mutated. The virus was stronger; it killed faster. It reached the States and people began dying by the thousands. The vaccine was rushed onto the market, but it only slowed the disease's progress, drew out the suffering for months. Your mother was trying to reach me but I had no idea. She sent emails and letters, called before the phones went out. It wasn't until I was quarantined that I discovered the correspondence in my office. A whole stack of letters was piled on my desk, unopened."

I remembered that time. The bleeds had gotten worse. She went through handkerchief after handkerchief, trying to keep her nose dry. She'd finally gone to sleep one afternoon, her bedroom dark as I wandered out. The house across the street was marked with a red X. The lawn beside it was dug up, the dirt turned over where they'd buried the first bodies. The quiet scared me. All the children were gone. A broken bicycle sat in the middle of the road. The neighbor's cat was outside, lapping at the end of a hose, as I approached the door. I'd walked in, looking for the couple I'd seen coming and going so many times before, the man with the brown hat. I remembered the smell, thick and foul, and the dust that had accumulated in the corners. *We need help*, I'd said, as I took a few tentative steps into the living room. Then I saw his remains on the couch. His skin was gray, his face partially sunken in from decay.

"You left us," I said, unable to hide the anger in my voice. "She was alone, she died alone in that house, and you could have helped her. I was waiting for someone to save us."

He covered my hand with his own, but I pulled away. "I would've, Genevieve—"

"That's not my name," I snapped. I clutched the picture to my chest. "You can't just call me that."

He stood and walked to the window, his back to me. Outside, the land beyond the wall was black, not one light visible for miles. "I didn't even know you existed until I read her letters." He sighed. "How could you be angry with me for that? They had to put soldiers at my door to prevent people from attacking me. I was one of the few government officials in Sacramento who survived. The people were convinced I had some magical cure, that I could save their families. As soon as the outbreak ended, as soon as I had the resources, I sent soldiers. I was setting up a new, temporary capital, and trying to assemble the survivors. I sent them to her house to find you both. You were already gone."

"Was she there?" I asked, my hands folded over the photo. I remembered her standing in the doorway, blowing me a kiss. She had looked so fragile, her bones jutting out beneath her skin. Still, it didn't stop me from imagining that things could've been different. That maybe—against all logic—she could've survived.

"They found her remains," he said. He turned and came toward me. "That's when I started searching for you, in the orphanages at first, and then, when the Schools were assembled, I looked at the rosters there. But there was no girl named Genevieve at any of them—you must've started going by Eve already. It wasn't until they sent back the graduation photos and I saw your picture that I knew you were alive. You look so much like her."

"I'm supposed to believe all of this based on this one picture?" I held it up.

"There are tests," he said calmly.

"How am I supposed to trust anything you say? My friends are in those Schools still. They're all there because of you."

He walked around the table, letting out a deep breath. "I don't expect you to understand it yet. You couldn't possibly."

I let out a tiny laugh. "What's to understand? There doesn't seem to be anything complicated about what you're doing. They're all there, against their will, because of you. You're the one who started the labor camps and the Schools." I shook my head, trying not to notice the way our noses both slanted to the left, or how we shared the same heavy-lidded eyes. I hated his thinning hair, the subtle cleft in his chin, the deep creases at the corners of his mouth. I couldn't believe I was related to this man—that we shared history or blood.

His skin glistened with sweat. He covered his face but I watched him, refusing to look away. Finally he turned and pressed a button on the wall. "Beatrice, please come now," he said, his voice low. He brushed a piece of lint off the front of his suit jacket. "You've had a trying day, to say the least. You must be tired. Your maid will see you to your room."

The door opened. A short, middle-aged woman came in, clad in a red skirt and jacket, the New American crest on the lapel. Her face was lined with deep wrinkles. She smiled when she saw me and curtsied, a "Your Royal Highness" escaping her lips.

The King put his hand lightly on my arm. "Get a good night's rest. I'll see you tomorrow."

I started walking to the door, but he grabbed my hand and brought me into a hug, squeezing me close. When he pulled back his expression was soft, his eyes fixed on mine. He wanted me to believe him, that much was clear, but I steeled myself against it. I thought only of Arden's bound ankles, her body writhing as she tried to free herself.

I was relieved when he finally dropped my hand. "Please show Princess Genevieve to her suite and help her out of those clothes."

The woman looked at my tattered pants, the blood on my arm, the bits of dried leaves tangled in my hair. She smiled sweetly as he disappeared down the hall, his shoes snapping against the shiny wood floor. I stood frozen, my heart loud in my chest, until the room was silent, all traces of him gone.

twelve

"AND THIS IS WHERE YOU'LL HAVE YOUR AFTERNOON TEA," Beatrice said, gesturing at the massive atrium. Three walls were all windows, and the glass ceiling exposed the starless sky. We had passed the formal dining room, the sitting area, the locked guest suites, and the maid's kitchen. It had all gone by in a blur. *He is your father*, I repeated to myself, as if I were a stranger delivering the news. *The King is your father.*

No matter how many times I turned over the thought, it seemed impossible. I felt the hardwood floors beneath my feet. I smelled the sickeningly sweet cider boiling on the stove down the hall. I saw the sterile white walls, the polished wooden doors, heard the *clack clack clack* of Beatrice's low heels. But I still couldn't believe that I was here, in the King's Palace, so far away from School, Califia, and the wild. So far from Arden, Pip, and Caleb.

Beatrice walked two steps ahead of me, telling me about the indoor pool, rattling off the thread count of the sheets. She went on about the fresh meats and vegetables that were delivered to the Palace daily, the King's personal chef, and something called air conditioning. I didn't listen. Everywhere I looked I saw a locked door with a keypad beside it.

"All the doors need a code to open?" I asked.

Beatrice glanced at me over her shoulder. "Only some. Your safety is obviously very important, so the King has asked that I not share the code. You can call me on the intercom if you need anything, and I'll take you wherever you need to go."

"Right," I muttered. "My safety."

"You must be relieved to be here," Beatrice went on. "I wanted to say how sorry I was about all you've been through." I watched as she punched in the code to the suite, trying to catch as many numbers as I could. She pushed open the door, exposing a wide bed, chandelier, and a serving cart with a covered silver platter. The faint smell of roast chicken filled the room. "I've heard what happened in the wild—how that Stray took you, how he murdered those soldiers right in front of you."

"A Stray?" I asked. The photograph of my mother trembled in my hands.

"The boy," she said, lowering her voice as she led me into the bathroom. "The boy who kidnapped you. I guess it isn't public yet, but the Palace workers have all heard. You must be so grateful to Sergeant Stark for bringing you back here, inside the walls. Everyone's talking about his upcoming promotion."

My stomach felt hollow. Stark's words in the elevator returned, his promise that he would never let me forget what happened that day. He must've known how I felt about Caleb. He had seen how concerned I was on that ride in the Jeep, could hear the panic in my voice as I begged him to stitch up Caleb's leg. It all became sickeningly clear: As the King's daughter, I could never be executed in the City. But Caleb could.

"You have it wrong. Caleb didn't kill anyone. I wouldn't have survived if it wasn't for him." I tried to look her in the face, but she turned away. She stood in front of the sink and twisted on the faucet, waiting until the water was hot and steaming.

"But that's what everyone's saying," she repeated. "They're searching for the boy in the wild. There's a warrant out for him."

"You don't understand," I managed. "They're all lying. You don't know what the King has done out there. He's evil—"

Beatrice's eyes widened. When she finally spoke her voice was so low I could barely hear it over the running water. "You didn't mean that," she whispered. "You cannot say such things about the King."

I pointed to the window, the land stretched out for hundreds of miles. "My closest friends are imprisoned right now in those Schools. They are being used like farm animals, like they never imagined or hoped for anything different."

I let the photograph fall to the floor and put my head in my hands. I heard Beatrice shuffling around the bedroom, opening and closing drawers. The tap was still running. Then she was beside me, tugging the sour, sweat-soaked shirt from my body, helping me step out of the muddy pants. She set a hot, soapy cloth on the back of my neck and ran it over my shoulders, working the dirt off my skin.

"Maybe you misunderstood or misheard," she said

matter-of-factly. "It's a choice the girls have at the Schools—it's always a choice. The ones who are part of the birthing initiative volunteered."

"They didn't," I said, shaking my head. "They didn't. We didn't . . ." I bit my bottom lip. I wanted to hate her, this foolish woman, who was telling me about *my* School, *my* friends, *my* life. I wanted to take hold of her arm and squeeze, until she listened. She had to listen—why wouldn't she just listen? But she worked the washcloth over my back, gently lifting up the thin straps of my tank top. She wiped the dirt from my legs and out from between my toes and rubbed at the mud behind my knees. She did it with such care. After so many months on the run, of sleeping in the cold basements of abandoned houses, her tenderness was almost too much to bear.

"They hunted us," I went on, letting my body relax just a little. "The troops hunted me and Caleb. They stabbed him. And my friend Arden was dragged back to that School. She was screaming." I paused, waiting for her to argue, but she was kneeling beside me, the washcloth hovering over the gash on my arm.

She turned over my hands, staring at the bluish-red line around my wrist where the restraints had been. The cloth slipped over the mark, working at the raw skin, the blood now a thin, purple crust. "We shouldn't be talking about the troops this way," she said slowly, less assured. "I can't." She looked up at me, her eyes pleading with me to stop. Finally, she turned away and picked up a nightgown she'd laid out on the bed.

I took the ruffled dress from her hand and slung it over my head. I wanted to cry, to let my body heave with sobs, but I was too exhausted. There was nothing in me left. "He can't be my father," I mumbled, not caring if she was listening. "He just can't be." I lay down on the bed and closed my eyes.

Beatrice sat down beside me, the mattress springs creaking underneath her. She pressed a clean washcloth to my face, wiping around my hairline, my cheeks, then folded it and placed it gently over my eyes. The whole world was black.

The day had been too much. The hope of seeing Caleb, the soldiers' attack, Arden and Ruby and the King with his declarations—the weight of it fell on me, pinning me down. Beatrice was right beside me still, her gentle fingers rubbing at my temples, but she seemed so far away.

"You're not feeling well," she offered. "Yes," she repeated to herself as I drifted off. "That must be it."

thirteen

THE KING STEPPED OUT ONTO THE OBSERVATION DECK AND gestured for me to follow. My legs were unsteady as I stared at the tiny world a hundred stories below. The wall wrapped around the City in a giant loop, stretching for miles beyond the central cluster of buildings. Expansive crop fields sprouted up in the east. Old warehouses spread out to the west. The land at the edge of the wall was covered with fallen buildings, garbage heaps, and rusted, sun-bleached cars.

"I suppose you've never been this high up before?" the King asked, glancing at my hands, which were curled tightly around the metal railing. "Before the plague, there were buildings like this in every major city, filled with offices, restaurants, apartments."

"Why did you bring me here?" I asked, staring at the short rails in front of me, the only thing preventing a fall. "What's the point of this?" I'd spent the day in the top floors of the Palace. My arm was stitched and bandaged. I'd soaked in the bath, clogging the drain with dirt and bits of dead leaves. The King had insisted I accompany him to this immense tower, all the while rambling on about *his* City. *My* City now.

He moved easily around the narrow deck. "I wanted you to see the progress for yourself. This is the best view in the entire City. The Stratosphere used to be the tallest observation deck in America, but now we use it as the army's main lookout tower. From up here a soldier can see for miles. Sandstorms, gangs. In the event of a surprise attack from another country or one of the colonies, we'll have plenty of warning."

Inside, the glass tower was swarming with soldiers. They peered through metal scopes, scanning the streets below. Some sat at desks, headphones on, listening to radio messages. I saw my reflection in the windows. The skin beneath my eyes was puffy. I'd woken in the middle of the night, trying to decide what to do about Caleb. I knew

I could put him in even more danger just by mentioning his name. But I also knew Stark wouldn't stop searching for him. I couldn't let him be punished for what I'd done. "There's something you should know," I said after a long while. "Stark lied to you. The boy who was in the wild with me—he wasn't the one who shot the soldiers."

The King froze by the metal railing. He turned to me, squinting against the sun. "What do you mean?"

"I don't know what Stark told you, but that boy helped me in the wild. He saved me. I was the one who shot the soldiers when they attacked him." My throat was tight. All I could see was the soldier's body hitting the pavement, the blood pooling beneath him.

"You can't punish him," I continued. "You have to call off the search. It was self-defense. They were going to kill him."

The King turned, his head cocked slightly to one side. "And what if they did? Who is he to you? This Caleb person, the one you sent the message to that night."

I stepped back at the sound of his name, knowing that I had revealed too much. "I didn't know him well." My voice was unsteady. "He acted as my guide over the mountain."

He narrowed his eyes at me. "I don't care what he

told you, Genevieve. Strays can be incredibly manipulative. They're known for taking advantage of people in
the wild." He pointed out over the horizon, to where the
mountains touched the sky. "There's a whole ring of them
who trade women just like you. Any girl they can find."

I wiped the sweat from my forehead, remembering
Fletcher, that truck, the metal bars that seared my skin.
There was truth to what he said, but if it hadn't been for
the King none of us would've been on the run in the first
place. There would've been nothing to escape from. "Is
that any better than what you've done? What's the alter-
native? Fill our heads with lies and send us off to some
building to have children we'll never see grow up, never
get to hold or feed or love?"

"I made choices," he said, his face suddenly flushed.
He glanced back at the building, looking at the soldiers
stationed at the metal scopes. Then he resumed, his voice
much lower than before. "You've seen only a fraction of
this world, and yet you stand in judgment. I was the one
who made the difficult decisions." He pressed his finger to
his chest. "You don't understand, Genevieve. The Strays
who live in the wild, even some people inside these walls,
they speak about what I haven't done. What I could've
done, how dare I choose this or that for the people of The

New America. But this world is not the same anymore. Riots broke out everywhere. The Northwest was threatened with floods. Hundreds of acres in the South went up in flames. Those who did survive the plague died when the fires ripped through. They say they wanted choices—but there were no choices. I did what I had to do so people could survive."

He guided me to the edge of the platform, the wind whipping through our hair. "We discovered we could use the Hoover Dam and Lake Mead in the restoration. We had to protect ourselves from other recovering countries that might see us as vulnerable. We made the decision to rebuild here, using power from the dam." He pointed beyond the main strip. "A hospital was restored within the first two years. A school, three office buildings, and enough housing for a hundred thousand people. The hotels were converted into apartments. The golf courses were turned into vegetable gardens, three factory farms went up the following year. People no longer have to worry about animal attacks or gang raids. If anyone wants to attack the City, they'll have to trek through the desert for days, then get past the wall. And every day, improvements are being made. Charles Harris, our Head of Development, has been restoring restaurants and shops and museums, bringing all the life back to this country."

I stepped away from him. It didn't matter how much good he'd done or how many buildings had risen from the dust. His men were the same men who'd hunted me.

"We were able to restore an oil well and refinery." He followed me, leaning down to look into my face. "Do you have any idea what that means?"

"And who works at these refineries?" I shot back, thinking of Caleb and all the boys in the dugout. "Who did the construction on those hotels? You've been using slaves."

The King shook his head. "They've been given housing and food in exchange for their work. Do you think anyone would've taken those children into their homes? People could barely feed their own families. We've given them a purpose, a place in history. There's no progress without sacrifice."

"Why do you get to decide who to sacrifice? No one gave my friends a choice."

He leaned in so close I could see the flecks of blue inside his gray irises. "The race is on now. Nearly every country in the world was affected by the plague, and they're all trying to rebuild and recover as quickly as possible. Everyone's wondering who will be the next superpower."

He kept staring at me, refusing to look away. "I decide because this country's future—because our lives—depend on it."

"There had to have been another way," I tried. "You forced everyone—"

"People weren't having children after the plague," he said, a low laugh escaping his lips. "I could've spoken about the population decline, statistics, appealed to their reason, offered incentives. No one wanted to raise a child in this world. People were just trying to survive, just trying to take care of their own. Yes, that's changing now, little by little. Couples are having children again. But this country couldn't afford to wait. We needed new housing, a capital, a thriving population, and we needed it immediately."

I stared at the sun-bleached buildings before me, their facades faded to creamy pastels—blues, greens, and pinks. It was easy to see what had been restored on the main strip: The colors were brighter, the glass gleaming in the midday light. The paved roads were cleared of debris, weeds, and sand. Then there was the stretch of land out by the wall, so different from everywhere else. Desolate buildings were half covered in sand, their roofs caved in. Signs had fallen over. Rotted palm trees littered the street. In the farmlands, cows, shifting ever so slightly in their tight-packed pens, made the ground look like a black, undulating mass. Rusted shells of cars were lined up in an empty parking lot. From high above, the improvements were clear—buildings were either restored, or sand-battered and broken. The King had either saved them, or they'd been left to rot.

"I can't forgive you for what you've done. My friends are still prisoners. Your soldiers killed good people when they hunted me; they didn't even flinch when they shot them." I thought of Marjorie and Otis, who had given us shelter along the Trail, hiding us in their cellar before they were killed.

The King turned back to the tower. "In the wild, the soldiers' first priority is to protect themselves. I'm not justifying it—I won't. But they've learned from experience that encounters with Strays can be deadly." He let out a deep breath and pulled at the collar of his shirt. "I don't expect you to understand, Genevieve. But I found you because you're my family. I want to know you. I want this City to recognize you as my daughter."

Family. I turned the word over in my mind. Isn't that what I'd always wanted, too? Pip and I had lain awake at night, talking about what it would be like to be sisters, growing up in the world before the plague, in some normal house on some normal street. She'd remembered a brother, two years older, who had carried her on his back through the woods. I'd wished for that, hoped and wanted it in those last days, alone with my mother in that house. I'd craved someone there beside me, to sit with me by her door, listening to the quiet rustling of her sheets, someone to help me endure the sound of those horrible, hacking coughs. But now that I had family I didn't want it anymore—not like this. Not the King. "I don't know if I can do that," I said.

He rested a hand on my shoulder. He was so close I could see the thin dusting of sand on his suit. "We've planned a parade for tomorrow," he said finally. "It's time the people know you're here, time that you take your place as Princess of The New America. Will you consider joining us?"

"It doesn't sound like I have a choice," I said. He didn't answer. My stomach quaked. Arden was in some cold room and I was here, high above the City, the King's daughter, discussing a parade. "You have to release my friends," I said. "Arden, Pip, and Ruby are still in that School. You have to call off the search for Caleb. I was the one—"

"We can't discuss this anymore," the King said, his voice low. He turned back to the building, where a soldier was staring through the metal scope at something beyond us. "Two soldiers are dead. Someone needs to be held responsible." He narrowed his eyes at me, as if to say, *And it won't be you.*

"At least tell me you'll release my friends. Promise me that."

Slowly, his expression softened. He wrapped his arm around my shoulder. We stood there looking out at the City below. I didn't pull away. Instead, I let him believe that we were one, the same, united side by side. "I understand where you're coming from. Let's enjoy the parade tomorrow, give ourselves some time. I promise I'll consider it."

fourteen

THE BLACK CONVERTIBLE CREPT ALONG THE MAIN ROAD, speeding up, then stopping, like a frightened cockroach. I rode in back with Beatrice, the King in the car ahead of us. There were nearly half a million people in the City, and it seemed as if all of them had turned out for the parade. They stood, hands outstretched over the barricades that lined the street, cheering and waving. A sign hung down the side of one building, WELCOME, PRINCESS GENEVIEVE painted in tall red letters.

We rolled forward. The Palace was just ahead, the cluster of giant white buildings a hundred yards away. A marble pedestal was set up in front of the fountains. A wooden podium faced out over the largest crowd of all, gathered on the street just in front of it. I couldn't stop thinking of Caleb, of the troops tracking him through the wild. I hadn't slept. My head ached, a dull, constant pain.

"Princess! Princess! Over here!" a girl cried. She couldn't have been much older than me, her hair a tangle of black curls. She bounced up and down on her heels. But I looked right past her, at the man hovering over her shoulder. His hair was so greasy it stuck to his forehead, his chin rough from days without shaving.

The car idled, waiting for the King to exit his vehicle in front of the Palace steps. The man pushed through the crowd. I gripped the seat, suddenly looking for the soldiers who were stationed along the parade route, guns in their hands. The nearest one was five feet behind me, his eyes locked on the King's vehicle. The man pressed closer.

Then his hand was up, hurling a large gray rock through the air. Time slowed. I saw it coming toward me in a clear arc. But before it reached me the car lurched forward. The rock whizzed behind my back and ricocheted off the far barricade, panicking the crowd.

"He threw it at her!" a heavyset woman with a blue scarf yelled to the soldier, as the rock skidded across the pavement, settling by the curb. "That man threw a rock at the Princess!" She pointed to the man across the street. He was already pushing into the crowd, away from the Palace, toward the vast stretches of land beyond the City center.

"Are you all right?" A soldier ran at the car, resting his hand on the door. Two more took off after the man.

"Yes," I said, my breath short. Three soldiers surrounded the car as we moved closer to the Palace. "Who was he?" I asked Beatrice, scanning the crowd for more angry faces.

"The King has made the City a great place," Beatrice said, smiling at the soldiers who now walked beside the car. "But there are still some who are unhappy," she said, her voice much lower. "Very unhappy."

One of the soldiers opened the door of the car, letting us out in front of the giant marble stairs. The screaming crowd drowned out my thoughts. People leaned over the barricades, their hands reaching out for me.

Beatrice stooped to grab the train of the red evening gown I wore, and I kneeled beside her, pretending to adjust my shoe. "What do you mean?" I asked, remembering what the King had said about the people who questioned his choices. Her eyes darted up to a soldier standing just a few feet away, waiting to escort me to my seat. "Are you unhappy here?" I whispered.

Beatrice let out an uncomfortable laugh, her eyes returning to the soldier. "The people are waiting for you, Princess," she said. "We should go." In one swift motion she stood, fluffing the train of the dress.

I climbed the stairs, the soldiers surrounding me. The crowd fell silent. The midday sun was scorching. The King stood to greet me, pressing his thin lips once against each cheek. Sergeant Stark sat beside him. He'd traded his uniform for a dark green suit, medals and badges marking its front. Beside him was a short, plump man, his bald spot pink and sweaty from the sun. I sat down in the empty seat next to him as the King took his place at the podium.

"Citizens of The New America. We have come together on this glorious day to celebrate my daughter, Princess Genevieve." He gestured to me and the people cheered, their applause echoing off the giant stone buildings. I looked straight ahead, taking in the crowd, which expanded across the City sidewalks and into alleyways. Spectators hung out of the top floors of apartment buildings. Others stood on the overpass, their palms against the glass.

"Twelve years she was inside one of our prestigious

Schools, until she was discovered and returned to me. While Genevieve was there, she excelled in every subject, learned to play the piano and paint, and enjoyed the security of the guarded compound. She, like so many of the School's students, received an unparalleled education. The Teachers spoke of her commitment to her studies and her boundless enthusiasm, describing it as the very spirit on which our nation was built so many years ago, and on which it has now been rebuilt.

"This is all a testament to the success of our new education system, and a tribute to our Head of Education, Horace Jackson." The short man bowed his head, taking in the burst of applause. I looked at him in disgust, his shoulder just inches from mine. Sweat ran down the sides of his head and caught in the thin ring of gray hair.

The King kept speaking of my return, how proud he was to bring me here, to this City that had been established on the first of January over a decade before. "The Princess was lucky. On her journey to the City of Sand she was escorted by this nation's brave soldiers, among them the fierce and loyal Sergeant Stark. It was Sergeant Stark who found her, who put his own life at risk to bring her back to us." Stark rose to receive a medal. The King went on about his service and commitment, detailing his accomplishments as he promoted him to lieutenant.

I closed my eyes, retreating into myself. The shouts, the cheers, that booming voice I'd heard on the radio so many times before, all of it disappeared. I remembered lying beside Caleb that night on the mountain, the thick, musty sweaters we wore an unwelcome wall between us. He had pulled me to him, my body resting against his to keep warm. We'd stayed like that all night, my head on his chest, listening to the quiet drumming of his heart.

"And now to conclude," the King said cheerfully. "I'd like to introduce you once again to the Golden Generation, the bright young children who came directly from the birthing initiatives. Every day, women are volunteering their service to support The New America and help restore this country to its fullest potential. Every day our nation becomes stronger, less vulnerable to war and disease. As we grow in numbers we come closer to returning to our rich past, to becoming the people we once were—the nation that invented electricity, air travel, and the telephone. The nation that put a man on the moon."

At this, people broke out into wild applause. A chant started somewhere in the back of the crowd and rippled forward, a great ocean of feeling. "We will rise again!

We will rise again!" they repeated, their voices blending together into one.

The crowd in front of him looked vulnerable and desperate. Their faces were thin, their shoulders stooped. Some were badly scarred, others had leathery, sunburned skin, deep creases in their foreheads. A man standing on top of a hotel awning was missing an arm. The Teachers had often spoken of the chaos in the years after the plague. No one went to hospitals for fear of the disease. Broken arms were splinted with the leg of a chair, the handle of a broom. Wounds were stitched up with sewing thread, and infected limbs were amputated with handsaws. People looted stores. Survivors were attacked on the way home from supermarkets. Their cars were raided, their houses burglarized. People died fighting over a single bottle of water. *The worst was what they did to the women*, Teacher Agnes had said, staring out the window, its frame pitted and broken from where the bars had been removed. *Rapes, kidnappings, and abuse. My neighbor was shot when she refused to give her daughter to a gang.*

The King cleared his throat, pausing before resuming the speech. "Becoming your leader has been the greatest honor of my life. We have embarked on a long road, and

I *will* see you through to its end." His voice cracked. "I will not fail you."

The King took his seat beside me. He grabbed my hand, squeezing it in his own. Looking out at the crowd, it was easy to believe he was right—that he *had* saved the people inside the City walls. They seemed calm, happy even, in his presence. I wondered if I was the only one who thought now of the boys in the labor camps, or the girls who were still trapped inside the Schools.

There were children assembled behind us on risers. They were all about five—the same age as Benny and Silas—but much smaller. The boys were dressed in crisp white shirts and pants, the girls in the same jumpers we'd worn at School, gray dresses with the New American crest pasted over the front. "*Amazing Grace*," a girl with a long auburn braid sang into the microphone. "*How sweet the sound, that saved a wretch like me. I once was lost but now am found . . .*"

The chorus joined in, swaying back and forth as they sang, their voices cutting clear across the City. Their mothers might've been the girls who had graduated five years before me. Pip and I had watched them from our upstairs window. We loved how they walked, how they tousled their hair, how they seemed so womanly and beautiful striding across the lawn. *I want to be just like them*, Pip had said, leaning her head over the stone ledge. *They're so . . . cool.*

The crowd was overcome. Some wrapped their arms around friends, others stood with their eyes closed. A woman lowered her head to cry, blotting her face with the sleeve of her shirt. I almost looked away, but something behind her caught my eye. A man was standing just a yard away from the metal barricade. Everyone else was engrossed in the music. He was in the center of them all. He didn't move. He wasn't paying attention to the children behind me, to Lieutenant Stark, or to the King. He was looking only at me.

Then he smiled. It was barely noticeable—just a tiny curl of the lips, a brightness in his pale green eyes. His head had been shaved. He was thinner, yes, clad in a dark brown suit. But my whole body knew him, the tears coming fast as we stared at each other, letting the truth of it sink in.

Caleb had found me.

He was in the City of Sand.

fifteen

THE SONG ENDED. I KEPT STARING AT HIS FACE, AT HIS HIGH cheekbones, the mouth I'd kissed so many times before. I had to force myself to look away. Caleb was alive, he was here, we would be together. The thoughts came at me all at once. Then I stared at the King's hand covering my own. Stark's presence, just two seats away, made my stomach seize. The troops were after him. Everyone wanted him dead.

The King stood, reaching for my arm. I let him take it, my legs trembling, uncertain, as we turned toward the Palace. It was a moment before I realized he was leading us back inside, up to the highest floors, far above the City. Away from Caleb.

I couldn't stop myself. "Wait—I'd like to greet the crowd."

He paused next to the fountain, studying my face as though my features had rearranged themselves. I hoped he hadn't seen the desperation in my eyes, the way my gaze was drawn back to where Caleb was standing, a cap now hiding his face. "That is a fine idea." He brought my hand to his mouth, kissing it, a gesture that stiffened my spine. Then he motioned for the Lieutenant and the Head of Education to continue inside.

Soldiers surrounded us. As we started down the stairs, I peered into the crowd. Caleb was there, just a few yards in, sneaking glimpses of me as he pressed forward, moving closer to the barricade to shake my hand.

The palms above us offered no relief from the heat. I glanced back. The Lieutenant disappeared into the Palace, swallowed by the sea of small children, their Teachers ushering them toward the Palace mall with promises of ice cream.

"Princess Genevieve!" a woman with crooked glasses called, nearly tipping over the metal barricade. "Welcome to the City of Sand!" She was in her thirties, clad in a faded flowered dress. Her skin was pink and damp from the midday sun.

I reached out, taking her hand in my own. "I'm happy to be here," I said, the words suddenly feeling true. The King stood beside me, patting a twelve-year-old boy on the head. He was no more than a foot away from me, occasionally smiling, sometimes resting his hand on the small of my back. I kept scanning the crowd, tensing as Caleb shifted in its depths, his hat inching toward me. "Pleasure to meet you."

Caleb was only two yards away now, the gap between us closing with every passing minute. A man asked me to sign a scrap of paper for him; another asked how I found the City, if I'd been to the top of the Eiffel Tower yet, the miniature version that was just across the street. I answered in half sentences, silently wondering if the King knew what Caleb looked like. It wasn't too late. I could still turn around before he came any closer.

But I didn't. Instead I stole glimpses of him through the mass of people, taking in the angular chin I had once held, now clean of all stubble. His skin wasn't the deep reddish brown it had been in the wild. He seemed thinner, but healthy, his lips fixed in a subtle smile.

A soldier paced in front of the barricade. He dragged his baton down the metal rungs, letting out a horrible *bap-bap-bap-bap* sound. I followed his gaze, taking in

ANNA CAREY

the scene as he did, wondering if he noticed the young man
in the dark cap. But he settled his sights on a woman in a
tight white dress, her breasts spilling over the neckline.

Caleb inched closer as I moved down the row, shaking
hand after hand. I kissed a baby boy on the head, smelling
the powder on his skin, enjoying how his soft hair grazed
my neck. I reached out for a woman deeper in the crowd,
feeling Caleb's eyes on me as he approached. Her doughy
hand gave under my touch, the bright midday light revealing the faint freckles on her pale skin. The King was still
beside me. His voice was clear as he thanked a man for
his support.

I took an older woman's hand in my own, stepping
away from my father. Caleb was right over her shoulder,
not two feet back. "Pleased to meet you, Princess," he
said, stretching his hand for me to hold.

"Yes, thank you," I said, offering a slight nod. We
stayed like that for just a moment. I wanted to thread
my fingers through his, to pull him close to me, so close
that his chin was on my shoulder, his face nestled into my
neck. I wanted his arms around me, pressing our bodies
together so we were one again.

But the soldier turned back toward the crowd. He left
the woman with the white dress and circled me, yelling

at a man who was standing on a trash can to get a better view. The King stepped away from the metal barricade and signaled for us to return to the Palace. A young blond boy reached out, over Caleb's arm, begging to say hello.

Caleb released me to them.

I stood there, strangers' voices in my ears, my hand still warm from his touch. It took me a second to process the tiny piece of paper tucked between my fingers, folded so many times it was smaller than a penny. I clutched my chest, pushing it into the neck of my gown.

"Welcome, Princess," the teenage boy said as he gripped my hand. "We're so happy you're here."

I stayed there, frozen in my father's stare, as Caleb backed away. Then, as suddenly as he'd appeared, he pulled down his cap and was gone.

sixteen

AN HOUR LATER, THE CONSERVATORY WAS FILLED WITH PEOPLE. Women in ball gowns strolled through the indoor garden, admiring the peach-colored roses and blooming hydrangeas. Giant balloon sculptures drifted over the crowd. After the parade ended, many of the Outlanders, as the King had called them, had disappeared into the far reaches of the City, where the land was barren except for a few houses and motels. Others had taken the elevated trains back to their apartment buildings. Only a small group—members of the Elite—had been invited to the parade reception. Some waited on lines to ride the giant balloons. A few climbed up into the baskets beneath them and lifted up to the glass ceiling.

I stood there watching it all, unable to stop smiling. Caleb was alive. He was inside the City's walls. I pressed my fingers to the neck of my dress, feeling for the tiny slip of paper, just to be certain it was real.

"Isn't it incredible?" A young man strode up beside me. He had a thick mop of black hair and a strong, angular face. A cluster of women turned when he approached. "It's become one of my favorite spots in the Palace mall. In the morning it's quiet, nearly empty. You can actually hear the birds in the trees." He pointed to some sparrows on a branch above a small fountain.

"It's impressive," I replied, only half paying attention. I stared straight ahead as the King greeted the Head of Finance and the Head of Agriculture, two men in dark suits who always seemed to be whispering to one another. I didn't mind them now. I didn't hate the crowd congratulating the Lieutenant. Everything seemed more certain now, the whole City a more manageable place. I'd slipped into the bathroom after the parade, savoring a few solitary moments in the cold space. Caleb had drawn a map on one side of the paper. The line snaked out of the Palace and across the overpass, where the land was less developed. An X was scrawled on a dead-end street. I'd run my fingers along the message, reading it again and again.

Meet me at 1 AM, he'd written at the bottom of the page. *Take only the marked route.*

The man was still looking at me, his lips twisted in quiet amusement. I turned to him, for the first time noticing his clear blue eyes, his flawless, creamy complexion, the way he stood with one hand in his pocket, so self-assured. "I think *you're* impressive," he whispered.

The heat rose in my cheeks. "Is that right?" I knew it now, the playful tone in his voice, the way he leaned forward as he spoke: He was flirting.

"I read about your adventure in the paper, how you were lost in the wild all those days. How you survived after being kidnapped by that Stray."

I shook my head, careful not to reveal too much. "So you've read one article and now you think you know me?"

I stared out into the conservatory gardens, at Reginald, the King's Head of Press—the very man who'd written the story. He was tall, with chestnut skin and cropped graying hair. The King had briefly introduced us the day after I arrived at the Palace. Reginald never bothered to ask about the pink marks on my wrists or the stitches on my arm. He didn't ask me much at all. Instead he'd completely fabricated a story about how I'd escaped the School to find my father, who I didn't even know was the King. How I'd traveled through the wild until I was kidnapped by some vicious Stray. The article ended with a quote from Stark detailing how I'd been "saved."

"I've never understood Strays." The man shook his head. "Who would choose that life when they could have this?" He gestured around the room.

My thoughts drifted to Marjorie and Otis at their kitchen table, content to live by themselves, free from the King's rules. "A lot of people."

The man narrowed his eyes at me, as if he wasn't sure he'd heard me correctly. I was about to excuse myself when the King started toward us.

"Genevieve!" he called out, his face breaking into a genuine smile. "I see you've met Charles Harris. He's the one I was telling you about." He gestured at the domed ceiling, the planted gardens and marble floor. "His family has overseen nearly every building and restoration project inside the City walls. The City of Sand wouldn't be what it is without him."

So this was the Head of Development. He seemed surprisingly normal with his crisp buttoned shirt and huge blue eyes. Every inch of him seemed to imply he was decent, nice even—a person to be trusted. I wondered if he was the one who worked the boys in the labor camps, or if he made someone else do it.

"I was just telling Genevieve how incredible it is that she arrived here safely. A testament to her strength, I'm sure."

"I'm happy she's home." The King held a glass in his hand. "Charles here has been in the City since it was founded. His family was one of the lucky ones—both his parents survived the plague. They donated assets to help fund the new capital. His father was the Head of Development until he passed away last year." I studied Charles, his shiny, clean-shaven face and mop of thick black hair. He couldn't have been more than five years older than me. So little separated him from the boys in the dugout—their parents had died, and his hadn't.

"It's been an honor to take over my father's legacy," he said matter-of-factly.

The King gestured at the domed ceiling above us. "This was Charles's first project. He spent a good six months studying the recovered plans for the conservatory, looking at pictures from before the plague to get it all just right. With a few improvements, of course."

Charles pointed to the far end of the dome. "A small plane had crashed into that side of the conservatory, leaving a giant hole in the ceiling."

The string quartet in the corner struck up a song, and a few couples ventured into the center of the room to dance. People clinked their glasses together, toasting. The King raised his hand, waving two women over. The younger one seemed about my age, with straw-colored hair and thin, glossy lips. The other woman looked similar but older, her eyelashes clumped together with thick mascara. Her hair was styled in a stiff gold bob. "Perfect timing," the King started, resting his hand on the older woman's back. "Genevieve, I'd like you to meet my sister-in-law, Rose, and my niece, Clara. Rose was married to my late brother."

The King had mentioned them the day before—my aunt and cousin. I offered my hand to the girl but she looked away as if she didn't notice. Rose quickly took it in hers instead. "We're happy you're here, Princess," she said slowly, as if it took great effort to get each word out.

Clara's eyes darted from Charles to me, then back to Charles again. She sidled up next to him, resting her hand on his arm. "Let's go on the balloon ride, Charles," she said softly. She turned to me, surveying the satin gown Beatrice had helped me into, the shoes with the gold clasps on their sides, the low bun my hair had been twisted into. I'd been in her presence for less than five minutes, but I could tell, with complete certainty, that she hated me.

Charles stepped forward. "I was just about to ask Genevieve," he said. "She hasn't been yet, and it's a novelty every new citizen should experience. I promise I'll take you later." He offered me his arm. Clara glared at me, her cheeks flushed.

"I actually wanted to look at the greenhouse," I said, pointing to the enclosed glass room on the other side of the conservatory, the lush flowers filling every inch of it.

"Charles can go with you," the King said, urging me toward him.

"I'd prefer to go alone," I said, nodding to Charles in apology. His arm was still outstretched, waiting for me to take it.

It took him a moment to recover, a low laugh escaping his lips. "Of course," he looked at the group as he spoke. "You must be exhausted from the parade. Another time." He studied me as though I were some exotic animal he'd never come in contact with before.

The King opened his mouth to speak, but I turned and took off through the conservatory into the greenhouse, relieved when I was finally alone again. Outside the glass ceiling, the sky was already orange, the sun dipping behind the mountains. The reception would end soon. In a few short hours I'd be on my way to see Caleb, all of this—the Palace, the King, Clara, and Charles—receding behind me.

Caleb is alive, I repeated to myself. That was all that mattered. I reached my hand to the top of my gown. The tiny square was still inside my dress, pressed against my heart.

seventeen

WHEN I RETURNED TO THE SUITE, I GOT TO WORK, SEARCHING the closet for something discreet to wear. The hangers were heavy with silk dresses, fur jackets, and petal-pink nightgowns. I dug through the drawers below, settling on a black sweater and the one pair of jeans I'd been allowed, even though Beatrice had warned me not to wear them outside of my room. I stepped out of the gown, finally able to breathe.

I unfolded the tiny paper map, one side printed with directions, the other with the note from Caleb. He said he had a contact in the Palace, someone who'd left a bag for me on the seventh floor staircase. If I could get out, I'd travel ten minutes off the main strip, to the building he'd marked with an *X*.

If I could get out.

It was a foolish idea. I knew that. I buttoned my jeans, slipped on my socks and shoes, and fastened my hair back. I arranged the pillows and duvet to look as though it contained a sleeping body. It was foolish to think I could get out of the Palace unnoticed, that I could find my way through the City. Because of the strict curfew—the streets were clear from ten at night until six in the morning, a rule the King had established to keep order—I'd be one of the only people on the sidewalks. If anyone followed me, I'd lead them right to Caleb.

But as I crept toward the door, listening for any sound in the hall, I couldn't think of doing anything else. He was here. Only a few streets separated us. I had let him go once, and I wouldn't do it again.

I lifted the metal cover of the keypad on the wall. The code started with 1-1, I knew that much. Those were the easiest numbers to catch. I'd thought I'd seen a 3 and another 1 at the end, but it was hard to know for sure; Beatrice's fingers always moved so quickly whenever she was coming and going. I pressed my ear to the door. I couldn't hear anything. She was probably down the hall now, dropping empty glasses in the sink as she spoke to Tessa, the cook. Still, my hands shook as I entered the 1, then another 1, a 2, an 8, and finally the 3 and 1 at the end.

It beeped twice. I tried the door but it was locked. I rested my forehead on the wall, desperately trying to remember. It could've been a 7, not an 8, that I'd seen. It could've been a 2, not a 3. It could've been anything.

Numbers, combinations, codes ran through my head. Then I had a sudden flash of the King at the podium, before Stark had received his medal. *We've made tremendous progress*, he'd said, *Since the day the first citizens arrived here, January first, two thousand and thirty-one.*

Before I could second-guess myself, I punched in those six numbers: 1-1-2-0-3-1. Nothing happened. The lock didn't beep. The metal lid fell shut. I turned the knob and for the first time it gave. The door swung open, releasing me into the quiet hall.

It felt good to be free of the suite, with its sealed windows and cold, tiled bathroom, the couch that was so stiff it was like sitting on a cement block. Outside, the lights in the corridor were dimmed. I heard a clanking noise from the kitchen, where the staff was cleaning up for the night. I looked right, then left, moving along the wall, nerves knotting my stomach as I inched closer to the east staircase.

I peered through the small rectangular window in the door. The stairwell was empty. Another keypad was on the wall. I typed the same code, moving slowly, careful not to make any sound. The lock opened and I ran through the door, trying to ignore what lay beyond the narrow railing—an open shaft that dropped fifty stories to the ground. I took the stairs two at a time as I began the long descent.

When I was four flights down a door opened somewhere above me. "Where are you going?" a voice called. I froze, pressing myself against the wall, out of sight. Everything echoed in the concrete staircase. Even my breaths betrayed me. "I can hear you!" That voice, her tone—I knew in an instant it was Clara. Then I heard the *clack* of her shoes against the cement floor as she came after me.

I took off. I flew down the stairs, not stopping until I had cleared another ten flights. The footsteps quieted. I inched away from the wall and gazed up. I could just make out Clara's hands gripping the railing, her fingernails painted bloodred. "I know you're there!" she yelled again. I kept going, leaving her there, in the top of the tower, calling out my name.

When I reached the seventh floor a bag sat waiting for me, as Caleb had promised. Inside was a Palace uniform. I changed quickly, pulling the cap over my eyes, and continued down the staircase. The flight opened into a wide hallway, metal doors on either side. From one of the small windows I could see into the Palace mall. The ceilings were painted blue, white spongy clouds stretching out across them. The shops were all closed, one reading TIME & AGAIN JEWELRY in fat letters, another GUCCI RESTORED. A soldier paced the length of the stores, his back to me. Two others stood watch at the revolving doors.

I moved down the wide hallway to the EXIT sign. Caleb's contact had lodged a ball of paper into the doorjamb, making it impossible to lock. The knob gave easily. Outside, the air was cooler, the wind covering everything with a fine layer of sand. The route Caleb had marked was just in front of me. Troops were stationed at the Palace's front entrance and along its back. I could see them through the narrow trees, five soldiers huddled together, only occasionally glancing behind them. I took off, ducking behind the fountain, half covered by the high wall of shrubs.

I turned back every now and then to make sure the troops weren't following me. A knot lodged in the back of my throat. Clara had seen me. At this very moment, she could be waking the Palace from the top down, alerting the soldiers stationed on each floor. I kept my head low, calmed by each steady step. I was out, moving through the City, already on my way to Caleb. What was done was done.

The streets were dark, the high buildings casting an eerie glow on the pavement. I heard the Jeeps patrolling the other end of the City center. High above me, windows sparkled with light. I crossed the overpass as the map showed, keeping close to the buildings on the other side. Dried-out palm trees lined the narrow street. A few of the buildings still hadn't been restored. A restaurant sat abandoned, tables and chairs gray with dust.

Every time I heard a Jeep on the street beside me, the map would show a turn, and I would head in the opposite direction, the noise of the engine fading into the background. The building Caleb had marked was nearly a mile east of the monorail, the entrance in an alleyway behind a theater. As I neared it my steps were lighter, my body floating along, alive with nerves.

The alley was dark, the air thick with the smell of rotting garbage. I entered through the door marked on the map. Inside it was pitch black. I felt my way along the wall and down a narrow set of stairs, into the building's underbelly. Smoke lingered in the air. Somewhere, someone was singing. The murmurs of faraway voices swirled around me. I crept along, stumbling over the last few steps, until I was at the bottom of the staircase, in front of another door.

A woman was on stage, clad in a silver-sequined gown, a three-person band behind her. She sang into a microphone like the one the King had used at the parade. A sad, slow song drifted to the back of the room. A man on a saxophone leaned forward, adding a few low notes. Couples spun around on a cramped dance floor, a woman nuzzling her face into a man's neck as he shifted his weight back and forth, his hips swaying with the beat. Others huddled in cozy booths, laughing over half-empty glasses. Lit cigarettes sat in plastic trays, the smoke spiraling up to the ceiling.

The walls were covered with painted canvases. One showed the City's buildings dotted with bloodred lights, making each skyscraper look sinister. A massive painting hung behind the bar. Rows of children were shown in crisp white shirts and blue shorts just like the ones the Golden Generation wore, but their faces were flat and featureless, each one interchangeable with the next. I scanned every person in the room, looking for Caleb at the bar, or in the pack of men huddled by the door. In the back, to the right of the stage, a figure sat alone in a booth. His face was hidden under the brim of his cap. He was twisting something between his fingers, lost in quiet concentration.

The song ended. The woman in the sequined dress introduced some of the band members and made a joke. A few people behind me laughed. I stood rooted in place, watching him play with the paper napkin, how he bit down hard on his bottom lip. Suddenly, as if sensing me there, he looked up, his gaze meeting mine. He stared at me for a moment, his face brightening in a smile.

Then he was up, closing the space between us. As the woman started singing again, he reached me, pressing his face into my neck. He wrapped his arms tightly around my shoulders, pulling me so close my feet lifted off the ground. We stayed there as the music swelled around us. Our bodies fitted together perfectly, as though we were never meant to be apart.

 eighteen

"I WAS GETTING WORRIED," HE SAID, WHEN HE FINALLY SET ME down. He gently pulled strands of hair away from my wet lips. "I thought I'd been stupid to give you that note, to tell you to come." He held my face between his hands, tilting my chin up so he could see beneath my cap. "You should know better than to keep a boy waiting," he laughed. "It was torture."

"I'm here now." I held onto his wrists and pressed down, feeling the bones just beneath the surface of his skin. He smiled, his eyes wet. "I'm really here."

He buried his face into my neck, his lips against my skin. "I missed you so much." His arms tightened around me. I stroked the back of his head. There was something about the way he held me—clinging to my sides, squeezing the breath from my body—that startled me.

"I'm okay," I said softly, trying to reassure him. His breathing slowed. "We're here, together. We're okay," I repeated.

He looked at me, running his finger over my cheekbones and down the bridge of my nose. Then he pressed his lips to mine, letting them rest there for a moment. I savored the familiar scent of his skin, his stubble against my cheek, his hands in my hair. I clutched his sides, wishing we could stay like this always, the moon forever in the sky, the earth paused on its axis.

After a long while we slid into the booth where Caleb had been waiting. The woman in the sequined dress was still singing, the melody slow and sweet as she described a midnight train to Georgia. A few men studied us from the bar as they swigged tiny glasses of black liquid. The candlelight danced on our faces. Caleb kept hold of my hand. "Where are we?" I asked, adjusting my cap so it hid my eyes.

"It's a speakeasy," Caleb said. "They serve their own alcohol. People come here to drink, smoke, go out after curfew—all the things the King has outlawed in the City."

I brought my hand to my face, afraid someone would recognize me from the parade. "Is it safe? Do they know who you are?"

"Everyone here is guilty of something." He lowered his voice, pointing to a man in the far corner playing cards. A gold watch was set on the table in front of him, along with some silver rings. "Gambling, alcohol consumption, smoking, exchanging goods 'off record,' they call it. Goods that aren't bought with the government-issued credit cards are supposed to be traded through the newspaper. You could be sent to jail just for coming in here." He picked up the napkin he'd been playing with. It was twisted into a small white rose. "Well, maybe *you* wouldn't get arrested, *Genevieve*." He smiled, tucking it behind my ear.

I put my hand on his right leg, where he had been stabbed. I could feel the scar through his thin pants, the line that slanted inward, toward his opposite knee. "What happened to you?" I finally asked. "All that time before you came here. I thought of you every day. I shouldn't have let you leave. I was so scared . . ."

"You did the right thing—we both did." Caleb inched closer and wrapped his arm around me, massaging the aches from my neck. "It's strange, but I always knew you'd come back to me. The how and when of it wasn't clear, but I knew."

"I hoped," I said, keeping my hand on his leg.

Caleb shook his head and smiled. "Could any day have been more perfect than today?" He kissed me once, then twice, his lips settling by the hollow of my ear. "I woke up and the City was talking about the new Princess, the King's daughter who'd returned from the Schools. I ran all the way from the Outlands to the City center like a complete idiot. Everyone thought I was just another one of your fans. I kept thinking, she's come back to me."

I pulled myself closer to him. "Tell me what happened when you left Califia. I need to know everything."

Caleb squeezed my hand. "I stayed in San Francisco, in a house just over the bridge. It was hard for me to walk, even with the wound stitched up. For a while I lived off figs and berries from the local park. But then a day passed, and another, and I was too weak to walk anymore. I was trapped.

"At some point, when I was really desperate, I tried to go just a block to find food. I collapsed on the sidewalk. I'm not sure how long I was there—one day, maybe a few. I just remember a horse coming toward me. I tried to crawl into a storefront, to hide myself, but it was too late.

A man was hauling me onto the horse, and then I passed out. I woke up hours later. He was giving me water. Then he finally mentioned Moss."

"Moss?" I asked, remembering the name. "The one who organized the Trail?"

"He's operating from inside the City now," Caleb said, his voice barely audible. He looked quickly around the room before speaking. Just one couple was dancing, the woman's hand resting on the man's heart. "He was working on the inside when the report came in about the troops killed at the base of the mountain. That soldier said where he'd last seen me, how I'd been stabbed, who I was with. Moss knew I must've been taking you to Califia. He came and found me. He forged my paperwork to make it look like I was just another Stray seeking refuge in the City. He's been organizing people inside the walls, the dissidents."

"The dissidents?" I kept my voice low, thankful when the trumpet blasted a few loud notes. Everyone around us was absorbed in their own conversations, clinking their glasses together in cheers.

"There's opposition to the regime. Moss brought me here to lead a build—we're constructing tunnels under the wall to bring in more people to help fight. Eventually we'll smuggle weapons in from the outside. There are three tunnels in all. Moss is talking about a revolution, but without guns we're helpless against the soldiers."

Caleb kept his lips close to my ear as he told me about the Outlands, the vast, barren blocks beyond the City's main street, where old motels were being used as housing for the lower class. Some lived in warehouses, others in run-down buildings without hot water or even plumbing. The regime had designated housing based on the assets individuals were able to contribute after the plague. Jobs were assigned by the government. Most Outlanders worked cleaning the luxury apartments and office buildings in the City center, staffing the shops in the Palace mall or running the new amusements that were opening up throughout the City. The King had established endless rules: no drinking, no smoking, no weapons, no trading without his consent. No one was to be out after ten o'clock. And the City was enter-only— no one could leave.

"All of the workers here are trapped. The regime decides their weekly allowance, what jobs they have. They keep telling everyone that the conditions will improve, that the Outlands will be restored just like the rest of the City, but it's been years. Now there's talk of expansion, of conquering the colonies in the east, of restoring and rebuilding there."

"The colonies?"

"Three large settlements to the east that the King has visited. Hundreds of thousands of survivors are there. He considers them part of The New America already, but until the colonies are walled in, until troops are stationed inside, they're technically separate."

"They're looking for you. Stark, that scared *kid*—" I stumbled over the word. "He told them you were the one who killed the soldiers. What if they find you here?"

"Without a shirt on I'm just another one of the workers." Caleb pressed his hand to his shoulder, where his tattoo was. I'd noticed it the first day I met him, the circle with the New American crest in it. Every boy from the labor camps had one, like a stamp, marking them as property of the King. "They're looking for me in the wild, not working in the Outlands like every other slave."

"And Moss? Where is he?" I asked.

"It's better if you don't know." Caleb pulled the brim of his cap down to hide his eyes. "A dissident got caught a few months before I arrived here. They think he was tortured. He gave up names. Suddenly people were disappearing, being taken away to prison."

"Was the man killed?" I asked, my throat tight.

"One of our contacts is working as a janitor inside the prison, but he couldn't get to him in time. It was a real blow. The dissidents consider one another family—if one person is in trouble, everyone is. They would've done anything to help him."

I squeezed Caleb's hand as I told him about the last three months: my time in Califia, Arden's arrival, our escape and capture, my days in the Palace with the man who called himself my father. When I was done the crowd had thinned out. Half the booths were empty, strewn with glasses and smoldering ashtrays.

Caleb tucked a few stray hairs back under my cap, so gently it nearly made me cry. Then he pulled a folded paper from his pocket and spread it out on the table, revealing a map of the City with routes outlined in different colors. He explained how the troops had their routines, specific streets they patrolled in ninety-minute blocks. The dissidents had learned their patterns and used them to avoid being caught. He copied one route down on a napkin, marking the path back to the City center, how to reenter the Palace and which staircase to take. Then he copied another for me to use in two nights' time.

"Let's meet here," he said, pointing to a spot on the

second map. "There's another dissident who works that building at night who will point you in the right direction." He studied my face and smiled. "I have a surprise for you."

"What is it?" I asked.

"If I told you, it wouldn't be a surprise, would it?" He laughed.

I stared at the place he'd marked; it was right on the main road, diagonally across from the Palace fountains. "But you could get caught."

"I won't get caught," Caleb said. He smoothed down the corners of the paper with his palm. "I promise. Just be there."

"How long will it be before the tunnels are completed? Can't we hide out until then?" He said the other dissidents were concerned about his meeting me, that it might compromise them, but he'd assured them I could be trusted.

Caleb shook his head sadly. "We don't know. The one that's furthest along is at a standstill. We need blueprints to continue. And if you turn up missing . . . they'll know you're somewhere inside the walls. They'll come looking." He put his hand to my cheek. "It's a good sign that you made it here tonight, though. We'll just have to meet like this until things are more certain."

We sat there for a while, my face nestled against his

chest, until the singer sang her last song. The band packed up their instruments. Glasses clinked together. Slowly, we made our way out.

Caleb's hand rested on the small of my back as we climbed the stairs, feeling our way in the dark. The Outlands were quiet. Figures moved behind a curtain in the window of an old motel. We passed a parking lot lined with rusted cars, a dried-out pool, a long strip of empty houses. "I can walk you to the corner," he said, clutching my hand. He nodded to the street just one block away.

I felt the map in my pocket, each step bringing us closer to good-bye. I would see him again soon. Still, I cringed at the thought of lying alone in that bed, between the cold, crisp sheets. "It's just two days," I said aloud, unsure who I was trying to comfort.

"Right," Caleb agreed. He kept his eyes on the road as we approached it. "It's not that long, really," he said, but he didn't sound convinced.

We were almost to the corner. He would turn right, further into the Outlands, and I'd turn left, back toward the Palace. When we were just a few yards away, Caleb pulled me into a doorway set off the narrow street, the two-foot threshold just deep enough for us both to press inside. He held my face in his hands, his expression barely visible in the darkness. "I guess this is good-bye," he whispered.

"I guess so," I said softly.

He kissed me, his fingers hard against my chin. My arms gripped his back as I pulled myself closer. His hands were in my hair. My heart sped up as his finger dipped inside the neck of my sweater, tracing lines over my collarbone. He leaned down and I kissed his closed eyelids, that tiny scar on his cheek.

Somewhere in the distance a Jeep backfired, the *boom!* startling me from my waking dream.

"I have to go—we have to go," I breathed.

I pulled away first, knowing that if I didn't leave then I never would. I turned to go, giving his hand one final squeeze.

nineteen

CLARA DROPPED HER PLATE BESIDE MINE, SPATTERING TINY droplets of tomato sauce on the white tablecloth. "You look tired," she said coolly, her eyes searching mine. "Late night?" Her short blue dress was too tight, the silk puckering along the seams.

"Not at all." I straightened up. At most, Clara had seen my back as I darted inside the stairwell door. She couldn't have known for certain that it was me.

Charles and the King had just cut the red-and-blue ribbon of the new marketplace, a giant outdoor restaurant built around the Palace's expansive pools. People ate at tables set up on the stone patio or strolled past various stands. Columns towered over us, holding up verdant topiaries and hanging purple flowers. Statues of winged lions and bucking horses perched above. The fabric stalls—called "cabanas"—had all been converted to storefronts where vendors sold Moroccan olives, Polish sausages, and fresh crepes with strawberries and whipped cream.

Rose sat across the table, looking as though her face might melt off. Pink blush had settled in her wrinkles, and there were faint dark circles under her eyes. She stared down at Clara's half-eaten plate of pasta. "Know when to say when," she whispered, resting her hand on Clara's fork. "You're too beautiful to let yourself go." Clara looked away, her cheeks going a deep red.

"We're thrilled with the final product," the King said loudly as he strolled toward us, Charles by his side. He addressed Reginald, the Head of Press, who was clutching a notebook. "When we restored Paris, New York, and Venice we wanted them to be tributes to the great cities of yesterday's world. This marketplace is an extension of that, a place people can experience all the delicacies we enjoyed before. You can't just hop on a plane and be in Europe, South America, or India anymore." He gestured to a corner of the wide marketplace. Tents were filled with steaming carts of dumplings, meats, and tiny rolls of sticky rice and fish. "My favorite is Asia. Did you ever think you would have sashimi again?" the King asked.

I watched him, noticing how easily he slipped into his public persona. His voice was louder, his shoulders back. It seemed as though every word had been rehearsed beforehand, every slight nod and gesture carefully designed to inspire confidence. "Our Head of Agriculture is working on ways to produce seaweed. The trout is all farmed from Lake Mead. It's not an ideal substitute, but it will suffice until we get the fishing fleets back on the oceans."

They sat down beside me, Reginald still scribbling in his notebook. Charles's eyes followed me. He kept staring until I met his gaze. "Don't say hello or anything," he said, playfully raising one eyebrow. "You know, I'm starting to take it personally."

"I think your ego can handle it," I offered, as I cut into the yellowish dumplings I'd found at the Polish storefront.

The King reached over, squeezing my hand so hard it hurt. "Genevieve is kidding." He laughed. He offered Reginald a subtle wave, as if to say, *Don't write that down.*

He cleared his throat and continued. "This is only the beginning. The City has proven a workable model for others in The New America. There are three separate colonies in the east. Every day people in those colonies worry about where their next meal will come from, if they'll be attacked by their neighbors. There's no electricity, no hot water—people are just surviving. In the City of Sand we aren't surviving—we're thriving. This is what *living* is."

He pointed at the blinding white marble and the clear blue pools. "There's so much land for the taking, and Charles and his father have proved we can develop quickly and efficiently. In six months we'll start walling in the first colony—a settlement in what was formerly Texas."

"I can't wait to see what you'll do with it." Clara slid her chair closer to Charles. "I've been listening to people talk about the global marketplace for the last few months, and I never imagined it would be as incredible as this."

"A lot of this we owe to McCallister," Charles said, waving to the Head of Agriculture, a man with glasses who stood by a giant mural of the old world, each country painted a different color. "If it wasn't for the factories he built in the Outlands, or the new methods of farming he developed, we wouldn't have any of this."

"You're being modest. This was your vision," Clara cooed. She pointed at Reginald. "I hope you're writing that down. Charles has been imagining this since before the Palace was even completed, before most of the buildings were restored. You've been going on about it since as long as I can remember, how you wanted to bring the diversity of the world inside the City walls."

I could barely look at her. Teacher Agnes's voice was in my head, her warnings about men and the deceitful nature of flirtation. *Charm is a verb*, she'd said, *something men do to control you*. But I wished she could see this now: Clara leaning in, resting her fingers on Charles's arm, tucking her blond hair behind her ears. It was the first time I'd seen a woman flirt so blatantly. I covered my mouth to stop myself from laughing, but it was too late. A slight chuckle escaped my lips. I turned away, trying to pass it off as a cough.

"Is something funny, Genevieve?" the King asked.

Clara narrowed her eyes at me. A subtle smile crossed her lips as she looked around the table. Everyone had gone quiet, their attention fixed on me. "So what *were* you doing out last night?" she asked loudly, tilting her head as though it were the most innocent of questions.

"You left your suite?" The King turned to me. I slipped my hands under the table, clutching the skirt of my dress to steady them. I'd studied his face at breakfast that morning, wondering if he'd returned to my suite at night, if he'd discovered the mound of pillows beneath the covers. But he seemed so calm, his voice even as he spoke of the day's events.

"No." I shook my head. "I didn't." I turned back to my food, plunging the fork into the dumplings, but Clara continued on.

"I saw you in the east stairwell." She planted her elbows on the table and leaned forward. "You were going downstairs. You were wearing a black sweater. You stopped when I called your name."

The King turned to me. "Is that true?"

"No," I insisted, trying to steady my voice. My throat was suddenly dry, the heat of the day too much, my hair sticking to my face and neck. "It wasn't me. I don't know what she's talking about."

"Oh," Clara said, her voice singsong. "I think you do . . ."

Everyone's eyes were on me. The sun beat down on me, the air stifling and still. The King was studying my face, his expression dark. It had been worth it, even for a few hours with Caleb, but I suddenly wished I hadn't paused in the stairwell, that I had ignored Clara's calls. I offered a slight shrug and turned back to my plate, the words lodged in the back of my throat.

The King leaned over, his hand heavy on my arm. "You are not to be going out," he whispered. "It's for your own safety. I thought that was clear."

"Perfectly," I managed. "I didn't."

The table was silent. Clara opened her mouth to continue, but Charles interrupted her. "Have you seen the fountain outside the conservatory?" he asked, giving me a small smile. "I've been meaning to take you there. If we leave now we can make it for the next show." He glanced across the table at the King. "Do you mind if I steal your daughter for a little while?"

At the suggestion, the King's face relaxed. "No—you two go. Enjoy yourselves."

As they watched us walk away, Reginald turned to Clara, his notepad still in his hand. "Perhaps you saw one of the Palace workers?" he asked.

"I know what I saw," Clara hissed. She looked at Rose, who shook her head slightly, signaling for her to let it go.

I followed Charles through the marketplace, around the wide, sparkling pools, thankful when we were far from the table. He led me across the Palace's marble lobby, where the old gaming machines still stood, shrouded in gray cloths. All the while two soldiers trailed behind us, their steps keeping time with ours, their rifles swinging on their backs. "I'm sorry about that," he said as we stepped into the sun. We crossed a narrow bridge to where a massive fountain spread out toward the sidewalk.

"What are you sorry about?" I asked.

"I have a feeling I had something to do with that." A tuft of thick black hair fell across his forehead. He smiled, combing it back with his fingers.

"Not *everything* has to do with you," I snapped. A cluster of people on the street turned, studying us, the soldiers gesturing for them to stay back.

"I think what you mean is, Thank you, Charles, for rescuing me from that inquisition." He threw his hands up in defense. "I'm just saying. I think maybe—just maybe—Clara has a little bit of a crush on me. At least that's how it's seemed since . . . always."

I looked at him. Charles's face was so sincere, his pale cheeks flushed. I couldn't help but laugh. "Maybe you're right," I admitted. Even if Clara had seen me leave last night, I doubted she cared what I did with my free time. She seemed to take more issue with Charles sitting beside me at meals, or the way he leaned forward when he spoke to me, so there were no more than a few inches between us.

"We grew up together in the City," he added. "The

last ten years we've been the youngest people living in the Palace. Clara is incredibly smart. She's talked about studying at the teaching hospital to be a doctor. Her mother is steering her in a different direction, though." He raised his eyebrows, as if to say, *Toward me.*

"I see." I nodded, thinking of the cold, calculating look Clara had given me when we first met.

People gathered along the rim of the great fountain. I stared at our reflection in the water, two shadows rippling with the wind. Charles didn't take his eyes off me. "So how have you found the City? You don't seem in love with it the way everyone else is."

I thought of Caleb's arm around me last night, how music and smoke had filled the room. Our bodies pressed together in the doorway. I smiled, the heat rising in my cheeks. "It has its advantages."

Charles inched closer to me, his shoulder pressing against mine. "Can you keep a secret?" He studied my face. "My father would have chosen nearly any city over this one. Despite what he told the King, he wasn't convinced until a few years into the restoration that Las Vegas would work. It was my mother who knew this was the right place. Most of the hotels were empty at the time of the plague. The buildings were easily stripped of advertisements. It's so separate from everything else—a haven. She always knew."

"Women's intuition?" I asked, remembering a phrase I'd heard at School.

"Must've been," he said. He stared out over the fountain. A little boy with a plaid cap was kneeling on the stone ledge, peering into the water. "She's been having a hard time without him. She keeps to herself a lot. As bad as this sounds, part of me wants to know what it's like to love someone that much."

I stared at the tiny stones piled up in the bottom of the fountain. I'd thought of saying it to Caleb before, of saying those three specific words—the ones the Teachers had warned us about. I'd decided in the stillness of Maeve's house, the quiet night surrounding me, that I meant those words for Caleb. Nothing was as persistent, as relentless, working its way through me, pulling at every thought.

When I turned, Charles was still looking at me. "Sometimes it's terrifying, though. The idea of being so close to someone." He searched my expression. "Do you know what I mean? Am I making any sense?"

The question hovered in the air between us. I remembered my first days in Califia, how I'd watched the shadowy city over the bridge, imagining what Caleb was doing there, if he'd gotten in contact with the Trail. The nightmares came soon after: Caleb standing by the water, blood running down his leg, turning the entire bay a rancid purple. "I do," I said. "So many things can go wrong."

Charles stared into the water. "See all of those?" he asked, pointing at the pebbles. "They made this into a memorial of sorts. People would bring stones here and throw them into the fountain, one for every loved one they lost in the plague."

He walked over to the shrubs that lined the conservatory building and plucked several tiny rocks from the ground beneath, rubbing the dirt off with his fingers. "Do you want a few?" he asked, offering them to me.

"Just one." I took the smooth brown stone in my hand. It was shaped like an almond—one side slightly wider than the other. I ran my fingers over it, wondering what my mother would've thought if she knew I was standing here, inside the new capital, imprisoned by the man she'd fallen in love with so many years before. I could nearly see her face, smell the mint balm she always smeared on her lips, leaving slippery smudges on my cheeks when she kissed me. I let the pebble slip through my fingers into the water below. It settled at the bottom, disappearing among the others, the surface still rippling in its wake.

We stood in silence for a minute. The wind whipped around us, a fleeting relief from the heat. Two older women approached the edge of the fountain, clutching worn photos in their hands. They watched as others lined up along the stone ledge. "What exactly is everyone waiting for?" I asked.

"You'll see . . . ," Charles said. He checked his watch. "In three . . . two . . . one . . ." Music sounded on the main road. Everyone stepped back. Water burst through the surface of the pool and rocketed toward the sky. It rose and rose and rose, nearly twenty feet in the air. The little boy stood up on the stone ledge and clapped. Charles's face was lit up like a child's. He hooted loudly, throwing his fist in the air, a sight that made even the soldiers laugh.

The wind shifted, blowing the spray at us and soaking the front of my dress. The cold water felt good on my skin. I closed my eyes, the claps and cheers swelling around me, and enjoyed those last few moments away from the Palace.

twenty

CLARA AND I STARTED UP THE LONG SPIRAL ESCALATORS TO the gallery on the second-floor mezzanine. I still hadn't gotten used to the moving metal stairs; I never knew whether to climb them or just stand there, holding the rail and gliding along. Light streamed in from the atrium above us. I took in the ceiling murals and the giant statues of robed women, the towering marble pillars, the horse statue below, leaping in midair, the fountains that shot up from still, turquoise pools. In some horrible way, the Palace was just as Pip had always imagined it—a gleaming model of perfection.

I kept my eyes on the scenery, trying to pretend I was alone. This morning, the King had suggested Clara take me on a tour of the art gallery. He said it would be nice for us to spend time together so I could get to know my cousin. I knew neither statement was true but I obliged, hoping it would make me seem happy with my place in the Palace. Like a girl with no secrets.

"How was your date with Charles?" Clara asked after a long while. The soldier always trailing just a few steps behind us stepped off the escalator.

"It wasn't a date," I said, an edge to my voice. I remembered that term from School; the Teachers had referred to it as part of the courtship period. They told us men sometimes acted like gentleman before revealing their true intentions.

We strode past the low railing. Below us shoppers wandered through the atrium, occasionally glancing up to see where we were headed. Above the gallery's entrance was a massive screen that changed every few seconds. First was an advertisement for the new global marketplace, OPENING THIS WEEK! Then it switched to a picture from yesterday's paper, of me in the back of a car with the caption: PRINCESS GENEVIEVE'S BMW CONVERTIBLE RESTORED BY GERRARD'S MOTORS: PROVIDING CUSTOM

RESTORATION AND DISPLAY OF AUTOMOBILES SINCE 2035.

"You know, you go around acting all annoyed, when you're the Princess of The New America," Clara muttered. "Anyone would kill to be in your position." The way she said it—the emphasis on *kill*—unnerved me.

"When was the last time you were outside these walls?" I asked. "Ten years ago?"

Clara's straw-colored hair was in a braid, which snaked around her head and curled up at the nape of her neck. "What's your point?" She narrowed her gray eyes at me.

"You can't speak to it, to whether or not I have a right to be angry or annoyed. You don't know what the world is like outside your bubble." With that I turned and started through the gallery's main entrance.

Inside, the room was cool, and empty except for a few schoolchildren clustered in the corner, their gray uniforms similar to the ones I'd grown up wearing. For a brief moment, the soldier and Clara were behind me, and I had the grand feeling of being alone. The open space comforted me. The wood floors were solid beneath my feet, the walls covered with familiar friends. I walked over to the Van Gogh painting I'd seen in my art books so many times before, the blue flowers that stretched across the canvas, growing toward the sun. *IRISES*, VINCENT VAN GOGH, a plaque beside it read. RECOVERED FROM THE GETTY MUSEUM, LOS ANGELES.

More paintings hung in a row, Manet and Titian and Cézanne, one after another. I walked beside them, remembering all the time I'd spent on the School lawn, the lake in front of me, dragging brush across canvas to replicate its glassy surface. I was examining the gash in the bottom of a Renoir, its canvas taped together, when Clara came up beside me.

"There are things I do know," she said, her voice tinged with anger. I could tell she had been preparing this speech for the last few minutes. Each word quivered with delight as she spoke. "I know how *unsavory* it is for a woman to be a man's *mistress*." She stared at the two figures in the painting. A man was helping a woman up a grassy incline.

"What are you talking about?" I asked, unable to stop myself.

"You weren't your father's firstborn," she said. "You were his last. I had three cousins before you, and an aunt, all of them lost in the plague." Then she turned, glaring at me. "I don't know what kind of woman would do that— have sex with a married man."

I smiled, trying to ignore the lump that had crept up the back of my throat. "You're mistaken," I managed. Clara just shrugged before she strode past me, toward a still life on the far wall.

My feet were rooted to the ground. I stared at the man in the painting, the hat that cast darkness on his face, the pink bulb of his nose, the way his eyes were painted with two black lines. He seemed to be sneering at me now.

She was his mistress, I thought to myself, my vision blurred by sudden tears. My mother, who had sung to me in the bath, wiping the suds from my eyes. I was five again, kneeling on the floor. She was sick. I saw the broken light underneath the bedroom door, her shadow moving as she rapped her knuckles against the wood, tapping out her kisses, because she couldn't risk pressing her lips to my skin. I had held my palm to the other side, keeping it there even after she went back to bed, her coughs breaking the night's silence.

I turned toward the door, the tears threatening to overtake me. I kept walking, past the irises and Manet's bullfight, the animal spearing the horse with its great and terrible horns.

"Your Royal Highness?" I heard the soldier ask, his

footsteps behind me. "Would you like to be escorted upstairs now?"

I kept ahead of him, barely listening as he ushered Clara out after me, toward the elevator. No matter what Clara said, I knew it wasn't my mother's fault, it couldn't have been, the woman who loved me so sweetly, who'd squeezed my toes one by one as she counted them, singing a silly song in my ear. Blowing on my soup to cool it before I even took one spoonful. *He* was the one who had had the other family.

I stepped inside the elevator. Clara came after me, making the car feel smaller and claustrophobic, the air stale and hot.

"Is everything all right, Princess?" the soldier asked as he pressed the button. I clasped my hands together, trying to steady them. I could only think of the King, that story he'd told me, the photo he'd held in his hands. He'd never said anything about his family. He'd taken so long to come for me, left me alone in that house. I spent so many days listening to her choked coughs, terrified when the room was silent for too long. She'd never felt further away than she did now, my only connection to her broken. "Princess?" The soldier repeated. He rested his hand on my shoulder, startling me. "What's wrong?"

"Nothing," I said, pressing the button for the bottom floor again. "I just need to speak with the King."

twenty-one

THE KING WAS AT A CONSTRUCTION SITE, WORKING ON A building at the edge of the City center. When he couldn't be reached, I demanded to be taken to him.

The car zipped down the empty street, past the massive City buildings. The fountains beside the Palace rocketed up into the air, spraying passersby with a fine mist. The view didn't hold any wonder for me now. I thought only of the smug smile on Clara's face as she told me about the affair. All those days at School, even the loneliest ones when I'd just arrived, I'd always had those memories of my mother. They'd stayed with me on the road, in the dugout, in the back of Fletcher's truck, even after the chaos of the cellar. But now everything was corrupted by Clara's words.

We turned right up a long driveway, toward a giant green building with a gold lion in front. The soldiers escorted me out of the car. Above the entrance was another giant billboard, like the one in the mall, flashing different announcements. A picture of two lions came up, the words THE GRAND ZOO: OPENING NEXT MONTH! beneath it. "This way," one of the soldiers said, leading me inside.

Three soldiers stood at the entrance to the main lobby. The giant room was sweltering, the air smelling of sweat and smoke. Spotlights illuminated different sections of the dark corridor. A few yards ahead, a boy was kneeling over a bucket. He was a year or two younger than me, his bare back dripping with sweat as he worked, smoothing wet plaster over the wall. He looked up, his face thin and sad. "He should be over here," the other soldier said, picking up his pace, his hand coming down around my arm as he ushered me quickly toward another hall.

I turned back, noticing two boys my age who were stapling down carpet. An older worker, maybe twenty, walked slowly down the corridor, carrying a giant wooden crate. When he passed one of the spotlights I made out his face, gaunt and sickly, his eyes sunk back into his skull.

His shoulder bore the same tattoo as Caleb's. Somewhere above us a terrible drilling sound split the air.

"Where is he?" I said, my voice flat. I walked faster, with purpose, thinking of all the boys in the dugout.

The soldiers strode in front of me, toward a glowing blue light. They glanced at one another, their faces uncertain, unsure if they should've brought me here or not. "Genevieve," a voice called out. Two figures appeared at the end of the hallway, silhouetted by the light. "What are you doing here?"

"I needed to speak with you," I said. The King was standing with Charles, who looked momentarily happy, his smile disappearing when he saw my face. I pushed past them, into the wide room. An eerie light filled the space. The walls were all glass, forming several enclosures with plants and giant, fake rocks.

"Would you give us a minute?" the King said finally. The men's footsteps receded down the hall. He stepped beside me, facing a tank filled with yellow grass. High above, a mountain lion lay out on a flat rock, its ribs jutting out of its side.

"She told me," I said, not turning to meet his gaze. "Clara told me about your wife. She said my mother was your mistress." My entire body felt hot. "Is that true?"

The King turned back to the corridor, where Charles and the soldiers had left. "This isn't the best time to talk about this," he said. "You shouldn't have come here."

"There will never be a good time to talk about it." I stared at him. "You didn't want me to come here because you don't want me—or anyone—to see how all of your projects are built."

His face flushed and his eyes went dark. He rubbed at his forehead, as if trying to calm himself. "I understand you're angry," he said. "Clara shouldn't have said anything. It was not her place."

He turned and walked the length of the room, his arms crossed over his chest. "I don't like that word—*mistress*. I know how it sounds and it wasn't the case. When I met your mother I was separated from my wife." He paused in front of a glass case titled GRAY WOLVES. Two giant dogs were tearing at red meat. Another gnawed at a broken bone.

"So she was your mistress," I said, unable to control my voice. "And you brought me here, telling me how you'd been looking for me for so long, how broken up you were without your daughter, and you just happened to leave out that you had a whole other family?"

The King cleared his throat. "I am sorry," he said,

laboring over each word, "that I didn't tell you about my other children. But it's not something I like to speak about. I'm more concerned with the future, just like everyone else in this City. We're all trying to move on."

The softness in his voice startled me, pulling me out of my own head and into his. I wondered how they had died, if their noses had bled like my mother's, if they had been together, as a family, or been separated in the hospitals. I wondered if he had held them, despite the warnings not to, if he had been the one to mash up their food and press it against their dry tongues.

"What were their names?" I finally asked. I had to know, just wanted to picture them, if only for a moment. I had siblings—at one point, if not now. The thought filled me with a strange sadness. "How old were they?"

He turned back to me. He had pulled a handkerchief from his pocket and was twisting it around his fingers, turning them pink. "Samantha was the oldest. She was eleven when she died. Paul went first—he was eight. And then Jackson, my little guy." A faint smile appeared and then was gone. "He wasn't even five years old."

I remembered the plate I'd prepared in the kitchen. How I'd sat leaning against her bedroom door, devouring the last of those mushy pink beans, comforted by her intermittent coughs. Before she had retreated to her room she had shown me how to open the cans, her hand around mine as we squeezed the metal gadget. They had been in a row, one for each day, over twenty cans long. *Only open one can*, she'd said, as she moved around the house, locking all the doors. *No more than one each day.*

"I'm sorry," I said softly. We stood side by side, and for that minute, in the stillness of that room, he was not the King. I was not the Princess, taken against her will to the City. We were two people trying to forget.

He rubbed his forehead with his hand. "I really loved your mother. And I was going to get a divorce. That was always the plan," he said. "But things were complicated between us. We were living different lives, in different cities. I never even knew she was pregnant. And then later, when the plague happened, it changed everything. I couldn't have left Sacramento even if I had wanted to. There was no way for me to help her. Everyone was just surviving."

"Did your wife know about her?" I asked, feeling sick even as the question left my mouth. "Did you ever tell her, or was my mother a secret?"

"I was planning on a divorce," he repeated. "I was just

waiting for the right time."

I turned and walked past him, starting down a tunnel with a glass enclosure on one side. There, just thirty feet away, was a grizzly bear like the one I'd seen in the wild. It lay there, seeming half alive, its head resting on a plastic rock.

"The only two people who can understand a relationship are the two people in it," he said from somewhere behind me. His shoes clacked against the broken stone floor. "You can't know what that time was like."

"I know that you lied," I said. "You lied to everyone." I stared at our reflections in the glass, the way our noses both slanted a little to the left, our cream-colored skin, the curtains of black lashes that fanned out over our eyes. We stood there, the two of us side by side, looking through ourselves into the small enclosure.

"I was happy when I was with your mother," he continued. I wasn't quite sure if he was speaking to me or not. He gazed up at the massive animal, his voice clear of anger. "It's hard for me to look at that picture, to see myself then. I was happier than I'd ever been in my life. She always seemed like she was vibrating at a different frequency altogether. She was nearly thirty when I met her. It was right after she'd taken a hiatus from painting."

I turned to look at him. "I never knew she was a painter," I said. Our house had slowly faded from memory. I could see only snippets of it—the old grandfather clock that sat in the hall, the beaten gold weights that hung inside it, making its hands move. The glow-in-the-dark stars on my bedroom ceiling, the stain on our couch from where she'd spilled tea. I couldn't remember even a single paintbrush, no canvases or art on the walls. "I learned at School."

"I know," he said, not elaborating on how. A smile crossed his lips, and he let out a small laugh. "I was with your mother on my fortieth birthday. She had planned this whole day. We went hiking along the beach, and she brought this miniature chocolate cake she'd made for me. She carried it the whole time, nearly four miles, just so we could eat it up there, overlooking the ocean. And she sang this silly song to me, this—"

"*Today, today*," I sang, unable to stop myself from smiling, "*is a very special day, today is somebody's birthday.*" I nodded my head, remembering how my mother used to hold my hands while we sang and danced in the living room, sidestepping around the coffee table and armchairs.

I wanted to hate him, tried to remember all the things

he had done, tried to picture Arden and Ruby and Pip in that brick building. He was the reason Caleb was in the Outlands, why we couldn't be together. But right then, we shared something that no one else in the world could: my mother. All her quirks, her silly songs, the way her hair smelled like lavender shampoo. He was the only other person who knew.

We walked silently through the corridor. Then he turned to me, leaning down so our eyes met. "I loved your mother. However complicated our situation was, however wrong it probably seems. I loved her. And our relationship gave me you." He shook his head, his fingers pressing against his temple. "That morning I went to your School, I was excited. I had the same feeling I'd had the day my other children were born. And when we arrived and the Headmistress told us what had happened, that you had left, I immediately ordered the troops to find you. You can think whatever you want, but you're my daughter—the only family I have left. I hated the idea of you out there, in the wild, alone."

I looked at his face, tense with worry. Then he stepped toward me, bringing me into a hug. For once, I didn't pull away. It was inescapable, irresistible, even after all he'd done. I saw myself every time he held his fingers to his chin when he was thinking, or smiled with his mouth closed. We argued the same way, our words short and even, had the same pale complexion, his hair was once the same dark reddish-brown hair as mine—though his was now peppered with gray. He was part of me, the connection undeniable, no matter how much I fought against it.

"Come now," the King said after a long while. "Let's get you back to the Palace." He led me through the long corridor, past enclosures filled with other creatures discovered in the wild—pythons, alligators, a tiger who had escaped from a zoo. We left through a side exit. The sun stung my eyes. Sweat beaded on my skin. A million thoughts rushed into my head as we walked toward the waiting car. But then I stopped, my feet rooted to the ground, the strangeness of the scene revealing itself to me.

Outside the front entrance, a few soldiers had gathered, their guns resting by their sides. They were all looking up at the electronic billboard perched high above the lobby entrance. There, in massive letters, were the words: AN ENEMY OF THE STATE HAS BEEN SPOTTED INSIDE THE CITY. HAVE YOU SEEN THIS MAN? IF SO, ALERT THE AUTHOR-ITIES IMMEDIATELY.

And below them, a drawing of a face so familiar, it was like looking at my own. Caleb was staring back at me.

His height, weight, and build were listed. Descriptions of the scars on his leg and cheek.

I felt as though all the blood had drained from my body. The King's hand was on my arm, urging me toward the car. "Genevieve," he said under his breath, his eyes fixed on the soldiers in front of the building. "This is not the time. We can discuss this in the Palace." I barely heard him as I read the last line on the billboard over and over again.

HE IS WANTED FOR THE MURDER OF TWO NEW AMERICAN SOLDIERS.

twenty-two

"I'M NOT FEELING WELL," I SAID, PULLING THE THICK COVERS around me. The sun had gone down. The upper floors of the Palace were quiet and dark. Beatrice sat at the end of the bed, her hand resting on the mound of my foot. "Will you bring me something to eat? I'm going to sleep but you can leave it by the door." I looked away before adding, "Please don't let anyone disturb me tonight, no matter what."

Beatrice combed my hair, running her fingers over my forehead. "Of course. You've had a very long day." I squeezed my eyes shut. I kept seeing Caleb's face on that billboard, hearing the soldiers muttering about the traitor who had killed one of their own, about what they would give to witness the execution. They knew he was inside the City walls. I needed to tell him not to come, that it was too dangerous, but there was no way to reach him. He was already moving through the Outlands, snaking down the empty streets to meet me.

"What's troubling you?" Beatrice whispered. She took my hand in hers, cradling it. "You can tell me."

I looked up at her kind, round face. *I can't*, I thought, knowing how much danger Caleb was already in. They were probably scouring the Outlands for him. "I'm just sick," I said, trying to smile. "That's all."

Beatrice kissed the top of my head. "Well, then I better get to it," she said, standing to go. Then she leaned over, looked directly at me, and pressed her warm palm against my cheek. "I will make sure no one disturbs you. You have my word." She remained there for a moment. Her brown eyes were alert, serious, like I'd never seen them before. *I know what you're doing*, she seemed to say, never taking her eyes off mine. *And I'll do whatever I can to help you.*

She stood and went into the hall. I kept staring at the door. It didn't shut all the way, and she didn't pull it closed and check the knob like she usually did. Instead it rested lightly on the frame, wood against lock, just slightly ajar.

I moved quickly. I'd hidden the uniform in the toilet tank, letting the plastic bag float on top of the water. I pressed the bathroom door closed and dressed as fast as I could, donning the wrinkled white shirt, the red vest, the black pants. Then I retreated into the hallway, down the east staircase, taking off my shoes so as not to make any sound.

It was still before curfew. The streets were just thinning out. I disappeared into the clusters of workers changing shifts, my stomach churning as I glanced over my shoulder to see if anyone was following me.

People strolled across the overpass, walking arm in arm as they made their way back to their apartment buildings. A Jeep came down the street, two soldiers hanging out of the truck's bed, scanning the sidewalks. I kept my head down, turning right to cross the main road, toward the building Caleb had marked. It was called the Venetian, an old hotel that had been converted into office buildings. A few restaurants had been opened, the gardens had been replanted, and the wide canals were filled with water once more. As I made my way over the arched bridge, a boat glided past, carrying the last of the day's passengers.

I was a few steps from the main entrance when I turned, noticing a figure standing on the dock. She was much shorter than me but wore the same uniform, her curly brown hair pulled away from her face. "Are you waiting for a gondola, Miss?" she asked softly, stepping under an overhang and into the shadows. She paused, waiting for me to respond.

I glanced down at the map, at the X Caleb had scribbled right by the dock, and nodded. I followed her to the edge of the water. "You should take off your vest, Eve," she whispered. As the light reflected off the water I caught glimpses of her delicate hands, the old cameo brooch she wore around her neck. "It'll look odd if one of the workers is out on the water. But keep your hat pulled down over your eyes."

I took off the vest and handed it to her just as a narrow boat glided past us. Caleb was standing on the stern, wearing a black shirt and white hat that shielded his face. I scanned the crowd leaving the garden, looking for soldiers. "Last ride of the night," he called out. He steered the boat with a long wooden oar, pausing at the dock so I could get in. Then he pushed off, into the open water, as the last few people meandered out of the Venetian's gardens.

I sat facing him, our eyes meeting as he paddled into

the center of the canal, away from where anyone could hear us. We drifted on the clear water, the Venetian's tower lit up behind us. It was a long while before either of us spoke. "They know you're here," I said. "We shouldn't be doing this. It's too dangerous now. What if someone followed me?"

Caleb scanned the bridge. "They didn't follow you," he said softly.

My hands were trembling. I tried not to look at him as I spoke. Instead I leaned back against the seat, letting it steady me. "The King might suspect something. Clara saw me leave the other night. Yesterday at the market-place, she said something in front of him." I looked at him, pleadingly. "I can't see you again, Caleb. They can't touch me—I'm his daughter. But you'll be killed if we're caught. Your picture is all over the City."

Caleb dipped the oar in the water, his muscles strain-ing with the effort. The lights danced on the surface of the canal as we glided toward the bridge. "What if I'm killed tomorrow?" he said, pressing his lips together. "What does it matter then? I'm *alive* here, today. I've been to the construction sites and talked to the people in the Outlands. Slowly, they're starting to see there's another way. We're talking about a rebellion. Moss needs me." He smiled, that smile that I loved, a dimple appearing in his right cheek. "And I like to think you do, too."

"I want you here," I said. "Of course I do."

"Then this is where I want to be." Caleb turned the oar in the water, steering us. "I can't sit around doing nothing. I already gave you up once before—I won't do it again."

He was silent for a long while. "Do you know Italy?" he finally asked. I nodded, remembering the country I'd read about in our art history books, where so many masters—Michelangelo, Leonardo da Vinci, Caravaggio—were born.

"I read once that Venice was the most romantic city in the world. That instead of streets there were waterways. That people played violins and danced in the main square, and boats brought them from place to place. I know I can never take you there, but we have this."

I stared at the golden tower above us, at the glassy canal, at the ornate arches beneath the bridge. The night was quiet. I could only hear the palms rustling in the wind, the boat slicing through the still water.

Caleb stepped down off the stern and came toward me, careful not to throw the boat off balance. "We're here now, together. Let's make the most of it."

He kept his eyes on me as the boat drifted under the bridge, into darkness. He pressed the oar into the water to slow us. Then he was right there in front of me, his face barely visible as his nose brushed against my cheek, his breath hot on my skin. I leaned my forehead against his. "I'm just scared. I don't want to lose you again."

"You won't," he said, taking off my cap. His hand found its way to the base of my neck, his fingers twisting in my hair. I let him hold me, my head resting in his palm. He dragged his fingertips along my spine, massaging my back through my shirt. Then my lips were on his neck, working against the soft muscles until they found their way to his mouth.

His hand stopped at my waist. He tugged gently at the bottom of the uniform shirt, as if asking me a question. He'd never touched me before, not like that, his fingers right against my skin. It was exactly what the Teachers had warned about in all their lessons, of the men who constantly tested your defenses, bulldozing one, then moving on to the next. They all wanted the same thing— to use you until you were all used up.

I'd spent so many years preparing for this moment, just so I could steel myself against it. But it didn't feel like that. Not now—not with Caleb. He was asking for permission, his face mirroring all the nervousness I felt. *I want to be closer to you*, he seemed to say, as he bit down on his bottom lip. *Will you let me?*

I climbed onto the bench beside him, wrapping my arms around his neck, our tangled bodies hidden beneath the bridge. His head fell back as I kissed him, the warmth of his tongue spurring me on. I nodded yes, guiding his fingers to my waist as he untucked my shirt. His cold hands pressed against my stomach, the touch stealing the breath from my body.

The boat floated on in the cool, dark tunnel. Water lapped at the bottom of the stone bridge. His hands wandered over my back as he pulled me closer to him, pressing his chest to mine. I rested my chin on his shoulder. He was saying something, each word muffled. I couldn't make it out until his mouth was right next to my ear, his lips tickling my skin. "I don't care what happens, Eve," he repeated. "This isn't something I can just walk away from. Not this time. I won't."

I stared at him, our noses nearly touching. I brought my hands to his face, wishing the City was deserted, that there were no soldiers patrolling the City center, no footsteps above us on the bridge, that we could drift into the open canal, his arms wrapped around me. "I know," I whispered, kissing him softly as we glided toward the end of the tunnel. "Nothing matters more than this."

I settled back down in my seat. He took his position on the stern, the five feet between us seeming so much further now. I pulled my cap back on as the light hit me. Slowly, the gondola drifted out of the dark, the oar dipping below the still surface of the canal.

"Can we go to the tunnels?" I asked, when we were far enough away from the bridge that no one could hear us. "I want to see where you've been spending your time, who all these people are."

Two soldiers strode by, their guns slung across their backs. Caleb pulled his cap down over his eyes. He grabbed the oar, pushing us farther out into the water. We were both quiet until they passed. "We can go there tonight," he said softly. "Meet me in the gardens after we dock. But first I have to tell you something." He rested his knee on the narrow bench in front of him, studying me. He smiled, his eyes so bright they looked like they were lit from within.

The boat pulled up beside the stone stairs. Caleb glanced at the cluster of people still lingering by the edge of the bridge, enjoying the last thirty minutes before curfew.

"I've fallen in love with you," he whispered, kneeling to kiss the top of my hand. He stayed there for a moment, smiling up at me, before helping me from the boat.

I started up the stone steps, every inch of me humming with a new energy. I wanted to scream it then—*I love you I love you I love you*—to grab his hand and run away from the Palace, these people, that bridge.

"Good night, Miss," he said loudly, as though I were any other stranger. "I hope you enjoyed your evening."

The woman who had greeted me was still standing beneath the overhang. I walked toward her, but not before turning back, my eyes wet. "I love you, too," I mouthed. It didn't seem stupid, or foolish, or wrong. I'd said something I'd always known, the admission sending me into the happiest, irreversible free fall.

His face broke into a smile. He studied me, not taking his eyes off mine, as he pushed off the dock and glided away.

twenty-three

IT TOOK NEARLY A HALF HOUR TO REACH THE AIRPLANE hangar. Caleb cut across the Outlands, through old neighborhoods waiting to be restored, the houses sitting with windows broken, sand piled up in their doorways. I trailed thirty feet behind him, keeping my head down, disappearing in the clusters of people rushing home to make curfew.

As I walked I replayed that moment: his eyes looking up at me, the whispered words only I could hear. I carried it inside me now, nestled somewhere inside my heart, a small, silent thing that we alone shared.

Finally the land opened up before us. Rusted, abandoned

planes sat on the pavement. Metal carts were strewn everywhere, some empty and bent, others piled with suitcases and crumpled, sun-scorched clothing. A metal sign above the building read McCARRAN AIRPORT.

Caleb hooked a right. I followed him across the sandy parking lot, turning back every now and then to check for soldiers. The airport was empty. A few faded playing cards blew past, somersaulting in the wind. He disappeared into a long stone building and I followed behind, waiting a few minutes before going in.

Inside, the shadowy planes towered above me, AMERICAN AIRLINES printed on their sides in red and blue letters. I'd only seen planes in children's books before, had heard the Teachers reference the flights that went from one coast to the other. "*Pssst*," Caleb's voice called out from the darkness. He was hiding behind a short metal staircase on wheels. I went to him. Keeping close to the wall, we started toward the back of the hangar, his arm around my shoulder.

"So this is where you come every day . . . ," I said, looking up at the massive planes, over a hundred and fifty feet long. Their metal wings were lined with rust, the white paint bubbling up in places.

"Some days. The construction is on hold now, but a

week ago there were nearly fifty people here each morning." We walked toward a door on the back wall. "Citizens come from all across the Outlands to take shifts, on top of the work they're expected to do in the City center. The regime has been running demolition a half mile east of here. During the day it's so loud you can barely hear yourself think, but it covers up the drilling or hammering sounds."

Caleb knocked five times on the door. A man with a full beard stuck his head out, a red bandana tied around his head. Sweat soaked the front of his T-shirt. "Aren't you supposed to have a hot date tonight?" he asked. Then he noticed me standing behind Caleb and a smile curled on his lips. "Ahhhhh . . . you must be the lovely Eve!" He made a big spectacle of bowing, dropping one hand to the floor.

"What a welcome," I said, bowing back. He hadn't called me Genevieve, and I immediately loved him for it.

"This is Harper," Caleb said. "He's been overseeing the dig while I've been at other sites."

Harper opened the door just enough for us to squeeze in. Lanterns lit the small room. Two others, a man and a woman in their thirties, stood at a table, hovering over a large sheet of paper. They looked up when I came in, their eyes cold.

"I haven't been outside since one o'clock," Harper went on. He was a shorter man with a gut that hung over his belt, his gray T-shirt two sizes too small. "Can you see the stars tonight? The moon?" His light gray eyes darted from Caleb to me.

"I didn't look up," I said, a little apologetically. I'd been too focused on keeping my eyes hidden, the cap pulled down over my forehead.

Harper wiped the sweat from his brow. "She didn't look up!" he teased. "The one thing that's hard about this City is the lights. Makes it difficult to see the constellations. You can get a good view from the Outlands though."

"Harper can tell direction by the stars. That's how he got to the City originally," Caleb put in. He rested his hand on my back as he spoke, his thumb grazing my spine. "What's that thing you always say, old man?"

Harper threw his head back and laughed. "Old man yourself," he grumbled, landing his fist into Caleb's arm. Then he looked at me, pointing at the ceiling for emphasis. "There are millions of stars, each one shining and burning out at the same time. They die like everything else—you have to appreciate them before they're gone."

"I won't forget," I said.

The wide office was empty except for the table and a stack of boxes. A hole nearly three feet across gaped open in the floor. I stood there, waiting for the other two to speak, but they were still perched over the paper, their faces half-lit by the lanterns. "No progress with the collapse?" Caleb asked them.

The man was tall and thin with cracked glasses. He wore the same uniform shirt as I did, except the sleeves had been ripped off. He shook his head. "I told you, I'm not discussing this in front of her."

Caleb opened his mouth to say something but I interrupted. "I have a name," I said, surprised at the sound of my own voice. The man kept his eyes on the paper, studying sketches of different buildings throughout the City, notes scribbled next to them in blue ink.

"We are all well aware," the woman said, glaring at me. Her blond hair was rolled into thin dreadlocks, her pants spotted with mud. "You're Princess Genevieve."

"That's not fair," Caleb jumped in. "I told you, you can trust her. She's no more the King's family than I am." My stomach tensed as I remembered this afternoon. I hadn't pulled away when he'd hugged me, had felt close to him when we'd spoken of my mother. A sinking part of me wondered if maybe I *was* guilty of something.

The couple returned to the sketches. "Give 'em time," Harper whispered, patting Caleb on the back. Then he looked at me. "If Caleb says I can trust you, then I trust you. I don't need any more proof."

"I appreciate that," Caleb said, grasping Harper's arm. "Harper was the one who started building the tunnels out of the City. He realized we could use the flood channels as a starting point. Parts of them have collapsed or are too unstable, mostly from all the King's demolitions. We're constantly digging through rubble, or finding parts of them blocked off. We've nearly gotten under the wall on this one, but then we hit a whole section that had collapsed."

Harper hiked up his belt. "It's too dense to dig through. We need to figure out an alternate route through the flood channels. Without maps of the drainage system we're just feeling our way in the dark."

"This is the entrance to the first tunnel," Caleb said, gesturing to the hole. Behind us, the couple hovered over their work. "We try to keep the hangar the way it was when we found it, just in case any troops come through. The rubble is taken out at the end of the night, a little at a time, and then the construction starts again the next evening—or at least it used to."

"Where are the other two tunnels being built?" I asked. "Who's working on those?" The man and woman raised their heads at the sound of my voice.

"Please don't answer that," the man said, his voice flat. He smoothed down the paper with both hands.

Every muscle in my body tensed. "You know I was an orphan," I said. "Up until a few days ago, I believed both my parents were dead. I'm not some spy. I have friends who are still locked up in those Schools—"

"You sat in that parade, didn't you?" the man with the cracked glasses interrupted. I could see my shadow in his lenses, a black figure against orange lantern light. "Were you not on that stage, in front of all the City's residents, that stupid grin on your face? Tell me that wasn't you."

Caleb stepped forward, raising his hand to shield me from the man's accusations. "Enough, Curtis. We're not going into this again, not now."

But I ducked under his arm, unable to stop myself. "You don't know me," I said, trying to keep my voice steady. I leveled my finger at his face. "Have you been in the Schools? Please, since you seem to know so much, tell me what it's like there." The man stepped back, but his eyes were still locked on mine, refusing to look away.

We could have stayed like that for hours, staring each

other down, but Caleb took my arm, pulling me away. "Let's get out of here," he whispered. He gave Harper a little half salute, and then we were back in the hangar, the door clicking shut behind us. "I shouldn't have brought you here. Curtis and Jo have been good to me since I've arrived—they were the ones who found me a place to stay, who backed me when the others were unsure about letting me lead the digs. They're not usually like that. They've just seen what can happen to dissidents who are discovered."

"I hate the way they looked at me," I muttered. We moved through the silent warehouse, under the rusted bellies of planes.

When we reached the door Caleb stopped, resting his palm on the side of my face. "I know," he said, pressing his forehead to mine. "I'm sorry. They may never completely trust you. But I do—that's what matters."

We stayed there for a moment, his breath warming my skin, his thumb grazing my cheek. "I know" was all I could manage. The tears were hot in my eyes. Here we were, miles from the dugout, from Califia, and there was still no place for us. We were bouncing between worlds, he in mine, I in his, but we'd never be able to truly be together in either one.

Caleb looked down at his watch, its glass face split in two. "You can take the second street parallel to the main strip. Turn through the old Hawaiian marketplace to get back. It's empty at this time of night." He looked into my eyes. "Don't worry, Eve," he added. "Please don't worry about them. I'll see you tomorrow night."

I pressed my lips to his, feeling his fingertips against my skin. I held them there, wanting the awful, uneasy feeling to subside, wishing we could be back on the dock, those three words floating between us. "Tomorrow night," I repeated as Caleb slipped another folded map into my pocket. He kissed me good-bye— my fingers, my hands, my cheeks and brow. I stayed there for just a moment. The rest of the world seemed far away.

But when I started across the City, alone but for the sound of my footsteps, Curtis and Jo's words returned. I found myself arguing my case to an imaginary room, explaining away my place in the Palace—something even I wasn't completely certain of. It wasn't until I passed the wide fountain, its surface glassy and still, that I thought of Charles. I saw his face in the conservatory that after-noon as he pointed to the glass dome, describing all his plans for the restoration.

I ran up the stairwell, taking the steps two at a time, ignoring the burning in my legs. Fifty flights went by quickly, my body energized by the sudden thought. Finally, there was something I could do.

twenty-four

"THE BUILDINGS THAT ARE TO BE RESTORED ARE FIRST determined by your father," Charles said, spreading the photos over the table. "We tour the place, take measurements, see what kind of shape it's in. Then I go through all the information I've recovered from before the plague—floor plans, blueprints, photos—to learn about the building's original condition, decide what can be restored and what we want to do away with."

I nodded, my eyes darting to the long drawers on the other side of the room. The suite on the thirtieth floor had been converted into Charles's office. The bed and dressers had been replaced with wide cabinets, and the desk sat in front of a glass wall overlooking the main strip. A long wooden table was set up with models, miniature versions of some of the sites I'd seen in the City center: the domed conservatory, the Venetian's gardens, and the Grand's zoo. A smaller room held more models, some piled one on top of another. I'd asked him for a tour of his office at breakfast that morning. Charles's face had brightened. The King had urged us to go, even though our plates sat on the table, the food still hot.

I picked up another photo of the roller coaster and arcade in the old New York, New York compound. "It's fascinating," I offered. The worn snapshot showed people strapped into the car, screaming, their cheeks blown back by the wind. It *was* fascinating to see the world as it once was, so many years before. But it was impossible to look at it without thinking of how we got here, now—of the boys in the dugout or the scars that crisscrossed the top of Leif's back.

"I'm relieved to hear you say that," Charles said. "I could talk about this for hours. Sometimes I worry I'm boring you."

I let out a low laugh, remembering one of Teacher Fran's sayings. "Only boring people get bored," I said softly. I turned a photo over in my hands, trying to decipher the smudged writing on the back. When I glanced up, Charles was looking at me. "The Teachers used to say that." I shrugged. "It's silly, I know."

"The Teachers," he said. "Right. I just realized we've never talked about your School."

"If you don't have anything nice to say, don't say anything at all," I added, pointing the photograph at him. "That was another thing they used to say." I looked through the doorway behind him. This one room contained so many documents—papers piled high in corners, blueprints of most of the buildings in the City center. There had to be more information here, something that would be useful to Caleb—I just had to find it.

"But you were the valedictorian." He plucked the photo from my grasp and set it down. I suddenly felt awkward, exposed even, now that I had nothing to do with my hands. "You must've enjoyed it somewhat."

"I did while I was there," I said, knowing I couldn't tell him the truth right now. About how our Teachers had twisted our lessons. About my friends who were still trapped inside. I walked over to his desk, pretending to look at a baseball resting on a stack of loose-leaf notebooks. Every surface was covered with maps. Scribbled notes were taped to the window.

"You like my paperweight?" he gestured at it. "You can still see the grass stains if you look closely. It's one of the few things I have from when I was a kid."

I held it for a moment, studying the faded red stitching that was coming undone in places. "Where did you grow up?"

He opened his hands, signaling for me to throw it to him. "A city in Northern California. There were government transports during the migration, trucks that made the trip here week after week. It took us nearly two days with stops. Everyone had to be cleared by a doctor beforehand."

I tossed it across the room in a slow arc. I thought of the quarantine wing at School, how lonely those first weeks were. The Teachers would only speak to us through a window in the door. I was so young, but I still remembered how I'd check myself every morning, searching my skin for any sign of the bruises symptomatic of the plague.

"They gave us these masks to cover our mouths," Charles went on. "I remember being fifteen and looking around at all these faceless people, most of them traveling to the City alone. It was surreal." He threw it back to me.

"What was the City like in those first years?" I turned the ball over, rubbing at the grass stain with my thumb.

"Depressing," he said. "Still so run down. People had come from all over. Some of them literally walked for weeks, risking their lives to get here. It wasn't the glimmering place they'd imagined. At least not then."

He walked over to the cabinets on the other side of the room. I followed behind, thankful when he opened one of the wide, flat drawers, exposing all the papers inside. "Those first few years we were here, all I saw was possibility. I knew I wanted to do what my father did, to work with him one day. The City center changed, building by building. You could feel the sadness lifting as people settled in, as the City began to look more like the world before. Obviously, it's still a work in progress. We're still putting the life back into it with restaurants and entertainment. But I've been tossing around some other ideas . . ."

Each drawer was labeled. A few read OUTLANDS with different directions beside it—northeast, southeast, northwest, southwest. Others were named after old hotels: two drawers each for the Venetian, Mirage, Cosmopolitan, and Grand. "When they started construction, they turned every lawn and golf course in the City into usable gardens. Which we needed, yes," Charles said, riffling through a stack of papers in the drawer. "But the public doesn't have access to those. We have clean water now, the ability to sustain plants. I wanted to create outdoor space for everyone." He spread a sheet of paper down on the table.

I stared at the wide expanse of green, broken in places by winding pathways. Trees were drawn in intricate detail, their limbs spread out over ponds and rock gardens. The giant lake in the center was surrounded by three stone buildings. I ran my fingers over the light pencil marks. It was as good a drawing as any of the ones I'd made in School. "You sketched this?"

"Don't be so surprised." Charles laughed. "It'll be four hundred acres if it's ever built. The largest park inside the City's walls."

Every tree and flower was carefully drawn. Boats floated along a pond. Red and yellow blooms were clustered around the shore. One of the buildings was labeled RECREATION CENTER; another, NATURAL HISTORY MUSEUM. A third had a patio and chairs. "A library," I said, unable to stop from smiling. "There's none in the City?"

"We restored one off the main road, but it's small and always overcrowded. This would be four stories, with a view of the water. It's just a matter of sorting all the recovered books. There's a whole building full of them just three blocks east." Charles pointed to the room behind him. "I have the model somewhere—would you like to see?"

He stared at me, his blue eyes wide. He looked like one of the dolls on Lilac's bed in Califia, with his square jaw and strong features, his mop of black hair perfectly in place. I knew he was objectively handsome. It was clear from the way Clara stole glimpses at him, or how clusters of women whispered when he passed. But every time I saw him I was reminded of my father, of the City walls that rose up around us, locking us in. "I'd love to," I said.

As soon as he disappeared into the cramped room, I walked over to the cabinets, running my finger down the labels on each drawer. The first one contained papers from the old hotels. The next had blueprints from a hospital building, another from the two schools that had been restored inside the City. There were ones marked for something called Planet Hollywood. I knelt down, studying the last few drawers. Charles shuffled around in the other room, searching through the stacked models, his footsteps quickening my pulse.

"Where *is* it?" I whispered, reading the labels. Three of the lower drawers were marked EMERGENCY PLANS. I pulled the first open and started flipping through its contents, papers showing the gates in the walls, inventories of the warehouses in the Outlands—medical supplies, bottled water, canned goods. None of them showed the flood tunnels.

Charles's footsteps stopped for a moment, then started again, growing louder as he came toward the door. I pulled the last drawer open. I didn't have time to think, simply rolled the whole stack of papers up as tightly as I could and squeezed them down the side of my boot. I slid the drawer shut and stood just as Charles came back into the room.

"This," he said, setting the model down on the table, "should give you the full idea."

I wiped at my forehead, hoping he didn't notice the thin layer of sweat that had settled on my skin. The miniature version of the park took up half the table, the buildings crafted out of thin pieces of wood. Blue paint had hardened to form the still ponds. A green, moss-like fuzz covered the ground. Charles kept looking at me, then at the model, as if waiting for some kind of approval.

"It's great, it really is," I said, trying to keep my voice even. But with the plans tucked away, I just wanted to be alone again.

"There's more," he added, pointing over his shoulder, at the side room. "I used to build these with my father. I can show you the others—"

"That's all right," I said quickly, stepping away. "I should really get back."

Charles's face changed, his smile suddenly gone. He looked stricken. "Right. Some other time then," he said, taking a deep breath. His eyes searched mine, looking desperately for something more.

"Another day," I finally offered, giving in to the lingering guilt. I tried to remind myself that he worked for my father. That we'd only spent a few hours together—if that—and that he probably had his own motivations for seeking out my company. "I promise."

I started out the door, leaving him there, his face half lit by the sun streaming through the blinds. A soldier waited for me in the hallway. He followed me into the elevator and up to the top floors of the Palace.

When I was alone in my suite I sat down on the floor

and pulled off my boots. As I sorted through the thin sheets, any guilt I felt about deceiving Charles disappeared. There, just ten papers into the stack, were sketches of tunnels. LAS VEGAS DRAINAGE SYSTEM typed across the top in beautiful, perfect print.

twenty-five

"YOU DIDN'T HAVE TO DO THIS," CALEB SAID WHEN WE reached the top of the motel stairs. He grabbed my hand, pulling me to him, his arms wrapped around my shoulders. "But I'm glad you did."

The faint sounds of music drifted from a room at the end of the corridor. We'd traveled through the Outlands to Harper's apartment, looking for Jo and Curtis. Now we stood on the upper landing of the run-down motel. Faded plastic chips were strewn everywhere. Broken chairs covered the patio. A man bathed his small son in the half-empty hot tub below, using an old juice carton to rinse the soap from his hair.

Caleb led me through the corridor. We stayed close to the wall, hidden below the awning. A few lights were on in the other rooms, visible through windows covered with tarps and ripped sheets. Caleb knocked five times on the last door in the hall, the same way he had at the hangar. Harper was inside, his hearty laugh breaking the silence.

"You two again." Harper grinned, opening the door. He wore a long blue robe, a tight gray tank top visible just underneath it. "What are you doing out here?" He ushered us in, checking to make sure no one had seen. The room was crammed with worn mattresses and stacks of the City's newspapers. Curtis and Jo were sitting on warped wooden boxes, drinking from a jug of amber liquid. Curtis set the jug down when he saw me. His eyes were tiny black specks behind his thick glasses.

"I have a present for you," I said, unable to stop from smiling. I kneeled down and unzipped my boot, handing the roll of papers to him.

Jo helped Curtis spread them out on the floor. "Are these what I think they are?" she asked, flipping through the pages.

"Where did you find them?" Curtis pulled one from the bottom of the stack, tracing his fingers over the sketches. He glanced sideways at Jo, his face breaking into a smile. He covered his mouth as if trying to hide it. "I don't believe this."

"I think what you mean to say is 'Thank you,'" I corrected. Harper let out a little laugh and winked at me in approval.

"That's where the collapse is," Jo whispered, pointing to a spot on the map. She moved her finger across to the other side. "We need to access this tunnel to the east. All this time we've been thinking we should keep digging north."

A pot was boiling on a hot plate next to the refrigerator, the steam filling the air with a strong, spicy scent. Harper moved around the makeshift kitchen, taking another jug and emptying it into glasses for Caleb and me. "You did good," he whispered, handing me one.

"Eve stole them from Charles Harris's office," Caleb added, as if that provided some greater understanding.

Even Jo laughed. "*The* Charles Harris? The King's Head of Development?"

I nodded, taking a sip of the drink. It tasted similar to the beer they made in Califia. "I brought them to you as soon as I could." I stared at Curtis, waiting for him to respond—to say thank you, to apologize, anything—but he kept his eyes on the papers, studying the new route. It was a long while before he even looked up.

We were all watching him. He glanced around the room and shrugged. "You're the King's daughter," he said, adjusting his glasses on his nose. "What do you expect?"

Jo looked up at me, her eyes rimmed with thick black eyeliner. "We made a mistake." She glanced sideways at Curtis. "It's hard to know who to trust. We just lost some of our own because of leaked information."

Harper sat down beside me, wrapping his arm around my shoulder. "That's their code for 'sorry,'" he whispered. He took another swig of his drink.

"With the new plans, it can't be more than a week off," Caleb offered. He kneeled down beside Curtis and traced the distance to the wall. "I've already alerted Moss to let him know that construction will move forward tomorrow. He's contacting the Trail."

"I can get thirty workers by the afternoon," Jo said, looking at her watch. Her blond dreadlocks were tied back with a strip of red fabric. "I'll get the contacts coming off the night shifts."

"Curtis, I'll trust you to run construction while I'm at the other site tomorrow morning," Caleb added. Curtis rolled up the papers and tucked them in his knapsack. He nodded, his eyes moving from Caleb to me.

"Which means," Harper said, jumping up from the mattress, "instead of commiserating, we should be celebrating." He went over to a stereo on the dresser and popped in a disc like the ones I'd seen at School. The room filled with low music, a silly song with a man speaking the lyrics. *He did the mash*, it played. *He did the Monster Mash. The Monster Mash. It was a graveyard smash!*

Caleb laughed. "What is this, Harper?" he asked.

Harper kicked a few crumpled shirts out of the way to clear a dance floor. "This is the only CD I have that works. Halloween songs or not, it's still music."

Harper spun around, his beer sloshing in the glass as he pulled Jo along in his wake. She sidestepped some crumpled newspapers, laughing the whole way. I sat on the mattress, watching as Caleb joined in, halfheartedly shaking his hips, to Harper's delight. "Woohoo!" Harper yelled. "Atta boy!"

It took me a moment to realize Curtis had sat down beside me. "I doubted you," he said, so low I could barely hear it over the music. "We've been working on that tunnel for the last three months and because of you, we just might finish." He offered his hand. "You're one of us now."

I took it in my own. "I always was," I said. "The King may be my father, but I've been in the wild, the Schools. I know what he's done."

The music filled the small room. Curtis was quiet for a moment, considering what I'd said. "It just takes me a long time to trust someone. Most people in the Outlands don't even know my real name."

"Enough of your yapping!" Harper interrupted us. He grabbed my arm, pulling me up from the floor. He twirled me once, quickly, his limbs loose from all the beer. "Let's enjoy ourselves for one night. Come on, Curtis—on your feet, man! Otherwise I'll do it—I will," he threatened, grabbing the straps of his robe, ready to open it.

Curtis held up his hands in surrender. He joined in, shuffling awkwardly around the cramped room. Caleb took my hand, spun me around, and dipped me so fast my stomach felt light. His green eyes met mine, our faces just inches apart as we stayed there for a second, listening to the silly chorus.

He leaned in, his lips brushing against my ear. "Do you want to go?" he asked.

He smiled at me, the same smile I'd seen so many times before. I loved every part of him. The smell of his skin, the scar on his cheek, the feel of his fingers pressing into my back. The way he could tell what I was thinking just by looking at me.

"Yes," I said finally, my skin hot beneath his hand. "I thought you'd never ask."

twenty-six

CALEB'S HANDS WERE COVERING MY EYES, HIS PALMS SWEATY against my skin. I held onto his wrists, loving the way his arms felt around me, his feet on either side of mine, his steps guiding me forward. We were inside, that much I could tell, but I didn't know where. "Now?" I asked, trying to keep my voice low. "Not yet," he whispered in my ear. I shuffled along in darkness.

Soon, he stopped, turning me to the right. Then he dropped his hands. "All right," he whispered, resting his chin on my shoulder. "Now you can look."

I opened my eyes. We were in another airplane hangar, much bigger than the one where the tunnel entrance was hidden. Airplanes sat in rows, some large, some smaller, all lit up by the moonlight streaming in through the hangar's windows. "This is where you've been living?" I asked, looking at the plane above us.

He grabbed a metal staircase and dragged it over, its rusted wheels squeaking and groaning with each turn. "Harper found it for me—he thinks I'll be safer here. It's on the other side of the airport from where we were yesterday." He gestured at the steps. "After you."

I started up the metal stairs, dwarfed by the plane. It was so much bigger when you stood right beside it, with wings ten people could lie across. I remembered the day we'd read about a plane crash in *Lord of the Flies*. Teacher Agnes had told us about the planes that flew over oceans and continents, how crashes were rare but deadly. We'd made her tell us everything—about the "flight attendants" who rolled carts down the aisles, serving drinks and miniature meals, about the televisions nestled in the back of each seat. That afternoon Pip and I had lain on the grass, staring up at the sky, wondering what it was like to touch the clouds.

Caleb opened an oval door marked EMERGENCY EXIT, pulling it out and up with both hands. Seats were lined up, row after row after row, stretching all the way back to the plane's tail. The plastic shades were drawn. Lanterns were perched on trays in the seat backs, giving the whole place a warm glow.

"I've never seen the inside of one of these," I said, following Caleb down the front rows. The seats were wider. Two were folded down like beds, musty blankets piled on top of them. A knapsack full of clothes and some old newspapers sat on the chair beside it. The top one had the picture of me from the parade, PRINCESS GENEVIEVE GREETS CITIZENS written below it.

"Look at all this room!" I spun around with my arms out and still didn't touch anything.

Caleb pushed past me, to the front of the airplane, landing a kiss on my forehead as he did. "Where would you like to fly to? France? Spain?" He grabbed my hand, leading me into the front cabin, which was covered in metal panels and a thousand tiny dials.

"Italy," I said, putting my fingers over his, as he moved a control in the front seat. "Venice."

"Ahhh . . . you want a *real* gondola ride." He laughed. He slid a tab over our heads, then another, pretending he was preparing the plane for takeoff.

I picked up one of the headsets and covered my ears. I turned a switch on our right, then another, as I settled into one of the chairs. "Fasten your seatbelt," Caleb said. He pulled the buckle around my waist, one hand resting on my hip.

He leaned forward and gripped the controls, pretending to fly. We gazed out the front window, scanning the dark hangar as though it held the most spectacular view. "We'll have to stop over in London first," he said, his voice booming in the small metal room. "See Big Ben. Then maybe Spain—then Venice."

I pointed at the ground below. "Everything is so tiny from up here." I leaned over him to get a better look at the imaginary world below. "The Stratosphere tower is an inch tall . . ."

"Look," Caleb said, pointing out the side window. "You can see over the mountains." He rested his hand on my leg and smiled.

"We're finally on our way." The plane was lifting off, my body sinking into the soft cushiony seat, and the City was growing smaller, the buildings shrinking until they vanished in the distance. We were drifting up, over the clouds, the sun beaming down on us.

After a long while, Caleb leaned in and brushed the hair away from my temple, kissing my forehead. He unbuckled my seat belt and stood, pulling me out of my seat, his hands on my hips. He was smiling to himself, his eyes bright in the lantern light, as if he knew something I didn't.

I took off the headset. "What is it?" I asked, trying to meet his gaze.

"Moss granted me leave from the City," he said. "As soon as the first tunnel is completed, he told me I can go. He thinks it's too dangerous to stay, to be leading the digs. They're narrowing their search. I'll return if he needs me."

My hands trembled. "So you're going to leave?" I asked, my voice thin with nerves.

"*We're* going to leave." He stroked the side of my cheek. "If you'll come with me. I want to go east, away from the City. It'll be a risk, but it's a risk everywhere. We'd be on the run again, which isn't what either of us want, but please, at least consider it."

I didn't hesitate. "Of course." I brought my hands to his face, watching the lantern light on his skin. "It's not even a question."

He pressed our bodies into one, his hands moving over my back, my shoulders, my waist, pulling me closer and closer to him. "I promise you we'll figure it out— we'll figure out some way to live." He breathed into my neck. "This feels right to me. It's everything else that's screwed up."

"So things begin now," I said. "I'm here. I'm with you. And in a week we'll leave. It's as simple as that."

Caleb lifted me up, letting my back rest against the metal wall. I wrapped my legs around his waist. He pressed his mouth to mine, his hands in my hair. My lips touched his, then found their way to the soft skin of his neck. His hands slipped down my sides, ran over my vest, and settled on my bottom ribs.

He carried me into the cabin. Every inch of me was awake, my cheeks flushed, my pulse alive in my fingers and toes. I couldn't stop touching him. My fingers ran down the knots of his spine, lingering on each one, a tiny knot below the surface of his skin. The plane was silent and still, his hands cradling my neck as we lay down on the makeshift bed, just big enough to fit us both. He pulled off his shirt and threw it on the floor. I ran my fingertips over his chest, watching goose bumps appear under my touch. He let out a small laugh. I circled over his ribs, then down to the square muscles of his stomach, watching his lips twist as my fingers moved.

"My turn," he finally whispered, reaching for the buttons on my vest. He popped them open one by one.

Then his hands moved quickly, pulling it from my shoulders and starting in on the crisp white uniform shirt. He didn't stop until each button had been undone, the fabric pulled back, exposing the black bra I'd found in my closet the first day I'd arrived. The folded map was still inside.

He kissed me, unable to stop smiling. My head rested in the crook of his arm, his cheek next to mine as I watched his hand move over my body. His fingertips touched down on my skin, the heat spreading out beneath them as they ran along my stomach, circling my belly button. He traced a line up the center of my ribs to the hard, flat space between my breasts. Then he brushed his hand over each one. He curled his fingers, his knuckles dragging across the soft flesh that spilled over my bra.

That was all it took. Our mouths pressed together, his breath hot in my ear, his whispered words barely audible. *I love you, I love you, I love you.* He kissed me again, his lips hard against mine as I clung to him. His hands were all over me, his body shifting on top of mine. Then the air went out of my lungs, and the world fell away.

The walls went first, then the seats. The floor dropped out from under us, the lanterns disappeared. The voices from School were silenced. I couldn't smell the musty cushions. We were suspended in time, his hands holding my sides, my legs wrapped around his, pulling him into me as we kissed.

twenty-seven

THE POUNDING WOKE US. THE PLANE WAS SO DARK THAT I couldn't see Caleb beside me. I could only hear him and feel his hands searching around my feet for his crumpled shirt. We'd only been asleep for a few minutes. We'd only just drifted off. "Who is it?" I asked, panic rising in my chest.

"I don't know," Caleb whispered. "Quick—we can go out the back exit." He reached around until he found my hand. The warmth of it comforted me.

We felt for our clothing on the floor. The pounding continued, each knock jolting my entire body. "Come on, man!" I heard Harper yell. He was jimmying the emergency door, trying to pull it out. "It's me. You don't have much time!"

Caleb yanked his hand from mine. The cushion gave beside me and he was up, his bare feet padding down the aisle. The door finally opened, throwing a long square of light into the cabin.

"I knew it," Harper spat. I pulled the blanket around me, ducking out of the light, scrambling to find my clothes. "I should've come earlier. I knew something was wrong when you didn't show at the hangar. It's nearly eight thirty. She's got to get out of here." I could only see his finger pointing into the depths of the plane. I pulled on my pants and socks and fastened my bra behind my back. I slipped my feet into the black boots, buttoning my shirt as I started toward the door.

Eight thirty. Beatrice must have already entered my room to wake me, was probably stalling now as the maids set up for breakfast. In less than half an hour the King would stride into the dining hall and sit down at the massive chair at the end of the banquet table. The meal always started at nine o'clock, not a minute later. Always.

"I'm going," I said, my throat dry. I ducked out the door, squeezing Caleb's arm in good-bye. "I'll just leave the way I came." Harper was wringing his hands together.

I darted down the metal staircase, fumbling around in my pockets, looking for the folded map.

"Wait!" Caleb called after me. He pulled his shoe on as he ran, hopping part of the way. "You can't go on those roads. There could be checkpoints set up. I'll take you." He reached out his hand for me to hold.

"You shouldn't." I shook my head as we started toward the door of the hangar. We ran under plane after plane, our footsteps echoing off the concrete floor. "There's more at risk for you. I don't want you getting involved in this."

But he followed anyway, striding behind me as I pushed out the door and into the blinding light. He reached for my arm, pulling me back. His eyes met mine for a brief second. "I can't let you go alone," he pleaded. He plucked the map from my hands and tore it in half. "Please just follow behind me. Stay a few yards back."

Then he was off, darting through the Outlands, the decrepit buildings spitting out the City's first shift of workers. The morning was colder than usual, the wind kicking up dust and garbage. A foil bag drifted past, DORITOS printed on its side. I kept my head down to blend in with everyone else. We were all moving toward the City center, wearing identical red vests, a quickness to our steps. We moved past another old hotel and an office building with burned-out windows. A row of houses was boarded up, the walls cracked, sand piled on the window-sills. In less than ten minutes we reached the City limit, and Caleb turned down a street lined with thin trees. I followed, the paved road hard beneath my feet.

As we got closer to the Palace the crowd thinned out. It was harder to avoid being noticed. A woman strode past with two small children. The little girl pointed at my face. "It's the Princess, Mom," she said, staring at me over her shoulder as I passed.

I kept walking, the wind pushing my hair away from my face. I was thankful when I heard her mother's frustrated *Shhhhhh*. "Enough, Lizzie," she chided. "Stop saying silly things."

Ten minutes passed, then twenty. Right now the King was sitting down at the table, staring at the empty seat beside him, his fork clinking nervously against the edge of his plate. Maybe he was searching my room. Beatrice would tell them I'd been there when she'd left me the night prior, and she wouldn't be lying—I had. I had stayed in bed until she was down the hall, in her own room, her door shut. I could make up a story. Needing a drink in the middle of the night, feeling claustrophobic in that suite. Maybe the door lock had broken, letting me out. But whatever happened, whatever story I chose, one thing was certain: From now on it would be nearly impossible to leave the Palace.

We were getting closer. Caleb walked confidently, unhurried, both hands in his pockets. He looked over his shoulder occasionally to make sure I was still there. We passed a baseball field I remembered from my walk home from the hangar. *We can't be far now*, I told myself, quickening my steps.

We started through an old parking lot and down a narrow road. The monorail flew by above our heads, the well-dressed citizens sitting comfortably in the train's wide cars. The wind was relentless, the sun hidden behind a flat gray blanket of cloud. As we crept along the old Flamingo hotel the intersection opened up before us to reveal a small patch of the main road. *One more block*, I thought, watching Caleb edge toward the corner, where the narrow street emptied out beside the Palace's front fountain. He would turn right and I would take the overpass to the other side of the road, blending in with the workers in the Palace mall.

When he was steps from the corner he kneeled down, pretending to tie his shoe. He looked at me, his mouth turned up in a half smile, his green eyes bright. We had made it. I didn't know when I would see him again, or how, but we would find a way. I touched the rim of my cap, a barely perceptible salute.

Then he stood. He took his last few steps, turning right on the main road to loop back toward the Outlands. I climbed up the overpass stairs, keeping my head down to avoid being seen. It took me a second to hear the soldiers' loud voices, to see the crowd that had assembled by the Palace's front entrance, workers and patrons alike, all trying to get inside. The troops had closed the building, blocking off the street just north and just south of it. We were trapped.

I froze on the overpass, watching Caleb's panicked face as he approached the Palace. He darted behind some workers, then turned, trying to go back the way we came, down the narrow street. It was too late. A soldier at the end of the checkpoint was already stepping out of line, his eyes fixed on the stranger in the wrinkled pants and partially untucked shirt—the only one who had come toward the Palace, then turned away.

I didn't think. I just ran. I pushed through the crowded overpass and down the stairs, darting across the street. Caleb was walking quickly in the opposite direction, his head down, trying to disappear into the crowd. The soldier was nearly on him. Then he reached out and grabbed Caleb's collar, yanking him back.

"It's him!" he called out to the others.

I pumped my arms as fast as I could, not stopping until I was right behind him. I jumped on the soldier's back, trying to pull him down, to give Caleb just a few seconds—a chance—but my body was too light to do damage.

Another soldier grabbed me from behind. "I've got the Princess," he called, and then we were in the center of all of them, soldiers swarming around us, one taking hold of my hands, another my legs.

"Caleb!" I yelled, straining to see through the men moving frantically around me. "Where are you?"

I twisted my wrists, trying to free myself, but the restraints were too tight. They dragged me back toward the Palace entrance, through the low row of shrubs, past the fountains and winged, marble statues. The last thing I saw was a soldier's baton, the black rod rising above the feverish crowd, then landing, with a terrible thud, on Caleb's back.

twenty-eight

"SO. CLARA WAS RIGHT THEN. SHE DID SEE YOU LEAVING THE
Palace that night," the King began. I didn't respond. He
paced the length of his office, his hands behind his back.
"How long have you been sneaking around like this, lying
to me, to all of us?"

As I was dragged into the Palace mall, he had been right
there waiting for me. He ordered the men to let me go so
they didn't scare the employees stuck inside the stores. A
woman in the restored jewelry shop peeked out from behind
a glass case of necklaces, watching them untie my hands,
my father keeping a firm grip on my arm. "Genevieve," he
said, his voice flat. "I asked you a question."

"I don't know," I managed. I rubbed at my wrists, the skin still red from where they had tightened the restraints. I kept seeing Caleb's body on the ground. The troops surrounding him. One soldier had turned away from the pack and spat on the side of the road. *Wish I could shoot him myself.*

The King snorted. "You don't know. Well, you're going to have to figure it out. You could've been kidnapped, held for ransom—do you have any idea how dangerous that was? There are people in this City who want me dead, who believe I'm ruining this country. You're lucky you weren't killed."

I stared out the window. I couldn't see the City. Beyond the glass the world was all sky, a gray expanse that stretched on forever. "Where is he?" I asked. "Where are they taking him?"

"That's not your business anymore," the King said. "I want to know how you got out, where you were last night, what you were doing, and who you were with. I want the names of the people who helped you. You have to understand, he was just using you to get to me."

"You have it wrong." I shook my head. I stared into the carpet, at the neat, vacuumed lines crushed by footprints. "You don't know him. You have no idea what you're talking about."

At this he exploded, his face turning a deep pink. "Do not tell *me* what *I* know," he yelled. "That boy has been living in the wild for years now, with no respect for the law. Do you know that these aren't the first soldiers he's attacked? When he escaped the labor camps he nearly killed one of the guards."

"I don't believe that," I said.

"You have to understand, Genevieve. People who live outside the regime have been perpetuating the chaos. We are trying to build, and they are trying to destroy."

"Build at what cost?" I asked, unable to stand it anymore. I twisted the cap in my hands, bending the brim until it nearly folded in half. "Isn't that always the question? When will you be satisfied? When every person in this country is under your control? My friends have given their lives. Arden and Pip and Ruby are still in there." The King turned away at the mention of their names.

The silence swelled around us. I stared at his back, the answer becoming clear before I even asked the question. "You aren't going to let them go, are you? You were never going to." He still wouldn't look at me.

He took measured breaths, each one slow, drawn out, keeping horrible time. "I can't," he said finally. "I can't make an exception for them. So many young women have given their service. It wouldn't be right."

"You made an exception for me," I tried.

He shook his head. "You are my *daughter*."

I felt like I was choking. I remembered Pip's face as she curled up beside me, her cheek pressed against my pillow. The lights had already gone out at School. Ruby was asleep. We stayed there, our hands clasped together, moonlight streaming in from the window. *Promise me as soon as we get to the City we'll find a dress store*. She pinched her collar, the same starched white nightgown everyone else wore. *I hope I never see another one of these again*.

"By blood," I muttered now. "I'm your daughter by blood. I don't belong here, in this place. Not with you."

Finally, he met my gaze. Something in his face changed. His eyes were small and calculating, looking at me as if it were the first time. "Where do you belong then? With him?"

I nodded, tears threatening to spill down my cheeks.

The King rubbed his temple, letting out a small, sad laugh. "That *cannot* happen. People expect you to be with someone like Charles—not some escapee from the labor camps. Charles is the type of man you're supposed to marry."

"Who are you to say what I'm supposed to do? Who I'm supposed to be with?" I shot back. "You've known me for less than a week. Where were you when I was alone in that house with my mother, when I was listening to her die?"

"I told you," the King said, an edge to his voice. "I would've been there if I could have."

"Right," I said. "And you would've told your wife about her—it just wasn't the right time. And you'll get to restoring the Outlands, to giving the workers proper housing, just as soon as you put up zoos and museums and amusement parks and restore the three colonies in the east."

The King held up his hand to silence me. "That is quite enough. Whatever they told you, Genevieve, whatever they said about me—they have an agenda that you cannot begin to know. They want to turn you against me."

"It isn't like that." I shook my head, hating how the certainty in his voice created so much doubt in mine. "Caleb would've died in that labor camp if he hadn't escaped. You don't know him."

"I don't need to," the King said, stalking toward me. "I know enough. Now, I'm going to ask you one more time. I need to know if he was working with anyone, if you heard anything about any plans to attack the Palace. Did anyone threaten you?"

I fixed Caleb's words in my mind, all the things he'd said that first night below ground, when he'd told me of the dissidents who'd been tortured. "He wasn't working with anyone," I said quietly, wishing the King would look away. "He was only in the City because of me."

"How'd you get out of your suite?" he asked. "Did Beatrice help you?"

"No—she had no idea," I said, my palms pressed together. "I figured out the code. A door in the east stairwell was unlocked. I stole the uniform from an apartment in the Outlands." I thought of the airplane sitting abandoned in the hangar, the blankets crumpled, the lanterns dark. They would change the code now, have soldiers stationed at my door. The Palace would be impossible to leave. This would've been unbearable, had Caleb still been in the Outlands. Had I any reason left to escape.

"Whatever he told you, Genevieve, whatever he said—he is using you. There are hundreds of dissidents in the City. Some of them are working with Strays on the outside. It's possible he knew you were my daughter before you did."

"You don't know anything about us." I stepped back, hating how easily all the warnings from School returned, filling my head, coloring everything past and present. Caleb had had that picture of me when we met. He'd stayed with me by the river, helping me hide, even though the troops were close behind us. It wasn't true, I knew it couldn't be, but the accusations hung in the air.

"You're no longer associated with him," the King said. "There is no 'us.' You are the Princess of The New America. It's bad enough citizens saw you apprehended outside the Palace the same time he was. He's committed a crime against the state."

"I told you, he didn't do it," I said. "He can't be punished for this."

"Two soldiers were killed at a government checkpoint. Someone has to be held responsible," the King said, his voice flat.

"I could explain what happened, how it was in self-defense."

"These laws exist for a reason—anyone who threatens one New American threatens all." He looked at me. "You can't defend him, Genevieve. You are not to speak to anyone about this."

"The people don't have to know," I tried. "You could

release him. What does it matter to you if he's outside the City? Everyone will believe he's dead."

The King paced the length of the room. I saw his momentary hesitation, the way his brows knitted together, his fingers working at the side of his face. I was still wearing the uniform, the same shirt Caleb had unbuttoned, the vest he'd pulled from my shoulders. I could still feel his hands running over my skin. Nothing had mattered in that moment—the rest of the world so far away, the Teachers' warnings losing all meaning.

Now, the rest of my life presented itself to me, an endless succession of days in the Palace, of nights alone in my own bed. The only thing that had carried me through in Califia was the possibility of finding Caleb, of being together again, in some future time and place. "You can't kill him," I said, my hands clammy and cold.

The King started toward the door. "I can't discuss this anymore," he said. He reached for the keypad beside it.

I raced in front of him, my hands on the doorframe. "Don't do this." I kept picturing Caleb in some awful room, a soldier striking him with a metal baton. They wouldn't stop until his face—the face I loved so much— was swollen and bloody. Until his body went horribly still. "You said we were family. That's what you said. If you care about me at all you won't do this."

The King pried my fingers from the doorframe and held them in his own. "He'll be tried tomorrow. With the Lieutenant's testimony it will all be over in three days. I will let you know when it's done." He leaned down to meet my gaze. His voice was soft, his hands squeezing mine, as if this small, pathetic offer were some sort of consolation.

The door opened. He stepped into the quiet hall and said something to the soldier stationed outside. The words seemed far away, somewhere beyond me. I was trapped in my own head, the memories of the morning returning to me. The darkness of the plane, Caleb's back as we walked through the City. The wind kicking up dust and sand, coating everything with a thin layer of grime.

It's over, I thought, the smell of his skin still clinging to my clothes. In three days, Caleb would be dead.

twenty-nine

THE STILLNESS OF THE SUITE WAS INTOLERABLE. LATE THAT night, I sat on the edge of the bed, the minutes passing slowly. The moonlight cast strange shapes on the floor, menacing black shadows that hovered around me, my only company. There was no more pretending. A soldier stood outside my door now. Caleb was somewhere beyond the City center, sitting in some cell, both of us waiting, each hour bringing us closer to the end.

Footsteps echoed in the hall. The knock on the door raised the fine hairs on my arms. The King came in, flicking the lights on, the brightness stinging my eyes. "They said you wanted to talk, Genevieve." He sat down in the armchair in the corner, his hands folded together, his chin resting on his knuckles as he watched me. "Did you think about what I said? It's a matter of safety—yours and mine."

"I did," I replied. Outside, the sky was flecked with stars. The sun had disappeared hours before, slipping behind the mountains. I picked at the thin skin around my fingernails, wondering if I could actually say it out loud. If I had the courage to make it real. "I can't let you punish Caleb for something he didn't do. I did it. I told you—I was the one who shot those soldiers."

The King shook his head. "I'm not having this conversation again. I won't—"

"You said I'm supposed to be with someone like Charles, that there are expectations for me as the Princess. But I can't spend another day here knowing Caleb is dead. That he was punished for something I did." My voice cracked as I said it. The soldiers were everywhere now, some wandering the hallways, others stationed beside my door. There was no way out. I took a deep breath, thinking of what would happen to Caleb after the Lieutenant testified, if he'd be tortured, how he'd be killed. "I'll marry Charles if that's what you want—if that's what you think I'm *supposed* to do. But you have to let Caleb go."

The King stared at me. "It's not just what I want—it's what the City wants. It's what makes sense. You would be happy with him. I know you would."

"So you'll agree to it?"

The King let out a long, rattling breath. "I know you can't see it now, but this will be the best for everyone. Charles is a good man, has been so loyal and—"

"Tell me you won't hurt him." My throat was tight. I couldn't listen to any more about Charles, as if marrying him would suddenly open up something inside me, a riptide of feeling, threatening everything I'd ever known. As if love were a choice.

The King stood and came toward me. He rested his hand on my shoulder. "I'll have the soldiers release him beyond the walls. But from now on, there will be no more talk of this boy. You'll pursue a future with Charles."

I nodded, knowing that tomorrow it would all feel much heavier. But right now, sitting in my suite, it was bearable. Caleb would go free. There was possibility in that—hope, even. So long as Caleb was alive, there was always hope. "I want to say good-bye," I said. "Just one last time. Will you take me to him?"

The King stared out the window, beyond the City. I closed my eyes, listening to the air coming through the vents, waiting for him to respond. All I could see was Caleb's face. Last night we lay awake, his head resting against my heart. The plane was silent. *I almost have it*, he'd said, his eyes half-closed. *One more time.* I slipped my hand beneath the blanket, pressing my finger into his back and dragging it along his skin, spelling the letters out one by one, slower than before. When I was finished he looked up, his nose practically touching mine, a smile curling on his lips. *I know*, he'd said, burying his face into my neck. *I love you, too.*

When I opened my eyes, the King was still standing there. He turned away from the window. Without saying a word he opened the door, his hand up, gesturing for us to go.

—+—

THE PRISON, A MASSIVE COMPLEX SURROUNDED BY A BRICK wall, was a ten-minute drive from the City center. Two of the seven watchtowers were in use, the guards stationed high above the ground, their rifles at the ready. They'd shown me into a concrete room with a table and chairs bolted to the floor. The King stood outside with a guard, both of them watching me. I sat there, my fingers rapping nervously on the metal.

A minute passed. Maybe two. Memories piled on top of one another—moments between us—the feel of the horse beneath us as we hurdled over the ravine, the dank, earthy smell of the dugout on our skin. He'd grabbed my hand that night as we walked through the cool corridor, the warmth of it sending a fiery charge up my arm. It spread out in my chest, shot down my legs, awakening feeling in every inch of me, electrifying even my toes. Until then I'd been half-alive, his touch the only thing that could wake me from that sleep.

A guard led Caleb inside. They'd ruined his face. A bloody gash stretched from his right brow to his hairline, splitting his skin. His cheek was pink and swollen. He was hunched over, still in the same wrinkled shirt he'd put on that morning, buttoned all wrong, blood dried black around the collar.

"Who did this?" I asked, barely able to get the words out. I pulled him close, hating that they hadn't untied his hands, that he couldn't touch my face or thread his fingers through my hair.

"All of them," he said, his words slow. He rested

his chin on my shoulder. I ran my hand along his back, wincing as I felt the welts where the baton had landed. I touched each one, wishing we could go back to the night before, wishing we could undo everything that had happened since we awoke.

"They told me they're releasing me outside the walls," he continued. "That I can't come within five hundred miles of the City again. What did you say to them?"

The King was just outside the door, his profile visible in the tiny window. I looked down at the concrete. "I'm sorry," I whispered. "It was the only way I could get them to let you go."

Caleb lowered his head. "Eve—tell me. What did you say?" he asked, his face screwed up with worry.

I leaned in, my arms wrapped around his sides. "I said I would marry Charles Harris," I whispered. "That if they let you go I would . . ." I trailed off, my throat tight. Standing by the fountain that day, Charles had appeared harmless, sweet even. The moment had been a welcome respite from the Palace. But now every word he'd spoken seemed steeped in ulterior motives. I wondered how many conversations he'd had with the King—if he always knew we were both speeding inevitably toward this, a future that bound us together.

Caleb shook his head no. "You can't, Eve," he said. "You can't."

"We don't have any other options," I said. The guard's eyes were on me, his stare boring into my skin.

Caleb leaned down, trying to meet my gaze. "We can find some way. Once you marry him there is no more you and me—there's no more us. You can't."

"I don't want this either," I said, my voice threatening to break. "But what other choice do we have?"

"I just need more time." His voice was pleading, desperate. "There has to be a way."

The King rapped twice on the door. "Time's up," the guard called. He stepped forward, glancing outside at my father. I leaned in, trying to pull Caleb to me one last time, holding the back of his head to bring his chin to my shoulder. I kissed his cheek, felt the tender skin around the gash, let my fingers stroke his temple.

"You have to stay away from here. Promise me you will," I said, my eyes watering. I knew that if he had any chance he'd use the tunnels to come find me. "We can't do this again."

The guard approached him, yanking his arm. Caleb leaned in, his lips right against my ear. He spoke so low I could barely make out what he said. "You're not the only one in the paper, Eve."

I looked at him, trying to decipher the meaning behind his words, but the guard was already taking him away. As he dragged him by the arm, Caleb shuffled backward, trying to keep his balance, his eyes searching my face for understanding.

thirty

CHARLES RESTED HIS HAND ON MY BACK. I COULD FEEL HIS fingers trembling through my thin satin dress. "Do you mind?" he asked, his voice tentative. He'd been like that for days, wanting to know if he could sit beside me, if I'd like to walk with him through the new Parisian storefronts or tour the upper floors of the Palace mall. It made me dislike him even more, his constantly asking permission, as if we were pursuing a real relationship. All of it would be tolerable if we didn't bother pretending to one another, if we could just say the truth out loud: I'd never be with him by choice.

"If you have to," I whispered, turning to the small

crowd who'd gathered around us. The restaurant was in the Eiffel Tower, a nearly five-hundred-foot replica of the Paris original, with lush red carpets and one wall of glass windows that overlooked the main road. A select few sat at tables covered in white linens, cutting into tender pink steaks. A few men sucked on cigars. The white smoke hung around us, making it seem as if I were seeing everything through a heavy veil.

Charles took my hand. He had the ring in his palm, the diamond catching the light. I hadn't eaten all day. My stomach seized thinking of the endlessness of it, the weeks that would drag on as the previous one had, the obligatory exchange of polite conversation passed back and forth between us. It wasn't his fault—part of me knew that—but I hated Charles for going along with it. He'd sat with me every evening at dinner, offering stories about life before the plague, how he'd spent summers on the beach by his parents' house, letting the waves carry him to shore. He told me of his latest project in the City. He never mentioned Caleb or our impending engagement, as if ignoring it would undo the facts. No matter what was said, no matter how much he tried, we were just two strangers sitting across from each other, on an awful collision course.

It had been eight days. The King took me back to the prison to show me Caleb's empty cell. He'd pointed to the exact spot on the map where Caleb had been let go, an abandoned town just north of Califia called Ashland. I'd pored over the pictures they'd taken of the release—the only proof I had that it had been done. Caleb was already halfway into the woods, a knapsack on his back, his face turned in profile. He wore the same blue shirt he'd had on the last time I'd seen him. I recognized the stains on the collar.

His words still haunted me. I had looked at the paper every day, waiting to hear that something had happened outside the City's walls, that Caleb had been spotted somewhere, despite the public "report" of his execution. But every day it was the same inane nonsense. They speculated about my growing relationship with Charles, if a proposal was imminent. People wrote in, saying where we'd been seen inside the City. I spent nights alone in my room, staring up at the ceiling, tears rolling down and pooling. In little more than a week my life had been drained of everything real.

The King rapped his fork against his glass, the clinking splitting the air. Clara stood across the room with Rose, her face ashen. She'd avoided me since Charles and

I had been announced as a couple. I only saw her at the obligatory social events—dinners and cocktail receptions in the City. Her eyes seemed permanently bloodshot. She spoke softly and always excused herself early. I'd heard that her mother was now pushing her toward the Head of Finance, a man in his forties who constantly spit into his handkerchief. Whenever I was certain there couldn't be anyone in the Palace as miserable as I was, I thought of Clara.

Charles reached for my hand, waiting until I rested my palm in his. Then he cleared his throat, the sound filling the quiet room. "Some of you may have noticed that things have been different for me lately. That I've been happier since Genevieve arrived in the Palace. Now that we've been spending more time together I can't imagine being without her." He kneeled down in front of me, his eyes focused on mine. "I know we'll be happy together—I'm certain of it." As he spoke, the rest of the crowd disappeared. He was only talking to me, saying all the things unsaid between us. *I'm sorry it had to happen like this.* He squeezed my hand, his lips still moving as he went on about when he saw me for the first time, about the afternoon by the fountain, how he had loved the sound of my laugh, the way I'd just stood there, not caring that the water soaked my gown. *But I'm still glad it happened.*

"All I really need now is for her to say yes." He let out an awkward laugh and held the ring up for people to see. I saw Clara out of the corner of my eye. She was hurrying toward the exit, squeezing through the crowd, trying to hide her face with her hand. "Will you marry me?"

The room was silent, waiting for my reply. "Yes," I said quietly, barely able to hear my own words. "I will, yes."

The King clapped. The others joined in. Then everyone surrounded us, their hands patting me on the back and grabbing at my fingers, asking to see the ring. "I'm so proud of you," the King said. I tried not to wince as his thin lips pressed against my forehead. "This is a happy day," he announced, as though saying it would make it true.

"Can we take a picture?" Reginald, the Head of Press, strode over. His photographer, a short woman with wiry red hair, was right behind him.

"I suppose that's all right," Charles offered. He rested his hand on my back. I tried to smile but my face felt stiff. The camera kept flashing, stinging my eyes.

Reginald flipped open his notebook, scribbling in the margin until his pen worked. "You must be thrilled, Genevieve," he said, half question, half answer. The King was right beside me. I spun the ring around my finger, not stopping until it burned.

"It is a joy," I said.

Reginald's features softened, as if my reply pleased him. "I've gotten tremendous feedback on the pieces I've run about you two. Forget the engagement—people are already asking when the wedding will be."

"We'd like to have it as soon as possible," the King replied. "The staff has already been talking about the procession through the City. It'll be spectacular. You can assure the people of that."

"I have no doubt," Reginald said. He pressed his thumb on the back of the pen, clicking it closed. "I look forward to running this piece tomorrow morning. Everyone will be thrilled."

The smoke circled my head. Here I was, standing beside Charles Harris as his fiancée, made up in a dress and heels, doing what I'd said I'd never do. I recounted that moment in the prison so many times, Caleb's bruised face, the raised knots along his back. They were going to kill him, I kept reminding myself. I'd stopped it the only way I could.

And yet now I was part of the regime, a traitor, no doubt, in the dissidents' eyes. I imagined Curtis reading about my engagement in the factory, holding it up to the others as proof that he'd been right about me all along. Even when the tunnels were completed, they would never help me escape now.

The Head of Finance signaled Reginald from across the room. He was in a cluster of men, his blond hair gelled back into a hard helmet. "If you'll excuse me, I have something I need to attend to." Reginald raised his glass once more. Then he strode off, maneuvering past a woman in a fur stole.

The restaurant was too hot. The smoke snaked through the air and flattened out across the ceiling. I covered my mouth, unable to breathe. "I have to go back to my room," I said, taking Charles's hand off me.

The King dropped his glass on a waiter's tray. "You can't just run off," he said. "All of these people are here for you, Genevieve. What am I supposed to tell them?" He gestured around the room. Some of the crowd had settled in their seats, others huddled together, speculating on whether Charles's mother would be well enough to attend the wedding.

Charles nodded to the King. "I can take her," he whispered. He reached for my hand, squeezing it so gently it startled me. "I think everyone will understand if we head out early. It's been a long night. Most of the guests will be leaving soon anyway."

The King glanced around the room, at the few people standing beside us, making sure they hadn't overheard our conversation. "I suppose if you leave together it'll be better. Just say a few good-byes, will you?" He shook Charles's hand and offered me a hug. My face pressed against his chest, his arms wrapped around my neck, suffocating me. Then he started through the crowd. Rose was waving him over, an extra glass in her hand.

Charles and I headed toward the door. We offered quick explanations to the guests we passed—all the excitement had been too much for one day. When we were finally outside in the open mall, away from the crowd, Charles still hadn't let go of my hand. His face was close, his fingers wrapped around mine. "What is it?" I asked.

"I keep waiting for something to change with us," he whispered, his blue eyes meeting mine. I glanced over our shoulder at the two soldiers trailing behind us. They were ten yards back, strolling past the closed home goods store, the windows displaying copper pots and pans. "I know this isn't ideal—"

"*Ideal?*" I said. The word made me laugh. "That's one way to put it."

He refused to look away. "I just think that we need more time. To really know each other. They told me you had feelings for him, but that doesn't mean this can't be more than it is. That it can't grow into . . . *something*." I was thankful he didn't say the word we both knew he was thinking: *love*.

I slipped my hand out from under his. It looked so strange with the glittering ring on it, like some picture from a book. "It won't," I whispered, walking ahead. I closed my eyes, and for a second I could almost feel Caleb beside me, hear his low laugh, smell the sweet sweat on his skin. We were back in the plane, his ear to my heart, clinging to each other in the dark. "I don't think that can happen more than once."

Charles followed me. "I don't believe that," he said. He stared at the marble floor. "I can't."

"Why not?" I asked, raising my voice. It sounded so foreign in the wide, empty corridor. "Why is it so hard for you to believe that someone wouldn't want to be with you?"

We descended the escalators. Charles stood on the step above me, his hand raking his hair. "You make me sound so awful," he muttered. "It's not like that. Ever since I can remember, people have talked about how I'll marry

Clara, as though it were a given. I was sixteen and everyone had my whole life planned out for me." The soldiers followed behind us. He lowered his voice, making certain they didn't hear. "And then you came to the Palace. You were different. You haven't spent the last ten years inside the City, doing the same thing every day, seeing the same people. I'm sorry if I like that about you. I didn't realize I wasn't allowed to have feelings about this whole thing."

"Have all the feelings you want," I said, an edge to my voice. "But that doesn't mean I can pretend that this is what I always dreamed of—not to you."

As we crossed the street toward the Palace, his gaze wandered to the fountains, the statues of the Greek goddesses that stood fifteen feet tall, carved from bone-white marble. All traces of the man I'd met in the conservatory were gone—he seemed so unsure of himself now. He spoke slowly, as if he were taking great care with each word he chose. "This is what I want. You are what I want," he said finally. "I have to believe that you'll want it, too—maybe not right now. But someday. Probably sooner than you think."

We took the elevator up the tower in silence. Two soldiers joined us, slipping in casually, as though they weren't watching my every move. I despised Charles then.

I could only think about the conversations that must have passed between him and the King, wondering if this was something that had been discussed all along.

When we reached his floor, Charles leaned in to kiss me on the cheek. I turned away, not caring if the soldiers saw. He stepped back, his face pained. I just pressed the button in the car, over and over again, not stopping until the doors shut behind him, locking him out.

thirty-one

BEATRICE MET ME AT THE ELEVATOR. SHE WALKED ME TO MY suite and helped me from the dress, all the while asking me about the party. It was a relief to be out of those skintight clothes. My face was wiped clean, my reflection finally recognizable without all the makeup caked on it. We sat down beside each other on the bed. I slid off the ring and set it on the nightstand, a faint pink mark on my finger the last reminder of what had happened that night.

"I never would've managed this long without you," I said, pulling at the collar of my nightgown. "A 'thank-you' doesn't seem like enough."

"Oh, child," she said, waving me off with her hand. "I've done what I can. I only wish I could help more."

"I can't live like this," I said. My lungs were tight at the thought of it, day piled on top of day, each one more stifling than the one before. I kept waiting for something to change, for the paper to reveal news of Caleb. But nothing happened. Now there would be plans for the wedding, ceaseless, senseless talk of bouquets and rings and which foods they would bring in from where. Did I want beige linens or white? Roses or calla lilies?

Beatrice pressed her palms together, her face strained with worry. "You *will* live like this," she said, "as we all have. With the memories of life before the plague. With the hope that it will one day be better."

"But how?" I asked. "How will it be better?"

She didn't answer. I put my face in my hands. I couldn't reach out to the Trail anymore. No one would trust me. I was under constant surveillance now. Caleb was gone, somewhere beyond the City's walls, with no promise of coming back. Even if the tunnels were built, how would I get to them? And if I managed to escape, how would I survive in the wild alone, with no weapons or food, the King's troops following just hours behind me?

Beatrice sat down next to me, working at the thin skin

on her hand. "Since you've arrived I've wondered . . . if it's possible for anyone to be truly happy here. You have to hold on to certain delusions, I suppose. Maybe hoping is foolish," she said, staring at a spot on the floor. "There have been rumors going around the Palace. The workers have been talking. Is it true, what you did for that boy?"

I offered a slight nod, knowing I could never truly answer that question.

"It was a brave thing," Beatrice said, resting her hand on my back.

I wiped my nose, the memory of Caleb's broken face coming back to me, the tender pink slice that ran across his forehead, the welt on his cheek. "It doesn't feel that way," I said. "I might never see him again."

Beatrice let out a deep breath. Her fingers wandered over the bedspread, digging into its soft gold fabric. The smell of cigar smoke still clung to my skin. "You do anything for the person you love," she said finally. "And then when you don't think you can give any more of yourself, you do. You keep going. Because it would kill you not to." She turned to me, her gray eyes wobbly. The room filled with the rush of the air-conditioning vents. "I've bargained with the King, too." A strand of gray hair fell in her face, shielding her eyes.

"What do you mean?" I asked.

"When they were doing the census you had to answer questions. Did you want to live inside the City? Did you want to live outside the City? What skills did you have to offer? What resources could you contribute? Some people had companies, warehouses full of goods. I had cleaned houses before the plague struck. I didn't have much money, and my daughter and I didn't have anything they wanted. We were put in the lowest category, with the most basic jobs and housing. We would've been living in the Outlands with all the others. After the chaos following the plague, people weren't sure what that would mean, if it would be more of the same—people fighting for food and clean water, more violent robberies.

"But I was told I was lucky. I was selected out of thousands. They said my application had been flagged, and I was offered a job in the Palace. But my daughter couldn't come with me. She would go to the Schools. We wouldn't be able to keep in contact, but she'd return to the City after she graduated, if that's the life she chose. Now I realize they probably just wanted more children for the Schools and the labor camps, as many as they could get. The Schools . . ." Beatrice let out a short, sad laugh. She rubbed her cheek. "They were supposed to be these places

of great learning, where girls could get a top-rate education. They told me they would give her much more than
a life in the City could. When I heard about the Golden
Generation, everyone assured me it wasn't mandatory,
that the members of the birthing initiative had volunteered. They said girls were given a choice. But then you
came here . . ."

"How old is she?" I asked. "Do you know which one
she's in?"

Beatrice shook her head. "I don't. I was pregnant when
the plague began. Sarah just turned fifteen last month."
She looked at me with pink, watery eyes, her lips twitch-
ing as she tried not to cry. "Do you know anyone there
still? Anyone you could talk to for me?"

I reached for her hand, my fingers shaking. I thought
of Headmistress Burns, her sagging, miserable face, how
she'd been aware of the Graduates' fate all along, how she'd
kept her hand on my back as I took those vitamins, how
she'd taken me to the doctor each month. I didn't know
what had become of Teacher Florence, if they'd discovered
she'd helped me escape. "I don't know," I said. "I can try."

Beatrice squeezed my fingers so hard her knuckles
were white. "That would be good," she said, her voice
breaking.

I enveloped her in a hug, feeling how small she was, her shoulders stooped, her hands clasped tight behind my back. "Yes" was all I could manage as we sat there in the stillness of the room. "I will try."

thirty-two

"WELL, LOOK AT YOU, CHARLES HARRIS!" MRS. WENTWORTH cried, poking Charles playfully in the chest. "You're looking more handsome than ever. It must be the glow of looooove," she drawled, swaying her big hips back and forth. I'd been told Amelda Wentworth was a prominent widow in the City, one of the original founders who had given the King access to her dead husband's assets, including his trucking company. She'd been like an aunt to Charles, watching him since he was a teenager, when he had first arrived in the City.

"And you, Your Royal Highness," she added, curtsying. "What a thrill this must be for you. One day you are living in the Schools and the next you're here, inside the City walls. Princess Genevieve." She was standing beside us, turning every few moments to glance around the crowded party.

We were in the penthouse of Gregor Sparks, one of the men who'd donated resources after the plague. The three-story apartment at the top of the Cosmopolitan building had a waterfall in the center of the room and recovered Matisse paintings on the walls. It was yet another engagement party, this one with delicate crackers dabbed with cheese and a full roast pig laid out on a silver platter. It was larger than the ones we had at School ceremonies, its haunches spread wide as a worker cut into its tender flesh.

"It's been a dream," I said, my smile tight as I took in her curls, stiff with spray, and the lipstick crusted in the corners of her mouth.

Some guests reclined on Gregor's long, S-shaped couch, their happy chatter filling the air. The women all wore gowns and silk shawls, while the men donned starched shirts, ties, and buttoned vests. It was a different world than the one beyond the wall, and at times like these, surrounded by the smells of mulled cider and lamb, the wild felt far away, another planet in some far-off galaxy.

"Baby lamb chop?" a waiter asked, presenting me with a silver tray.

I picked up a piece of the pink meat by the bone and brought it to my mouth, the sharp smell of mint stinging my nostrils. As I held it between my forefinger and thumb, a memory rose up: Pip and I on the School lawn, hovering over the gray mound we'd discovered in the bushes. A mound of fur, its tail hiding the rest of its body. Pip crept toward it, determined to pick it up, to figure out if it was sick or dead. She reached down and pinched its foot, then pulled, and the rotted flesh came loose. We started screaming, darting out of the bushes, but she had held it just one second—the thin, bloody bone.

Bile rose in the back of my throat. I could still hear Pip's scream. I dropped the lamb chop on the platter and stepped away.

"What is it?" Charles asked, his hand still on the small of my back.

"I'm feeling sick," I said, ducking away from him. I pressed a napkin to my forehead and lips, trying to calm myself. I had dreamed of her last night. Pip in those metal beds, Ruby beside her, then Arden. Another girl had appeared, a younger girl, her features faint in the haze of the dream. *When are you coming back?* Pip had asked, her stomach protruding nearly two feet, breasts swollen and red hair sticking to her forehead. *You've forgotten about us.*

"Would you like a drink?" Charles asked. "Water maybe?" He signaled to a server in the corner.

"Just space," I said, stepping away. "Give me one minute." I held up a finger. Then I ducked out of the crowded room, not stopping until I was down the hall, beyond the kitchen, my back resting against the wall.

I stayed there until my breath slowed. I had promised Beatrice. I'd promised her that I would help her find her daughter, and yet in the days that had passed I'd stood stupidly by Charles's side as he opened the zoo in the old Grand hotel. I'd attended parties and galas and hosted a brunch for the wives of the Elite.

"Are you all right, Princess?" Mrs. Lemoyne asked as she passed on the way to the bathroom. "You look ill." She was a mousy woman with rigid manners, always reprimanding someone for making some perceived misstep.

I patted my forehead with my napkin. "Yes, Grace, thank you. Just needed a breath."

"You should go by the window then," she urged. "Over there." She directed me into the formal dining room, where a server was hunched over the table, getting ready to serve the evening tea. Another was kneeling by a china cabinet, pulling cups and saucers from a shelf. Thankfully, the window was open, the cool night air rippling the curtains.

I stepped into the room, the murmurs of the party still audible down the hall. "I hope you don't mind," I said as I passed the man at the table. "I'll only be a minute."

A moment passed. He didn't answer. I turned around and he was staring at me. He wasn't wearing his glasses. His black hair was smoothed down and his body was rigid, his shoulders back, looking so different from the last time I'd seen him. I covered my mouth to stop myself from saying his name aloud.

Curtis balanced the tray on his hand. I glanced at the server kneeling just a few feet away, humming slightly as he arranged the cups on a silver tray. One of the chefs strode down the hallway with an empty platter. Mrs. Lemoyne returned from the ladies' room, smiling at me as she passed.

I looked into Curtis's stone-gray eyes, trying to decipher the meaning behind his silence. I wanted to ask if they'd heard anything more about Caleb's release. I wanted to know how far along the tunnels were, if they'd resumed work on the first one, if the plans had been correct. If they could reach me in the Palace I had a chance still—I could escape.

But he just leveled his gaze at me, his expression cold. "Tea, Princess?" he asked, holding out the tray. I reached down, my fingers trembling as I took a cup. He tilted the pot, letting the boiling water fall, the steam clouding the air between us.

In seconds he was gone, striding back down the long corridor, the china rattling against the silver tray. He never looked back. I stood there, the drink hot in my hands, until I heard the King calling from the next room.

"Genevieve!" he said, his voice cheerful and light. "Come now. It's time for the celebratory toast."

thirty-three

I STARED OUT THE WINDOW, FAR ACROSS THE CITY, TO THE point where the Outlands met the wall. From fifty stories up it seemed so small, an innocuous thing you could skip a stone over. All night I had been replaying that moment. Curtis's expression was the same as it had been the day we'd met in the hangar. I'd imagined him going back to the others and telling them I'd paraded around the apartment, chatting happily with Gregor Sparks, or how I'd stood there smiling stupidly as the King went on about the new royal couple.

I hated what he thought of me—what they all must've thought. That with Caleb gone, I'd returned to the Palace and set my sights on marrying Charles. There was no way to explain. Whatever I'd done to prove my loyalty didn't matter now. I was a traitor in their eyes. I accepted that a little more each day, and a sadness settled in— making every breakfast, every gala, every toast that much lonelier.

"Your Royal Highness," Beatrice said, curtsying as she entered the suite. "I've had the dresses delivered to the downstairs parlor. They're waiting for you."

I studied my reflection in the glass, wondering how anyone could believe I was happy. The skin under my eyes was swollen. My cheeks had the same hollow look they did those first days after I arrived. I blinked a few times, willing back tears. "You don't have to do that," I said finally.

"Would you prefer them in the upstairs sitting room?" she asked.

"No—the 'Royal Highness' nonsense," I said, turning to her. "It's unnecessary here."

Beatrice sighed. "Well, I can't go around the Palace calling you Genevieve. The King won't have that."

I picked at the hem of my blue dress, feeling satisfied when a loose thread gave, puckering the silk. I knew she was right. Still, I was desperate to hear my real name spoken out loud—not *Princess Genevieve*, not *Princess* or *Your Royal Highness*, just *Eve*. "I've been thinking about your daughter," I said. "I just need some time. I need to find out what School she's in, who the Headmistress is. Maybe after I'm married," I stumbled over that word, "I'll have a better chance at negotiating her release. Thankfully we have time before . . ."

Beatrice started toward me. "Yes, I know . . . ," she said, her voice a whisper. We stood there in silence, and then I took her hand, cradling it in my own. I squeezed, trying to stop the trembling in her fingers and the tears that pooled in her eyes, threatening to spill onto her cheeks. "We should go," she finally said, turning to the door.

The hallway was quiet. Charles and the King were in the City, visiting one of the new factory farms near the wall. The faint sounds of vacuuming came from another room.

The elevator opened up on the floor below, where giant white boxes were stacked in one corner. Rose and Clara sat in another, eating blueberry muffins and sipping coffee, a drink I'd yet to try. Rose was still in her silk pajamas, her blond hair pinned on top of her head, the day's paper in hand. Neither of them looked up when we walked in.

"So, these are the dresses," Beatrice said, walking over

to the stack. "They're all from before the plague, but they were treated and preserved, so the fabric is still bright. You'll see all the lace is intact. It's quite remarkable." She pulled the lid off a long box on the floor, revealing a white dress stuffed with paper. Its bodice was covered with tiny beads. I was supposed to be excited, I knew, but as my fingers touched the neckline, winding over the hard, puffy sleeves, I felt nothing but dread.

"Do you have to do this now?" Rose said, setting down her paper. "We're having breakfast." She swished her coffee around before taking another sip.

Beatrice let out a sigh. "I'm sorry, ma'am, but it's the King's orders. This must be done this morning, and I don't suppose we can move these boxes now."

Clara rolled her eyes. She pushed her plate away from the edge of the table and stood, leveling her gaze at me before heading out the door. Her mother followed behind her. Even after they turned down the hall I could hear their angry whispers, Clara muttering something about my nerve.

Beatrice pulled the first dress from the box. "That girl has wanted to be with Charles for years. Her maid says she's not handling this well, carrying on and whatnot."

As Beatrice closed the heavy wooden doors I stripped

down to my underwear, the air-conditioning raising goose bumps on my skin. I climbed into the dress and Beatrice zipped it up, spinning me around to face the mirror on the far wall. It plunged in a deep V in the front, sheer fabric with white beading clinging to my arms and chest. I pulled at the collar, nearly ripping it. "I can't breathe," I murmured.

"There are more, love," Beatrice said. She unzipped it and pulled another from its box. It was a puffy thing with a giant tail that followed behind me for nearly ten feet. I walked past the mirror, hating how it exposed the pale skin of my shoulders.

"What does it matter?" I said sadly, as Beatrice packed it away. "Any will do." Still, another was taken out. Another was put on. My thoughts drifted away from the room, from the Palace and the dresses and the incessant sound of zippers going up and down. Caleb must've reached a stop on the Trail by now. He would be back in communication with Moss soon. It wouldn't be long before he would be able to tell people inside the walls what had happened.

Beatrice buttoned up another dress. It was tight, the top of it squeezing my chest, suffocating me. "I'm sorry, Beatrice," I whispered. "Can I please take a break?"

"Don't apologize." Beatrice sighed, undoing the back of the dress. "Of course you can." She unbuttoned it halfway and released me, handing me the simple jumper I'd worn downstairs. I slunk toward the table, collapsing in Clara's vacant seat. "I'll ask the kitchen for some ice water," she said, disappearing out the door.

The morning sun streamed through the window, hot on my skin. I imagined myself in the wedding procession, the shiny car that would wind through the City streets, the cheering crowd reaching beyond the metal barricades, banging against the glass overpass. In one week I would be Charles Harris's wife. I would move out of my suite and into his. I would lie beside him every night, his hands reaching out for me in the darkness, his lips searching for mine.

I was staring at the newspaper, half in the room, half somewhere else, when the boldface type came into focus—PRINCESS TEA. The same words Curtis had uttered were now right in front of me, printed on one of the paper's back pages.

The advertisement section was the one place where citizens could post messages to one another. There they offered to trade or sell items that they'd made, brought to, or acquired in the City, under the consent of the King.

I ran my fingers over the bold font, knowing immediately what it was. The Trail often used coded messages to communicate. I remembered what Caleb had said at the prison, when he had leaned in and whispered in my ear. *You're not the only one in the paper.* I thought of Curtis's face in the dining room. His eyes had darted sideways as he spoke to me, his voice tense. It was strange that he'd said only those two words and nothing more. Now it all made sense.

I looked at the small type that described the tea—four boxes had been recovered from an old warehouse in the Outlands. The ad listed the year, the date on which they had been acquired, the brand and city they were from, and a desired price. *Perfect to celebrate the royal wedding,* the last lines read. *Enjoy with friends after watching the procession.* I kept staring at it, studying the way the letters lined up on top of each other, trying to figure out the code, if it ran vertically or horizontally.

Beatrice returned with two glasses of water, setting them down in front of me. "Do you have a pen?" I asked, counting every second letter, then every third, trying to find a pattern.

She pulled one from her vest and sat down beside me, watching as I counted every fifth, then every sixth character, copying them down next to one another to see if they spelled anything. Line after line was complete nonsense. I finally found the code running straight down the second to last column. *C, 1, N, P, R, $, N,* I copied into the paper's margins. *K, L, 1, 3, D.*

"Caleb's in prison," I repeated, ripping the advertisement out of the paper. "The King lied."

"Who's Caleb?" a voice asked.

I turned around. Clara was standing in the hall, her hand resting on the doorframe. Before I could think she rushed toward me, reaching for the ad. In one swift motion she yanked it from my grasp. I jumped up, trying to pry it from her hands, but I couldn't get a good hold on her. Then it was too late. She darted down the hall and into her room, slamming the door shut behind her.

thirty-four

I STOOD OUTSIDE, KNOCKING UNTIL MY KNUCKLES HURT. "Open the door, Clara," I yelled. "This isn't a joke." I glanced down the hallway. A soldier stationed by the parlor was watching me. Beatrice stood beside him, whispering something, trying to explain away the fight. I finally gave up, letting my forehead rest against the wood door. I could hear her pacing the length of her room, the muffled smacking of her bare feet against the floors.

She paused on the other side of the door. There was the familiar electric sound of the keypad. She opened it a few inches, revealing a sliver of her face. She no longer had the scribbled note in her hands. "Wow, Princess," she said, barely able to get the words out without laughing. "I never would've pegged you for a subversive."

I gave the door one big push, shoving my way inside. She rubbed her arm where the door had bumped her. "Where did you put that slip of paper?" I opened the top drawer of her desk, thumbing through a stack of thin notebooks. Beside them was a creased picture of a little boy and girl sitting in a wooden porch swing, a kitten curled up in the boy's lap. It took me a moment to realize that the girl was Clara. The boy looked just a few years younger, with thick black hair and ivory skin.

"Have you completely lost your mind?" she asked. She slammed the drawer shut, nearly closing my fingers inside. "Get out of my room."

"Not until you give that back to me," I said, scanning the night tables beside the bed. The fluffy pink comforter was covered with pillows of all sizes. Some were lace, others embroidered with delicate white lilies. There was nothing on the top of her dressers. Nothing in the trashcan beside the desk. She'd probably hidden it away somewhere, waiting until she had the perfect opportunity to expose me.

"What does it matter? I already read it." Clara crossed her arms over her chest. "It's that boy, isn't it? The one you were seeing at night?"

I shook my head. "Just leave it alone, Clara."

"I wonder what Charles would think about this. You sending messages through the paper." Her cheeks were red and blotchy, her fingers still rubbing the tender spot on her arm. "At least this time you can't call me a liar. Now I have proof."

I let out a long, rattling breath, unable to contain myself anymore. "Do you think I chose this? If it were up to me I never would've come to the City in the first place. I never wanted to be here."

Clara's thin brows were knitted together. "Then why are you marrying him? I was standing right there when he asked you. No one made you say yes."

I stared at my shadow on the floor, debating what to tell her. She already had enough to turn me in. The truth couldn't make things any worse. "Because they were going to kill him—Caleb. Agreeing to marry Charles was the only way I could stop it."

Clara walked toward me, her head cocked slightly to the side. "So help me understand this. You would leave the Palace right now if you could?"

"Of course," I said softly. "But I can't even leave my room. Everywhere I go someone is watching me. When I step into the hallway, Beatrice will be waiting there with the soldier by the parlor. Charles escorts me to every meal." I glanced at her window, which was open just a crack, the curtains billowing in the breeze. "Haven't you noticed I'm never alone?"

We stood there in the quiet room, facing each other. She looked more hopeful than she had in days. I straightened up, realizing I did have something to offer her, after all. "So if you want to tell Charles," I went on, "or the King, or your mother about that message, then fine. I'll marry Charles in a week and that will be it. But if you want me gone, those codes are my only chance."

I could see her considering it, weighing what she had to gain by outing me against what would happen if I escaped. She pursed her lips. "You don't love Charles?" she asked. Her eyes were clear when they met mine, the resentment in them diminished.

"No," I said. "I don't."

She walked over to a porcelain piggy bank on her nightstand. Its paint was chipped in places and one eye was nearly rubbed off. She held it up, a faint smile crossing her lips. "I've had this since I was three." She shrugged. "I wouldn't move to the City without him." She flipped it over, pulling a broken piece of cork out of the bottom.

The ripped newspaper was inside, my writing scribbled in the margins. She handed it back to me. "You have my promise, then. I won't tell anyone."

I ripped the square into the tiniest pieces I could, tucking them away in the pocket of my jumper. She'd given it back. She'd said she wouldn't tell. And she had no reason to—it would guarantee that I could never leave the Palace. She opened the door for me, and I started down the hall, turning over the scraps in my pocket, finally able to breathe.

thirty-five

THAT NIGHT I COULDN'T EAT. I SAT AT THE DINNER TABLE, thinking of Caleb in prison. I saw the gash on his forehead, a soldier landing another blow on his back, twisting his arm so it met his shoulder blade. They would want names. I knew they would. It was only a matter of time before they gave up, realizing he would never give them the information they needed. How much time did I have before they killed him?

"What's the matter, dear?" the King asked, glancing at my plate. "Did you want something else? We could have the chef prepare whatever you like." He reached out and put his hand on my arm. My entire body tensed at his touch.

I took a deep breath, trying to calm my voice. "I'm not hungry," I said. The roast chicken on my plate repulsed me.

The table was full. Clara and Rose sat next to the Head of Finance. Clara chatted happily with him now, her eyes meeting mine as she peppered him with questions about a new business venture. Charles was sitting beside me, talking to Reginald, the Head of Press, about an upcoming opening in the City.

"I'm glad that you two are getting along so well." The King offered a slight nod in Charles's direction. "I always thought you would." He squeezed my arm, then turned back to his plate.

I had the sudden urge to pick up my glass of water and throw it in his face. To plunge my fork into the soft flesh of his hand. He had lied. He thought I would never know, that I would walk through the wedding procession with a lightness in my step, content to imagine Caleb alive somewhere in the wild.

The King pushed away from the table and stood, signaling that he was ready to leave. I felt the piece of paper in the pocket of my cardigan, running my fingers over its blunt corners to comfort myself. After my conversation with Clara, I had gone back to the parlor and picked out a wedding dress. I chose the next one I tried on, not bothering to look in the mirror to see how it fit. I followed Beatrice back to the suite, stopping in the upstairs parlor to throw the ripped newspaper into the fire, watching as the advertisement and the message it contained twisted in the flames. Then I sat down at my desk and wrote.

I was careful with each word I chose, puzzling out the sequence so that the code could be applied backward, from the end of the text to the beginning, using every ninth character. It took me two hours of rearranging, moving words and phrases around, until I managed something. The piece was a formal address to the people of The New America, a missive about the great honor it was to be serving as their Princess. I spoke of the upcoming wedding, my great excitement about the nuptials, and how I had first come to meet Charles in the Palace weeks before. I reread it, lingering over the word *love*. A sickness settled in my stomach. I kept thinking of Caleb, alone in some cold prison, his skin crusted with blood.

KIN WE METE? the message spelled. NO TYM TO DLAY. I wished I had more to offer—a plan, a promise that I could secure Caleb's freedom. But if I confronted the King about the lies he would know I had a connection on the outside, telling me of Caleb's whereabouts. Everything I did would become suspect again, and all the work I had done in the past weeks to secure his confidence would be for nothing.

"Would you like to go down to the marketplace for dessert?" Charles asked as he helped me up from my chair. He'd been quieter in the past few days, seeming embarrassed by our conversation. Clara took off with the Head of Finance, glancing back over her shoulder at me.

I pulled the folded paper from my pocket. "Actually, I'd like to speak with Reginald." He turned when he heard his name.

"What for?" the King asked. He and Charles gathered around me, the room smaller in their presence. The Head of Education lingered by the door to eavesdrop.

I let out a deep breath. "I'd like to address the people of The New America for the first time. I'm here for good, as their Princess. I'd like them to at least know who I am." I didn't look at the King. I didn't acknowledge Charles. Instead, I kept my eyes on Reginald as I handed him the piece of paper.

"I suppose that's all right," the King said, his voice a little uncertain. "As long as there's nothing objectionable in it, Reginald."

Reginald pinched the sheet between his fingers, his eyes moving down the paper. His brows furrowed at some lines and relaxed at others. I swallowed hard, my chest seizing in panic. *He couldn't know*, I told myself, *he wouldn't be able to tell*. And yet the memory of that night at Marjorie and Otis's house returned. I saw Marjorie's trembling hands holding the radio, her questions, so urgent, as Otis threw the extra plates beneath the sink. *Which code did you use?* I heard her ask, then the sound of that first fatal shot.

Reginald pressed his lips together in thought. "Are you sure you want to print this?" His dark eyes met mine. The King circled around us, looking over his shoulder to review the content.

I breathed out, trying to slow the pounding in my chest. "I am," I said finally.

Reginald smiled and passed the paper to the King. "It's lovely," he declared. He bowed slightly to show his respect. "The people will be delighted to read this in tomorrow's paper."

thirty-six

THE GOLDEN GENERATION WAS BEING HELD IN A COMPOUND
northeast of the main road, a closed-in section of the City
that had once been called a country club. Its great lawns
had been converted to gardens and the large ponds were
used as reservoirs. Massive stone buildings now housed
the children's bedrooms, dining hall, and school. We
pulled up the long, curved driveway. Soldiers stood along
the perimeter, their rifles in hand.

"Princess Genevieve!" A voice called out behind me
as I started toward the glass doors. "Princess, over here
please!" Reginald's photographer got out of the car
behind us, a camera in her hand. She clicked it incessantly,

catching me as I ascended each step, the King trailing just a few feet behind.

I couldn't manage a smile. Instead I stared into the lens, thinking of Pip and Ruby and Arden. This visit had been my suggestion. I wanted to see where the children stayed, to meet them, to know the conditions of their everyday life. A big piece would run in the following day's paper about the former student turned Princess—the girl who understood the volunteers more than anyone else. I had planned to give Reginald another quote, another message for the dissidents. And yet now that the day was here and the stone building was right before me, it was difficult to take even one step.

"I think you'll be pleased," the King said to me when we reached the doors. Reginald followed behind us, along with three armed soldiers. "The sacrifices made by those girls have not gone in vain. The children are being raised properly."

I tried to smile, but a queasy, unsettled feeling rocked my insides. It had been three days since my address ran in the paper. People had written in praising my words and expressing enthusiasm about my upcoming union with Charles. As each letter was delivered to the Palace, the King softened a bit more. His laugh was heard more throughout the halls. His words were kinder, more enthused, as he relaxed into his lie. Caleb was still in custody. I was going to marry Charles. All was right in his world.

"We've been expecting you, Princess," a woman in a white shift dress said. She was only a few years younger than the Teachers at School, her thin skin like crepe paper. A tiny New American crest was pinned to her collar. "I'm Margaret, the head of the center."

"Thank you for having us," I said. "I spent my whole life at one of those Schools. I needed to come here to see this for myself." I stepped inside the marble hall, its walls echoing with the sounds of small children. In the foyer, a three-foot-high bouquet sat on a giant round table, its blooms exploding out in all directions, filling the air with the scent of lilies.

She pressed her palms together as she walked me to a door on the back wall. "We've worked hard these last years to ensure the children are well taken care of, provided with the best doctors. We make sure they receive proper exercise and eat a balanced diet."

The King and Reginald hovered behind me as I looked into the wide hall. Reginald withdrew his notebook from his suit pocket and jotted something down. Small children were huddled together on the floor, pushing around plastic cars and stacking blocks in short towers. In the corner a woman Margaret's age sat with a little girl whose face was swollen and tear-streaked, rubbing her back while she cried.

"This is our largest playroom," Margaret said. "It used to be one of the reception rooms. We keep the children here during the day in the hopes that citizens will come by and have a look. With a little luck many of these children will be adopted in the coming months." A girl with golden pigtails waddled over, her bottom thick from her diaper. She peered up at us with big sea-green eyes.

"This is Maya," Margaret offered. "She's two and a half."

I looked into her face, at her small, sweet nose and her flushed chubby cheeks. I touched her hand, and her tiny fingers curled around mine, her smile revealing two front teeth. "She's precious, isn't she?" Margaret asked. Behind us I heard the click of the camera.

As I stared into her eyes I could think only of Sophia in that awful room, her gaze meeting mine as I peered through the dirt-caked window. I thought of the girl who had cried out, her wrists straining against the leather, until the doctor had silenced her with a needle. Every one of these children had come from a girl just like my friends. Maybe Maya's mother had sat beside me in the School dining hall. She might have been one of the girls Pip and I had admired, taller than the rest, her glossy ponytail swinging back and forth as she strode by, a tray in her hands.

"We're hopeful that even those who aren't adopted will grow up happy and healthy, feeling as though they were always loved," Margaret continued. She strode over to a side door and unlocked it.

We started down a stone path, winding through a field of corn being farmed by a group of workers, to a building beyond the reservoir. "These children will become responsible citizens of The New America. They'll love this country and know the place they had in ensuring its future," the King added. "With every child born we grow in numbers. We become less vulnerable. We're closer to being the powerful nation we once were."

We climbed the stone steps and Margaret unlocked a second door, emptying us into another large room. Nurses wound through dozens of plastic beds. The babies were swaddled in tight blankets. Only their round, pink faces were visible. "These are our most recent arrivals," Margaret added. A staff member walked up and down the rows, cradling an infant in a dark blue blanket. "Would you like to hold one, Princess?"

"Yes," Reginald answered for me. "It would be nice to have a shot for the paper."

Margaret pushed into the room and maneuvered through the beds, choosing a sleeping baby bundled in a red blanket. She scooped her up and delivered her into my arms. My throat tightened just looking at the tiny creature, who had undoubtedly been shipped in on some truck, traveling for miles to this cold room, to wait for someone to want her.

It was true that the building was much different than I'd imagined. Cleaner, brighter, happier. Each floor was filled with staff members who spoke to the children in whispered words, who gently patted their bottoms to keep them from crying. But I couldn't look at any of it—at the beds and plastic pacifiers and the knit blankets—without thinking of my friends.

"Over here, Princess," Reginald's photographer called out. "Smile."

I looked into the lens and remembered the message, a quiet comfort. The dissidents had sent word in the paper the day after they'd run my piece, writing a reply under the familiar name Mona Mash. It was a long, flowery letter, a gushing account of the parade through one woman's eyes. She spoke of her excitement for the royal wedding, speculating on the best places to stand for the procession. It had taken me an entire day to figure out its meaning. Carefully recopying the letters nearly fifty different ways, I'd finally discovered the encrypted message: *We have a contact in the prison. A plan is in place that should secure his release. One tunnel complete.*

"Look how lovely you are," the King cooed as I held the baby in my arms. The photographer kept snapping photos, catching the morning light that streamed through the blinds. The little girl's face was calm. She cracked open her gray eyes, her lips puckering slightly. I didn't feel the stirrings of motherhood or some warm gushiness inside my chest. I could only think of the future before me, what would happen in the next week. It was only a matter of time, I kept telling myself. An end was coming.

Margaret took the baby from my arms and set her back down on the bed. "I'd love to show you one more thing," she said, starting out the door.

We followed her up the stairs, the King resting his hand on my shoulder. "These children will have real lives inside the City. Even the ones who aren't adopted fare better than any child could beyond the wall. They're raised here, given a proper education," he said softly. "They're taken care of. Their mothers' sacrifices have been honored."

"I can see that now," I lied, the words catching in my throat. "It all makes so much sense." Margaret strode out into the second floor. Reginald, his camerawoman, and the two soldiers followed behind her. For a moment the King and I were alone in the doorway.

He turned to me and rested his hand on my shoulder. "I know this hasn't been easy for you," he said, lowering his head to meet my eyes. "But I appreciate the effort you're making. I think you'll really enjoy life here, with Charles. Adjusting will just take time."

"It's getting easier," I said, not looking him in the eye. It was the first thing I had said that contained some bit of truth. Since discovering the message in the paper, things felt lighter. I could see an exit from this world and I was moving toward it, steadily, day by day. I had one more message to post in the paper, a response to my visit to the center, which would contain the seedling of a plan. If Harper and Curtis could help release Caleb, I'd meet him the morning of the wedding. With the City in such upheaval, we'd have the best chances of escape.

Beatrice had given me her word that she'd help. She would leave the bridal suite for an extended period of time, unlocking the door to the east stairwell to allow me access. I'd spent days watching Clara, waiting for her to divulge my secrets to Charles or the King. After seeing no signs of betrayal, I'd solicited her help. She would divert the soldier stationed outside my room so I could escape undetected. I tried not to be offended by how elated she was that I would be leaving the City forever.

The King kept his hand on my shoulder as we walked down the hall. "These are our adoption offices," Margaret said. She knocked on one of the doors and a middle-aged woman in a navy suit answered. They exchanged a few words and the woman stepped back, letting us inside. A couple sat in front of a desk. They were a little older than Beatrice, their hair showing the first signs of gray. They both stood when they saw the King and me, the man bowing, the woman curtsying.

"This is Mr. and Mrs. Sherman," Margaret said, gesturing to the couple. "They're starting a family."

"Congratulations," I said, looking into their faces. The woman's eyes were pink and watery. The man clutched a cap in his hand, curling the thin cotton brim.

"They're adopting two children," Margaret went on. "We've been in the process for a month now, and today is the day they're bringing them home."

"Two little girls—twins." Mrs. Sherman smiled, but her face looked pained, her forehead wrinkled in worry. "It's really a dream for us." Her husband wrapped an arm around her shoulder and squeezed.

"I was envisioning couples like you when I started the program," the King said. "People who wanted a second chance at life after the plague. This program was designed to grow The New America while allowing people to again experience the joy of having a family. We wish you luck."

"That means a lot," the man said softly, before kissing his wife on the forehead. He didn't wear a uniform, which made me think he was a member of the middle class. Some worked in the offices in the Venetian, others ran businesses in the Palace mall or the apartment buildings on the main strip. His clothes were gently worn, the hems repaired, a tiny hole visible in the elbow of his shirt.

Margaret stepped aside, leading us back into the hall, the door clicking shut. When we were a few steps away, she turned.

"It's hard," she said, her voice low. "Mrs. Sherman lost her entire family in the plague—a husband and two children, one only sixteen months old. Mr. Sherman lost his wife. Now that time has passed and they're established in the City, remarried, they want to start a family. But it opens old wounds, you know."

The King was quiet. "Of course," he said after a long pause. "We can all understand that."

We descended the stairs in silence, the sound of our footsteps echoing off the cold walls. When we returned to the main foyer we said good-bye to Margaret, the camera clicking as I shook her hand. We left Reginald at the front entrance, scribbling in his notebook. I thought of that baby, her sweet face, the way she had opened her eyes and looked at me for a brief moment. After I left the City there'd be no going back. The King would be after me, and Caleb and I would be forever on the run. I couldn't return to the Schools. I would never find my way back to Pip or Arden. They'd be trapped in that building, their children shipped off to this sterile center. I saw Ruby's face again, eyes glassy as she leaned on the fence.

I had to get word to them now, before I left.

I started down the steps, enveloped by the day's heat. The sun burned my eyes, seeming brighter, harsher even, as it reflected off the sandstone building. "Father," I said, conscious of the title that I had avoided for so long. The King raised his head. The cars pulled up the circular driveway. Soldiers lined up to escort us out. "I'd like to visit my old School, if just to see the younger girls there. I want to go back one last time."

Reginald and his team loaded themselves into the second car while the soldiers stood in the street, waiting for us. "I don't know if that's practical. You have the wedding to prepare for, and it might bring up—"

"Please," I tried. "I want to see it just one last time. I spent twelve years of my life there. It's important to me. Besides, I could speak to the students as the Princess of The New America." I tried to keep my voice even. The soldiers were all looking up, waiting for us to descend the stairs. A few people on the street had stopped to see the spectacle: the King and his daughter out and about in the City.

He started toward me, his arm around my shoulder. "I suppose it's not a bad idea," he said. "I've heard reports that the girls were very confused by your sudden disappearance." We slid into the cool car, his hand heavy on mine. "I suppose so, yes," he said. "But we'll have to send soldiers with you. And you'll take Beatrice."

I smiled, the first genuine smile of the day. "Thank you," I said, as the car started back toward the Palace. "Thank you, Father. Thank you."

thirty-seven

RAIN STREAMED DOWN THE JEEP'S WINDOWS IN NARROW, twisting rivers. Beatrice sat beside me, her hand on mine, as the dark wilderness spread out before us. I took it all in: the houses overgrown with ivy, the broken road that wound for miles, dotted with orange traffic cones. Old cars sat abandoned on the side of the highway, their gas tanks left open by travelers who'd tried to siphon fuel. Every part of it felt familiar, more like home than anything else—even the Palace, my suite, School.

"I haven't seen this in nearly a decade," Beatrice said. "It's worse than I remembered."

Two female soldiers sat in the front seat. The driver,

a young blond girl with an oval birthmark on her cheek, scanned the horizon, looking for any signs of gangs. "I love it," I said breathlessly, staring at the purple wild-flowers that sprouted up in the cracks of an old parking lot. A giant factory stood in the distance, HOME DEPOT written on its side in faded print.

We'd been traveling for hours, but the time slipped away easily. Trees snaked around one another, winding up toward the sky. Bicycle wheels were tangled with flowers and the rain accumulated in potholes, form-ing shallow, murky puddles. The other Jeep was right behind us, pitching over the same mounds of pavement that we had, slowing as we slowed, watching us from the back.

We would be in the woods again. The abandoned shacks and stores would provide cover as Caleb and I moved east, away from the City, the Schools, and the camps. The plan had been set in motion. The morning of my wedding, as I weaved through the congested City streets, blending in with the crowds, the dissidents would work with their contact inside the prison to secure Caleb's release.

Then we'd move through the tunnel, leave the City, and wait. We'd live in the eastern edge of the country, where the land was not visited as much by soldiers. We'd keep in contact with the Trail until the dissidents had mobilized, until the next steps were planned. For the first time in weeks I felt a sense of purpose, of control. The future was not just a string of dinners and cocktails and public addresses, of lies uttered with a tight, false smile.

"That's it up there," the soldier in the passenger seat said, pointing to the high stone wall. She was shorter than the other soldier, her machine gun resting across her muscular legs. The King had sent the few female troops he had along with us, knowing that Headmistress Burns would never permit men inside the compound.

Beatrice squeezed my hand. "They were juvenile detention centers before the plague." She pointed at the sharp, coiled wire that sat on the top of the building. "Holding cells for children who had committed crimes."

Rain battered the car. When we reached the wall, the soldiers exchanged paperwork with the female guards out front, their uniforms soaked through. After a few minutes we were let in. The Jeep pulled alongside the stone building where I'd eaten my meals for twelve years.

Now that we were inside, the excitement of the journey was gone. I stared across the lake at the windowless building, the place where Pip, Ruby, and Arden were all being held. The dinner churned in my stomach. I looked at the bushes beside the dining hall, the ones with the slight ditch underneath them. It was the exact spot I'd found Arden the night she escaped. When she revealed the truth about the Graduates.

My past rose up around me—the School, the lawn, the lake, all of it reminding me of my life before. Through the rain I could make out the library window on the fourth floor where Pip and I had sat reading, stopping sometimes to watch the sparrows outside. The apple tree was still there, across the compound. We would lie under it in the summer months enjoying the shade. The metal spoke jutted out of the ground where we used to play horseshoes. I'd tripped over it once, the top of it splitting my shin.

"I have a feeling . . . ," Beatrice began, peering out the rain-beaded window. The soldiers stepped out of the Jeeps to speak with the School guards. ". . . that just maybe . . . Who knows, right?" She didn't have to go on. She had asked me that morning, the question posed in half sentences, about whether her daughter could be at the School. It was possible, but improbable. I doubted that the King would've allowed her to come if her daughter was here, and I didn't remember any girl named Sarah. I had told her as much, but I could see now that she'd thought only of this as she stared out the window for all those miles, her fingers nervously twisting a strand of hair.

"There's always the chance," I said, squeezing her hand. "We can hope."

I looked out the side window, through the wall of rain, at the figure coming toward us. She stood under a giant black umbrella, her gray rain slicker falling past her knees. Even from twenty feet away I recognized her, her slow uneven steps, her square jaw, the hair that was always roped back into a tight bun.

Headmistress Burns.

She approached the side of the Jeep, staring at me through the rain. A soldier opened the door and helped me down the high step. "Princess Genevieve," Headmistress said, her voice slow and deliberate, lingering over my new title. "How delightful of you to grace us with your presence." She took another umbrella from her side and wrapped her hand around its neck, slowly expanding its cloth dome.

"Hello, Headmistress," I said, as the guard helped Beatrice out behind me. "It's delightful to be here." I kept my chin up, my shoulders back, careful not to reveal the terror I felt. I hated that she had this effect on me, even now, when I was no longer under her supervision.

Beatrice took the umbrella and held it above us. Her presence by my side comforted me. "This is Beatrice," I said as we started toward the dining building. "She'll be staying the night with me."

"So I've been told," Headmistress Burns said, looking straight ahead. "They've cleared out an upstairs bedroom for you two, as well as one for your armed escorts. It's nothing fancy, just the same beds you slept in when you were here. I hope you're not terribly offended by them now." Each word was tinged with malice. There was no way for me to respond.

She opened the door to the building and gestured for us to go inside. The hallway was quiet except for the low hum of the generators. I stamped the water off my feet as we hung up our coats in the closet. "The girls are waiting for you in the main dining hall," Headmistress continued. "You can imagine how confused they were when you disappeared the night before graduation. First Arden, then you. It raised a lot of questions for them, especially these younger ones."

"I understand."

"Your father reached out to me regarding this visit.

I've been told that you're speaking tonight on the value of your education and your royal duties in The New America. And that you will reassure these young women of the gift they have been given just by being here."

"That's correct," I said, the heat creeping into my cheeks. "Are these all the girls in the School?" I glanced sideways at Beatrice.

"Yes," Headmistress said, turning on her heel. "Shall we begin then? There's only an hour until lights out."

We went down the same tiled corridor I'd walked through hundreds of times before, Pip and Ruby arm in arm as we went to breakfast, lunch, and dinner. We'd crept in late one night, trying to sneak extra puddings from the kitchen, when Ruby had screamed, swearing a rat had darted over her feet. We ran all the way back up to the dorm room, not stopping until we were crowded in my cot, the blanket pulled over our heads.

Beatrice was wringing her fingers together. I set my hand on her back to calm her, but it didn't help. I could feel each breath, short and fast, beneath her sweater. We finally reached the main hall, a giant room with metal tables bolted to the floor. More than one hundred girls sat there, all over the age of twelve. The youngest ones had probably been given over by parents who now lived in the City—parents like Beatrice who'd believed their daughters would have a better life. The oldest were orphans like me.

They straightened up in their seats when they saw me, their whispers giving way to complete silence. "You all know Princess Genevieve," Headmistress Burns said, her voice drained of all enthusiasm. "Please rise and show her your respect."

The girls stood and curtsied at the same time. They were wearing the same jumpers I'd worn every day that I was here, the New American crest pasted unflatteringly over the front. "Good evening, Your Royal Highness," they said in unison. I recognized a black-haired eleventh year in the front. She'd played in the band the night before graduation, the music swirling in the air above the lake.

I gestured for them to sit. "Good evening," I said, my voice echoing in the room. I scanned the crowd, recognizing the faces of some of the students who had been below me in School. Seema, a dark-eyed girl with smooth, almond-colored skin, offered me a tiny wave. She'd helped Teacher Fran in the library, checking out the weathered art history books I'd loved. She was always apologizing for the missing volumes. "Thank you for inviting me back. I recognize many of you from my time here. For so many years this place was my home. I felt so safe here, and well loved." Headmistress Burns crossed her arms over her chest, watching me from the side of the room. Beatrice stood beside her, worrying the buttons on her dress as she scanned the crowd, studying each girl, searching each face. "I know my leaving School caused some confusion for all of you. And now you've heard the news from the City—my father is the King, and I am the Princess of The New America."

At that, the girls cheered. I stood there, trying to smile, but my face felt stiff. My stomach was twisted and tense, my dinner threatening to come up. "I've wanted to speak to you directly and tell you that there will be no greater champion for you inside the City of Sand. I will do everything I can to advocate for your needs." It was sincere. It was vague enough to invite interpretation. I couldn't lie to them, their excited faces reminding me of my own so many years before.

"I was given so much time for my studies. I became an artist, a pianist, a reader, a writer, among many other things. Take advantage of that." A hand shot up in the back of the crowd, then another, then a third, until a quarter of the girls had theirs raised, waiting for me to call on them. "I guess we're ready for questions," I said. *It's just a matter of time*, I kept telling myself, looking into their faces. The tunnels would be finished, the rest of the weapons smuggled through. The dissidents would organize soon. We just had to wait.

I called on a short girl in the back with a long black braid. "What are your duties as Princess?" she asked.

I picked at the skin on my finger. I wanted to tell her how all power had been taken from me the moment I'd stepped inside the Palace, how the King would only let me speak if it was to support the regime. "I've been visiting a lot of the people in the City, in all different places, to tell them about the King's vision for The New America."

"Who are your friends?" another girl asked.

I turned to Beatrice, who was standing beside Headmistress Burns. She bit down on her finger as she looked over the front row of girls, searching each face for Sarah. I couldn't speak, hardly noticed the girl's *Excuse me, Princess?* As Beatrice reached the end of the row her hands shook, her features twisting in a pained expression. Then she started to cry, the tears coming so fast she didn't have time to stop them. Instead she turned and ran out, wiping at her eyes with her sleeve.

I didn't think. I just darted out into the hall, past the two soldiers who stood on either side of the door. "Beatrice?" I called, starting down the tile corridor. "Beatrice?" But the only sound was my own voice, echoing in the hall, repeating her name in a question.

thirty-eight

"YOU'LL BE STAYING ON THE THIRD FLOOR," TEACHER AGNES said as we started up the stairs. She glanced every now and then at Beatrice, whose face was still swollen and red. "It's good to see you again," she added. Her gaze met mine.

Teacher Agnes's shoulders hunched forward as she conquered each step, moving slowly beside me, her knotted fingers clutching the railing. She had been a constant presence in my life, even after I'd left School. I heard her voice sometimes when Caleb touched the nape of my neck, when his fingers danced over my stomach. I had hated her, the fury coming to me as I remembered everything she had said in those classes, how she'd spoken of the manipulative nature of all men, how love was just a lie, the greatest tool wielded against women to make them vulnerable.

But now she looked so small beside me. Her neck was bent, making it seem like she was always looking at the ground. Her breaths were raspy and slow. I wondered if she had really aged or if it was the time that had passed, the months in the wild that allowed me to see her through a stranger's eyes. "Yes, it's been quite awhile," I said.

I reached out and took Beatrice's hand in my own as we started on to the third floor. I'd found her hiding in the doorway to the kitchen, her sweater pressed to her face, trying to quiet her sobs. Sarah wasn't here. There was nothing I could say, nothing I could do except hold her, her cheek pressed against my chest as she cried. After a few minutes I'd returned to the girls and Headmistress Burns, answered their questions and assured them my friend was fine, just sick from all those hours trapped in the Jeep's stuffy cab.

"The guards have brought up your bags." Teacher Agnes turned in to a room on the right, moving through it, lighting the lanterns on the bedside tables. The familiar sounds of the students filled the corridor. The girls were huddled in the bathroom, brushing their teeth, their laughs louder against the tile walls. A Teacher strode out of the bathroom, turning when she noticed me. We stared at each other a moment before her face broke into a smile, which disappeared so quickly I wondered if I'd imagined it.

It was Teacher Florence.

"I'll just be a minute," I said, holding up a finger to Beatrice, who had settled down on the bed. Teacher Florence was still in her red blouse and blue slacks, her gray hair wavy from the humidity. "I was wondering if I would see you." I glanced down the hall to the staircase to make sure Headmistress Burns was not in sight. "You're all right?"

We were standing in the hall, where I'd stood so many times, those nights when Ruby and I hovered outside the bathroom, waiting for a free sink. Teacher Florence gestured to a door at the end of the corridor—my old room—and we ducked inside. It was empty. She didn't speak until we were alone, the metal door shut behind us. "I'm doing well," she said. "And so are you, I hope." Her eyes searched my face.

I didn't answer. I couldn't stop looking at the room. They'd moved our beds so they were in a row against one wall. All three were unmade, strewn with tattered books and crumpled uniforms. A notepad on one bedside table was covered with doodles. Pinned to the wall above the desk was a paper with a black-and-white drawing of two girls, the words ANNIKA & BESS: FRIENDS FOREVER written below it in big puffy letters. All traces of Pip, Ruby, and me were gone.

"I am. Life's much different in the City," I said, ignoring the lump in the back of my throat.

"I didn't know you were the King's daughter," Teacher Florence stated. "It was something only Headmistress Burns knew." She sat down on a narrow bed, her fingers picking at the stiff gray blanket.

I wondered if that would've changed things—if she still would've helped me escape that night, taking me out through the secret door in the wall. "I figured as much," I said slowly.

"I heard that Arden was brought back, that she's on the other side of the lake now. Did you know?" she asked.

I sat down beside her. "I did." We both stared ahead, not meeting each other's eyes. "I saw her when I was in the wild. She saved me." I looked at the broken tile in the floor, the one that Pip and I used to hide notes under. The cracked piece was missing now, the dirty grout exposed.

She stood, fidgeting with the keys in her pocket. "I was the one who brought the girls to the graduation ceremony. Pip didn't want to leave. She started crying. She swore something had happened to you—that you never would've left. She kept asking Headmistress Burns to have the guards search outside the wall. It made me wonder about what I had told you . . ." She trailed off, her hand moving in her pocket, filling the quiet with the jingling of keys. ". . . maybe it could've been different."

I had replayed that moment in my head so many times before, recounting Teacher Florence's words, her orders that I must go alone. I had imagined all the different things I could've done, imagined myself waking Pip and Ruby, or hiding out somewhere beyond the wall. I imagined coming back the next day when they congregated on the lawn, yelling to them about the Graduates and all the King's plans.

Teacher Florence walked to the far corner, where a single chair sat against the wall. She slid it forward. "It wasn't until after the girls went over the bridge that I discovered this. I'd come back to clear out the room."

I kneeled behind the chair with her, my fingers running over the carved letters. EVE + PIP + RUBY WERE HERE, it said. I'd forgotten all about it. Pip had come into the room one morning after breakfast excited about Violet, another girl in our year who had written on her closet wall, behind the clothes where no one would discover it. She'd put our bed against the door as we sat there with a stolen knife, etching out our names. I stared at it now, my eyes blurry, remembering the way she had smiled that day, so satisfied when we'd completed our little masterpiece.

Before I could say anything, Teacher Florence's hand was in mine, pressing a cool object into my palm. She nodded at me as if to affirm what it was. Then she pushed my fist down, gesturing for me to put it away. I tucked it into the pocket, feeling immediately that it was a key. *The* key.

The door flew open, the metal banging against the cement wall. "You were too scared to ask her!" A girl's voice broke the silence between us. "You're such a chicken sometimes."

Two fifteen-year-old girls had come in, the fronts of their nightgowns wet from washing their faces. They froze when they saw us. One of the girls was blushing so much her ears turned red.

"Did you want to ask me something?" I said, smiling as I stepped out from behind the chair. The girls didn't answer. "This was my old room when I was at School. I hope you don't mind; Teacher Florence was showing me around."

The girl who'd been talking had thick black bangs that fell in her eyes. "No," she muttered, shaking her head. "Of course not."

I grabbed Teacher Florence's hand, wanting to thank her—for understanding, for helping me, for not asking me to explain anything—but then Headmistress Burns appeared in the doorway, her lips pursed. "I was looking for you, Princess," she said, her eyes darting to me, then Teacher Florence. "I'd like to speak with you in my office, alone." She turned to Teacher Florence. "Please see to it that these girls get to bed in a timely manner."

Then she disappeared into the hall, not bothering to see if I would follow her. I didn't dare look at Teacher Florence as I left. Instead, I felt the key in my pocket, turning it between my fingers, the weight of it calming me. Just before I crossed the threshold into the hall, I pulled it out and stuck it down the collar of my dress.

The hall lights shut off. Headmistress Burns held a lantern as we started down the stairs to her office. My cheeks burned at the thought of sitting in that room. No one went there unless they were being punished. I felt like a child now, nervous and afraid, wanting to confess everything I had ever done to displease her.

When we reached her office she set the lantern on the desk, then gestured for me to sit. The door slammed shut, making the light inside the glass flicker. I kept my eyes on her, my shoulders back, refusing to look away. "Can I help you with something, Headmistress?" I asked. "The trip has taken a lot out of me. I'm eager to get to bed."

She let out a small laugh. "Yes, Princess," she said, a hint of sarcasm in her voice. "I'm sure you are." She sat down in front of me, her plump haunches squeezed onto the corner of the desk. Her leg swung back and forth, back and forth, a metronome keeping time.

My hands were slicked with sweat. I kept my eyes on hers. She could accuse me of whatever she wanted. It didn't matter now. I thought only of Pip, Arden, and Ruby, and the key pressed against my breast—their only chance. "You must've thought you would outsmart us all," she said coldly. "That we were liars, that we had deceived you. But now here you are, your father's daughter, raving about the education you received."

"Do you have a point?" I asked. "Did you call me in here just to chastise me?"

Headmistress leaned down, her face level with mine. "I called you in here because I want to know who helped you. Tell me who it was."

"I didn't have help," I muttered. "I don't—"

"You're lying to my face." She laughed. "You expect me to believe that you got over that wall by yourself?"

So she thought I had scaled it. That was impossible—it was nearly thirty feet high—and yet I didn't correct her, saw my opening and went with it. "I had found rope in the Teacher's closet. Yards of it. I cut my arm on the wire on top." I showed her where the warehouse door had sliced my skin when I was trying to escape the Lieutenant. The scar was still pink.

She tilted her head as if considering it. "How did you know about the Graduates?" she asked.

"I'd always had suspicions," I said coolly. The control was shifting, my voice calmer as each question was answered to her satisfaction. "But it doesn't matter how I escaped. What matters is that I'm here. And I addressed the girls. I explained away my disappearance and spoke highly about your School. Tomorrow morning, I'd like to see my friends."

"That cannot be arranged," she said quickly. She stood and went to the window, her arms crossed over her chest. Outside, the compound was dark. A few lamps shone on the top of the wall, the barbed wire glinting in the light. "That would raise all sorts of questions. It would confuse the students."

"Wouldn't it be more confusing for them if I left for the City and never returned, if I didn't even want to see my friends to know how they were doing in their trade school across the lake?"

Headmistress Burns faced me. She let out a deep breath, her thumb running over the thick veins on the back of her hand. I stared at the figurines lined up on her shelf—shiny, garish children that seemed menacing now, their features contorted in a strange, unnatural ecstasy. She didn't speak for a long while.

"Do I have to remind you that one day I will be Queen?" I hardened my voice as I said it.

Her face changed then. She took a few steps forward, her nose scrunching as if she'd caught a whiff of something rotten. "Fine. You will see your friends tomorrow." She turned to the door and opened it, indicating that I should leave.

I stood, smoothing my dress. "Thank you, Headmistress," I said, trying to keep from smiling. I strode out the door and down the dark corridor, feeling my way as I had so many times before.

"But remember, Eve," she called when I'd nearly reached the stairs. She was still standing in the doorway, the lantern casting shadows on her face. "You aren't Queen yet."

thirty-nine

BY THE FOLLOWING MORNING, THE STORM HAD CLEARED. I took the bridge one step at a time, feeling the thin wood planks give slightly beneath my feet. It was just wider than my shoulders, with ropes strung up on either side; a lightweight thing extended over the lake's still surface. Joby, one of the School guards, followed behind me. I glanced back every so often at the girls studying on the lawn. Beatrice was standing by the dining hall building, talking to Teacher Agnes.

I imagined what it must've been like that day, with the chairs set up on the grass, the podium standing in front of the lake. The Teachers would line up along the shore, toes at the edge of the water, as they had every year before. Who had given the speech, telling the girls about the great promise of their future? Who had led them to the other side? I imagined Pip turning back, waiting for me, certain I would appear at the last possible moment.

When we reached the other shore the ground was still wet. Joby stepped ahead and circled around the building, gesturing me to follow. The two guards on shore pulled the rope to raise the bridge to the other side. We turned the corner and I saw the high windows, the ones I'd peered through the night I'd escaped. The bucket I'd stood on was gone.

"It must be strange to be back here again," Joby said, her long black hair tucked under the guard's hat. She met my eyes, as if to acknowledge the last day I'd seen her, in this same place, when Arden was being taken out of the Jeep and I was driven away by Stark.

I nodded, not wanting to risk a response. Before Joby had patted me down on the other side of the bridge, I'd slipped the key under my tongue. Now it sat there, waiting to be delivered to Arden, filling my entire mouth with a strong metallic taste.

She approached the high fenced-in section where they'd taken Arden. Joby opened the first door and led me across the short gravel driveway. We kept going, through the next door and into the grassy yard where I'd seen Ruby. Two stone tables sat outside, but there were no signs of the Graduates. "Wait here," she said. "She'll be out in a moment." Then she disappeared inside the building.

I walked the length of the yard, trying to calm my nerves. Just beyond the fence, by the closed gate, two more guards watched me, their rifles hanging at their sides. I rolled the key in my mouth. I hadn't slept. Instead, I'd imagined Pip as I'd last seen her, spinning around the lawn, the torches casting a warm glow on her skin. I remembered her teasing me as she stood beside me at the sink or hooting wildly, arms raised in the air, after she'd won a game of horseshoes.

The door swung open and Arden walked out, Joby following close behind. Her eyes were clear as she looked me up and down, taking in my short blue dress, the gold earrings that hung from each ear. My dark hair was brushed back in a bun. "I hope you didn't get all dolled up just to see me," she said, her cracked lips letting on just the slightest smile. The green paper gown fell just below her knees.

I looked down at my dress, wishing I was allowed to

wear more casual clothing in public. I didn't speak, but went to her, wrapping my arms around her and kissing her on the cheek. All the while I kept my eye on Joby and the two guards who stood by the closed gate, aware that they were always watching us.

I grabbed her hand and held it up in front of me. I closed my eyes as I kissed her palm, releasing the small key into it. Then I clutched her fist to my chest. "Of course I did." I laughed.

Arden sat down on the bench. Her hair had grown out, her scalp no longer visible. Her pale arms were covered with tiny circular bruises from all the injections. She kept her fist on the table, palm down, the key clutched inside it. "I'm relieved to see you," she said. "He hasn't hurt you, has he?" Behind her, Joby shifted to get a better view of us.

I shook my head. "I've been worried about you, too." I studied the plastic wristband she wore, covered with numbers. "Are you . . . ?" I didn't finish the sentence.

"Not yet," she said. "I don't think so." We sat in silence for a moment. I kept nodding, the tears in my eyes, thankful that she wasn't pregnant.

Joby checked her watch. I touched my fingers to the top of Arden's hand. "Remember when we used to play by the apple tree in the yard?" I asked, knowing that Arden would remember no such thing. We'd hated each other when we were here together, had made a point of avoiding one another those last few years. But the first nights we'd been in the dugout I'd told her how Teacher Florence had helped me, how I'd gone through a secret door. I wondered if she remembered, or if she'd been too sick to process the details. "We used to play right there, beside the wall. I loved when they let us out on the lawn."

Arden smiled, a faint laugh escaping her lips. She looked down at our hands, acknowledging the key beneath them. "Yeah, I remember that," she said.

I looked into her eyes, searching for recognition. She nodded. "I don't know when my next visit will be," I added, not looking away. "I have a lot of obligations in the Palace, duties to the King. I wanted to come now, because I might not be back for some time." My voice trembled as I spoke. "I wanted you to look after Ruby and Pip for me."

"I understand." Arden's eyes were red and wet. She covered my hand with hers, the stone table hot on our skin. "It's just really good to see you," she said, nodding. "I didn't know if I ever would again." She wiped her face with her gown.

We sat like that for a minute. Above us a flock of birds wheeled in the sky, their tiny bodies scattering, then coming back together, then scattering again. "I've missed you," I said. Arden would be able to get out, I kept telling myself. She'd gotten beyond the School walls once before. She had made it to Califia. If anyone would be able to get out of that brick building, if anyone could help Ruby and Pip escape, she could.

Joby stepped forward, gesturing for Arden to stand. "I'll bring the others," she said.

Arden hugged me. Her body felt much smaller beneath mine. With her back turned to Joby she brought her fingers to her mouth and slipped the key inside, like she was popping a sucking candy. Then she smiled, squeezing my hand before she walked away.

I stood there, watching her return to that building, her hands behind her back so Joby could see them. I thought of her subtle smirk as she flattened the key under her palm, as she listened to me speak of the apple tree and the wall beside it. She had understood. I knew she had. But looking around the fenced-in yard, at the guard's rifles, I wondered how long it would be before she escaped, if the days would pass too quickly. If, soon, she'd be stuck here indefinitely.

The door swung open, the rusty hinges letting out a terrible, screeching sound. Ruby appeared first. Her steps were even, her long black hair secured in a ponytail. "You came back," she said. She squeezed the breath from my body. Her stomach pressed against mine, the small lump not yet noticeable under her loose green gown. When she pulled back, her eyes were a little sad. "I knew you were still alive. I knew you hadn't disappeared. I had this memory of you. You were standing right over there, by the gate." She pointed to the place I'd last seen her, where she'd held onto the fence, staring vacantly beyond me.

"I did," I said, squeezing Ruby's arm. Whatever pills they'd given her then no longer had a hold on her. "I saw you that day. It was the day they brought Arden here."

"I kept telling Pip that I'd seen you." Ruby nodded. "I kept telling her but she didn't believe me."

Pip was walking out of the building, her head down. She kept her hands behind her back. The door banged shut, the sound loud enough that I flinched. She played with the ends of her curly red hair, which had grown so much longer in the months that had passed.

"Pip, I'm here," I said. She didn't respond. "I came to see you." She inched closer. I hugged her, but her body felt like stone. Instead she pulled back, freeing herself from my grip.

She rubbed her arm where I'd touched her. "That hurt," she said softly. "Everything hurts."

"Sit down on the bench," Joby said, guiding Pip by the elbow.

"Why are you wearing that?" Ruby asked, pointing to my dress. "Where have you been?"

My mouth was dry. I didn't want to tell them the truth—that I'd been living in the City of Sand. That I was the daughter of the same person who had put them here, in this building. The man who had lied to them—to all of us—for so many years. It wasn't how I wanted things to begin, this short meeting between us. "I was taken to the City of Sand," I said. "I found out I'm the King's daughter."

Pip lifted her head. "You went to the City of Sand without me." It was a statement, not a question. "You've been in the City of Sand this whole time."

"I know how this must seem," I said, reaching out for her hand. She pulled it away before I could touch her. "But it's not like that." I stopped myself, knowing I couldn't reveal too much in front of Joby. "I'm here now," I offered. But it sounded so small, so pathetic, even to me.

Ruby was staring at me. She bit at her nails. "Why are you here?" she asked.

To help you get out, I thought, the words dangerously close to leaving my mouth. *Because I don't know when I'll be able to see you again. Because I've thought of you both every day since I left.* "I had to come," I said instead. "I needed to know you were okay."

"We're not," Pip mumbled. She stared at the table, her finger making idle circles. Her cuticles were bloody and swollen. Her pregnant belly was visible when she sat down, the green gown jutting out around her mid-section. "We get to sit out here once a day, for an hour. That's all." She lowered her voice, her eyes darting to Joby. "Once a day. The girls who are on bed rest are strapped down. They give us pills sometimes that make it hard to think."

"They said it won't be long," Ruby offered. "They said we'll be released soon."

I tried to keep calm, feeling the guards staring at me. The King hadn't yet decided what would happen to the first generation of girls from the birthing initiative, but I'd heard it would still be years until they were released. I thought of the key that I'd given to Arden. Of the dissidents somewhere below the City, working on the tunnels.

Of the rest of the Trail, leading away from the Schools, winding through the wild, to Califia. Arden would get them out. And if she didn't, if she couldn't, I would find a way. "Yes, it's going to be all right."

"That's what they say," Pip continued. "That's what all the girls keep saying. Maxine and Violet, and the doctors. Everyone thinks it's going to be all right." She gave a sad little laugh. "It's not."

I watched her as she ran her fingers over the stone table, her knee bouncing up and down. She wasn't the same person who'd slept in the twin bed beside me all those years, who had done handstands on the lawn, who I sometimes caught humming to herself as she dressed, stepping to the side, then back, in a secret solitary dance. "Pip, you have to believe that," I tried. "It will be."

"Let's get you two back inside," Joby said, stepping forward. Pip kept staring at the table.

"Pip?" I asked, waiting until her gaze finally met mine. Her skin was pale, her freckles faded from so many hours indoors. "I promise everything is going to be okay." I wanted to go on, but they were already getting up, their hands crossed at the wrists behind them, ready to go inside.

"Will you come back?" Ruby asked, turning to me.

"I'll try my best."

Pip slipped inside the building without saying good-bye. Ruby followed after, glancing over her shoulder one final time. Then they were gone, the door falling shut behind them, the hollow *click* of the lock stiffening my spine.

forty

WHEN I RETURNED TO THE CITY, I GRANTED REGINALD MORE interviews. I spoke of my great excitement for the wedding, of Charles's commitment to The New America, and of my visit to the School, all the while comforted by the questions that would arise once I disappeared. People would have to wonder what had happened to me, their Princess, why I had gone missing on one of the biggest days in recent history. The King wouldn't be able to explain it away so easily, as he'd explained away everything else. Each day that I was out in the wild, on the run, meant one more day for the City to think about where I was, to question what I had said, to remember all the rumors that had circulated after Caleb's capture. Enough people had seen the soldiers grab me, had watched as my hands were bound and I was brought inside.

Harper had reached me through the paper only once more, to confirm the plan was in effect. Now I stood in the suite, staring out the window for the last time at the crowded City below. The morning sun reflected off the metal barricades lining the sidewalks, showing the extensive route that wound around the City center. People were already assembling on the main road. The streets were packed all the way to the Outlands.

The door opened behind me. Beatrice was in a cerulean blue dress, squeezing her hands together nervously. I stepped forward and pressed her fingers between my own. "I told you, you don't have to do this. You don't have to help me. It could be dangerous."

"I want to," she said. "You have to leave today—it's not a question. I just hid the ring." I wrapped my arms around her, not wanting to let go. In just an hour, the King would come to my suite, ready to escort me downstairs to the car, its engine running, waiting to start the long procession. He'd find the room empty, that silly white dress laid out on the bed. He'd move through the Palace, scouring the dining room, the parlor, his office.

On one of the floors he'd find Beatrice, in a search of her own, frantic to find my ring before the procession started. She'd tell him that she'd just left me in my room, that I'd insisted she look for the missing piece of jewelry, afraid that it had slipped off somewhere outside the suite.

"Thank you," I whispered, the words feeling inadequate. "For everything." I looked around the room, remembering how she had washed my scarred wrists when I'd first arrived, how she'd sat on the bed with me, her hand on my back as I fell asleep. "As soon as I reach the Trail I'll look for Sarah," I whispered. "We'll get her out in time."

"I hope so," she said, her face darkening at the mention of her daughter.

"She'll come back to you," I insisted. "I promise."

Beatrice smiled, then pressed her fingers to her eyes. "Clara's just down the hall—wait for her signal before you leave. I'll stay here for another forty minutes," she said. "All the entrances should be clear now. I won't let anyone come in." She fell back into the room, gesturing for me to go.

I crept toward the door. The lock had been plugged the same way the one in the stairwell had, a wad of paper lodged in its depths, preventing it from latching. I listened for the soldier. He stood right beside the door, his heavy breathing filling the air. My hand was on the knob, waiting to hear Clara's voice.

After a few minutes the sound of footsteps echoed against the wood floors. "I need help!" Clara called down the corridor. "You there—someone has broken into my suite."

I heard the soldier's muffled reply and the argument that followed, Clara insisting he go with her right then, that her very life was in jeopardy. As they started down the hall I opened the door a crack. Clara was walking quickly, holding up the hem of her dress, going on about the broken lock on her safe, how someone must've come into her suite during breakfast. The soldier listened intently, rubbing his forehead with his hand. Before they rounded the corner Clara glanced over her shoulder, her eyes meeting mine.

I darted toward the east stairwell. I wore the sweater and jeans I'd worn the first night I'd left the Palace, my hair secured in a low bun. I missed the cap I had pulled down over my eyes, feeling more exposed now, more recognizable as I started down the stairwell. I kept my eyes on my feet, careful to duck below the tiny windows that faced onto each floor.

Far below, the Palace mall was crowded with people. Workers were closing up their stores for the morning, pulling down large metal grates to cover their front windows. Shoppers emptied into the streets. Soldiers directed everyone out the various exits, clearing the main floor for the procession. I kept my head down as I started toward the same door I'd gone out of that first night, feeling the soldiers' eyes on me. "Keep moving!" one called out, his words tensing my entire body. "Go to the right when you reach the main road."

I followed the crowd, squeezed into the space between the Palace fountain and the metal barricades. The man next to me had his son with him, his arm around his shoulders as they took small steps, filing outside. I brought my hand to my face, trying to avoid being noticed by the two older women to my left, red-and-blue scarves tied festively around their necks. "Paradise Road will be the best view," one of them said. "If we're on the right-hand side, opposite the Wynn Tower, we can avoid the congestion. I'm not getting stuck behind the crowds like we were for the parade."

Finally we were down the Palace's marble steps, moving faster as we filed along the main strip and across the overpass. I broke off, relieved when I was away from the women, lost in the shifting current of the crowd. It would take time to get to the Outlands. I'd anticipated this, but it was even more apparent now, with everyone packed inside the barricades, shuffling along the sidewalks. Some streets were closed. The procession route was dotted with soldiers, many standing in the narrow road, scanning the roofs of the buildings, their rifles in hand.

I squeezed between people, ducking around a man who'd stopped to tie his shoe. When I passed a restaurant I checked the time against the clock inside. It was nine fifteen. Caleb had been led out of the prison by Harper's contact there. The dissidents should've met him in the Outlands by now. They were probably already at the hangar. With the soldiers concentrated inside the City center, there'd be less security near the wall. No one would come by the construction sites. It could be an hour or more before the handful of soldiers at the prison realized Caleb was missing and got word to the tower patrol.

The day was oppressively hot. I pulled at the neck of my sweater, wishing for an escape from the sun. All around me, people spoke excitedly about the wedding procession and the Princess's dress, and the ceremony that would be broadcast on billboards throughout the City. Their voices seemed far away, a chorus fading into the background, as my thoughts returned to Caleb. Harper had told me he hadn't been hurt. He'd said they would get him out. He had promised that Jo was securing places for us on the Trail, that they'd be waiting in the hangar for me when I arrived. As I crept closer to the Outlands, the minutes passed more quickly. I let myself imagine it, seeing him there, inside the open room. Our fingers laced together as we started through the dark tunnel, putting the City behind us.

I hurried my steps, weaving in and out of the crowd as I moved closer to the old airport. I didn't look at anyone. Instead I fixed my gaze on that spot in the south, just off the main road, where the buildings opened up to cracked pavement.

The Outlands were quiet. Across the gravel, two men sat on overturned buckets, passing a cigarette back and forth. Someone was hanging wet sheets out an upstairs window. I started across the airport parking lot, unable to keep from smiling. The King was probably at my suite. He had just realized I was gone. It was too late now. Here I was, minutes from the hangar, with Caleb so close. He was just inside that door, our packs filled, waiting for me.

I slipped into the old hangar, the planes towering above me. When I reached the back room the boxes had been moved aside, the tunnel exposed, but Jo was not there. I scanned the other end of the hangar, but there was no sign of Harper or Caleb. No maps were set out on the table. No lanterns were scattered about the floor. The light streamed in from a broken window, casting strange patterns on the concrete.

The silence was enough to raise the fine hairs on my arms. Two backpacks sat on the ground by my feet, unzipped, the contents riffled through. I knew immediately something had gone wrong. I backed out of the room. I took in the hangar—the rusted staircases that were scattered in the corners, the towering airplanes above. In the plane to the left of me, all of the shades were down except one. Something—or someone—moved inside. I turned and started toward the door, keeping my face down.

I was nearly at the exit when a familiar voice called out, echoing against the walls. "Don't move, Genevieve."

I glanced up. The first of the soldiers were exiting the airplane, their guns fixed on me. Their faces were covered in hard plastic masks. "Keep your hands where we can see them." Stark was in front, circling me at a distance.

Two more appeared from behind a staircase in the corner, while yet another emerged from the tunnel. They spread out across the hangar, moving along the concrete walls to either side of the entrance.

Stark was on me now, yanking my wrists behind my back and looping a plastic restraint around them. I kneeled down, afraid my legs might give out beneath me. I thought only of Caleb, hoping one of the dissidents had warned him of the raid.

As Stark took me toward the back room I heard footsteps nearing the door to the hangar. Someone was coming. The soldiers crouched beside the entrance, their guns in hand, waiting. Before I could act the door opened. Harper stepped inside. I saw him process the scene, just a second too late. He fell first. It happened so quickly I didn't realize he'd been shot. I just saw him lean against the doorframe, the open wound in his chest where the first bullet hit him.

I stood up from the floor. "Caleb! *They're here*," I shrieked, my voice strange as it left my mouth. "Turn around!"

Stark put his hand over my lips. Caleb was just rounding the corner, his face barely in view. His eyes met mine and then I heard the gun, the shot that ripped through his side. It sounded louder in the massive concrete space, ricocheting off the walls. I watched him stagger back. He lowered himself to the ground, his arm crushed beneath him, his face contorted and strange. I kneeled there, refusing to look away as he seized up, his eyes squeezed shut in pain. Then the soldiers moved in, the great mass of them swallowing him whole.

forty-one

THE JEEP MOVED QUICKLY, SPEEDING THROUGH STREETS ROPED off for the parade. Thousands of people leaned over the barricades, still cheering for their Princess, searching the route for signs of her. I was hunched over in the backseat, curled in on myself, unable to believe what had happened. My hands were scraped from when they'd taken me from the hangar. I'd struggled in the soldier's grip, trying to grab onto anything I could, but they'd dragged me away before I could get to Caleb.

Caleb has been shot, I told myself. I saw his face again as the bullet went through him. He was alone there, on that cold concrete floor, the blood spreading out beneath him.

We sped up the Palace's long driveway. They ushered me inside, past the marble fountains. The main floor had been emptied out for the wedding, our footsteps sounding down the hollow hall. Reginald was the only one there. He was pacing outside the elevator, that stupid notebook in his hand. He bit down on the end of his pencil.

"Stay away from me," I said, already imagining the story that would run the following day—how enemies of The New America had been caught the morning of the wedding. How the citizens were all so much safer now. "Don't even try."

"Can I have a moment with the Princess?" Reginald asked the soldiers, ignoring my comment. "She needs to be debriefed before she goes upstairs." The soldiers cut my restraints and stepped away, watching us.

"What do you want?" I asked when we were alone. I rubbed at my wrists. "Some quote about what a joy today has been?"

He rested his hand on my shoulder. His eyes darted to the soldiers, now stationed along the walls of the circular lobby. "Listen to me," he said slowly, his words barely above a whisper. His face was calm. "We don't have much time."

"What are you doing?" I tried to push him away but

he came closer, his hand still on me, his fingers digging into my skin.

"It's over," he said softly. "As far as you are concerned there is no Trail, there are no more tunnels. You never met Harper, or Curtis, or any of the other dissidents. As far as you know, Caleb was working alone."

"What do you know about Caleb?"

Reginald looked down. "A lot. Harper and Caleb died today, fighting against this regime."

I shook my head. "You don't know what you're talking about."

"Look at me," he said, squeezing my shoulder. He didn't stop until my eyes met his. "You know me as Reginald—but others know me as *Moss*."

He stepped back, letting his words sink in. I stared at his face, seeing him for the first time, the man who was always scribbling in that notepad, running stories in the paper, clipping quotes to suit his needs. This was the same man who'd helped Caleb out of the labor camps, who'd helped build the dugout. He was the one who'd organized the Trail. "Caleb's dead," I repeated. A numbness spread out in my chest.

"You have to continue on as though this never happened," he continued. "You have to marry Charles."

"I don't have to do anything." I struggled free from his grip. "What will that accomplish?" The sound of cheering swelled outside the Palace's front entrance.

"You need to be here as the Princess," he whispered, his lips an inch away from my ear. "So you can kill your father."

He stared at me intently. He didn't say anything else, instead flipping open the pad and pretending to make notes of our conversation. Then he signaled the soldiers back over, following us into the elevator in complete silence.

forty-two

WHEN I RETURNED TO MY SUITE, THE KING WAS WAITING FOR me. He stared at the wedding dress laid out on the bed, a bundle of papers clutched in his hands.

"You said you'd let him go. You showed me pictures, took me to his cell," I said, unable to contain my anger any longer. "You lied to me."

The King paced the length of the room. "I don't need to explain myself, certainly not to you. You don't understand this country. You knew about people who were building a tunnel to the outside and you didn't tell me." He turned, leveling his finger in my face. "Do you have any idea what kind of danger that would've put civilians in? Having an open passage into the wild?"

"The soldiers shot them," I said, my voice trembling.

The King crumpled the papers in his hand. "Those men have been organizing dissidents for months, planning to bring weapons and who knows what into this City. They had to be stopped."

"*Killed*," I snapped, the tears hot in my eyes. "You mean killed—not 'stopped.' Say what you mean."

"Do not speak to me that way." The blood rushed to his face. "I've had enough. I came here this morning, early, to bring you this," he said, throwing the bundle of papers at me. They landed on the floor. "I came to tell you how proud I was of you and the woman you're becoming." He let out a low, sorrowful laugh.

But I was barely listening, my mind instead running over the events of the morning. He'd ordered Harper and Caleb killed. But who had told him about the tunnel beneath the wall? How had Stark gotten there before me? The questions ran through my mind on an endless loop. *Caleb is dead*, I kept repeating, but nothing could make it feel real.

"There are nearly half a million people downstairs," he continued, "waiting for their Princess to come down the street with her father, to offer their good wishes before she is married. I will not keep them waiting." He headed to the door, his fingers pounding the keypad. "Beatrice! Come help the Princess get ready!" he yelled before disappearing down the hall.

The door slammed shut behind him. I let out a deep breath, feeling the room expand in his absence. I looked down at my hands, which burned now, my wrists red from where the restraints had been. I kept seeing Caleb, his face before he fell, the way his arm was crushed beneath him. I closed my eyes. It was too much. I knew he couldn't have survived, but the idea that he was gone, that he would never cradle my head in his hands again, never smile at me, never tease me for taking myself so seriously . . .

I heard Beatrice come in, but I couldn't stop looking at the scraped skin on my wrists, the only proof that the last several hours had really happened. When I looked up, she was standing there, staring at a spot on the carpet.

"It was Clara, wasn't it?" I said slowly. "What did she tell them? How much do they know?"

But Beatrice was silent. When she looked up, her eyes were swollen. She kept shaking her head back and forth, mouthing the words "I'm so sorry." She finally said it aloud. "I had to."

Something about her expression frightened me. Her

lips were twisted and trembling. "You had to what?"

"He told me he would kill her," she said, coming toward me, wrapping her hands around mine. "He came up early, just after you left. You weren't here. They'd discovered Caleb's empty cell. He said he would kill her if I didn't reveal where you were. I told him about the tunnel."

I pulled away, my hands shaking.

"I'm so sorry, Eve," she said, reaching out for me, trying to stroke my face. "I had to, I didn't mean—"

"Don't," I said. "Please go." She came to me again, her hand on my arm, but I slunk back. It wasn't her fault. I knew that. But I didn't want her comfort either, this person who had played a part in Caleb's death. I turned toward the window, listening to the sound of her choked sobs until they settled into silence. Finally, I heard the door close. When I was certain she was gone I turned, studying the crumpled papers on the floor.

I picked the first one up, calmed by the familiar handwriting. It was the same yellowed paper I'd carried with me since School. The old letter, the one I'd read a thousand times, was now sitting in a backpack off Route 80, outside of that warehouse. I would never see it again.

The sheet was worn around the edges. *Wedding day*

was scrawled along the front in wobbly letters. I sat on my bed, pressing the paper between my fingers, trying to smooth out the hard crease from where he'd crumpled it in his hand.

My sweet girl,

It's impossible to know if and when you will read this, where you will be or how old. In the passing days I've imagined it many times over. The world is always as it once was. Sometimes the church doors open up to a bustling street, and you stride out, your new husband beside you. Someone helps you inside a waiting car. Other times it's just you and him and a small crowd of friends. I can see the glasses raised in your honor. And once I imagined there was no wedding—no ceremony, no big white dress, none of the tradition—just you and him lying beside each other one night and deciding that was it. From now on, you'd always be together.

Whatever circumstance it is, wherever you are, I know that you are happy. My hope is that it is a big, boundless happiness that works its way into

*every corner of your life. Know that I am with you
now, as I've always been.*

I love you, I love you, I love you,
Mom

I folded the letter in my lap. I didn't move. I sat there
on the bed, my face swollen and pink, until I heard the
King's voice, as if startling me from a dream. "Genevieve,"
he said, his voice stern. "It's time."

forty-three

I STOOD IN THE BACK OF THE PALACE CATHEDRAL, THE GAUZY veil shielding me from a thousand staring eyes. The King was beside me, his face fixed in a grotesque smile. He offered me his arm. As the music started I threaded my hand through his elbow and took the first step toward the altar, where Charles waited for me, the wedding band already out, pressed between his thin fingers.

The string quartet played a long, sorrowful note as I took one step, then another. The eaves were crowded with people clad in their finest silk dresses, ornate hats, and jewels. Their plastic smiles were too much to bear. Clara and Rose were on one aisle, their hair done up in stiff, overblown waves. Clara's face was drained of color. She didn't look at me as I passed, instead wrapping her satin sash tightly around her fingers, squeezing all the blood from her hands. I scanned the pews for Moss, finally spotting him in the middle of the front row. We locked eyes for a moment before he turned away.

I was trapped here. The horrible, stifled feeling had returned. I closed my eyes for just a moment and Caleb's voice came back to me, the smell of smoke as real as it had been hours before. We were supposed to be out of the tunnel by now, moving through the abandoned neighborhood, our packs full of supplies. I took another step, then another, all the should-haves presenting themselves before me, one after the other. We were supposed to be leaving the City, going away from the wall and the soldiers and the Palace, moving east as the sun made its slow arc across the sky, finally warming our backs. We were supposed to be arriving at the first stop on the Trail.

We were supposed to be together.

But instead I was here, more alone than I'd ever been, the diamond tiara heavy on my head. The King paused in front of the altar and lifted the veil for a moment. He gazed at me, playing the role of the loving father, the camera flashing, freezing us forever in this terrible place. He pressed his thin lips against my cheek and let the veil fall back over my face.

Then—finally—he was gone. I stepped up the three short stairs and took my place beside Charles. The music stopped, the people were silent. I focused on my breathing, the only reminder that I was still alive. I steadied my hands, remembering Moss's words.

The ceremony was about to begin.

acknowledgments

A BIG HUG AND THANK-YOU TO ALL WHO MAKE THIS SERIES possible: funny man Josh Bank, for general awesomeness; Sara Shandler, for her spontaneous "I love Eve" emails, which are so supportive they make me want to dance; Joelle Hobeika, editor extraordinaire, for being able to talk character development and reality television with equal enthusiasm. To Farrin Jacobs, for all those aha! notes. And to Sarah Landis, the all-knowing "third eye," for seeing the things that we've missed (and then some).

To the sharp women who promote these books as if they were their own: Marisa Russell, for blog tours and retweets and signings; Deb Shapiro, for being the first to be All About Eve. To Kate Lee, my Twitter bestie, for all her good work and guidance. And to Kristin Marang, for her time and love spent on all things digital. That two-hour "conversation" was magical.

Much love and thanks to all of my friends, in so many cities, who offered everything from flash mobs to cocktail parties just to celebrate this series' release. Special thanks to those who've kept me afloat during this process: Helen Rubenstein and Aaron Kandell, who read early drafts of this book; Ali and Ally (the aptly named Allies) for understanding. To Anna Gilbert, Lanie Davis, and Katie Sise—my long-distance girlfriends—for talking it out; Lauren Morphew, right back at you. And to T.W.F., for making LA feel like home.

As always, endless gratitude to my brother, Kevin, and my parents, Tom and Elaine, for loving me first and best.

TURN THE PAGE TO READ WHAT
HAPPENS NEXT IN

An Eve Novel

BY ANNA CAREY

one

CHARLES RESTED HIS HAND FIRMLY ON MY BACK AS WE SPUN once, then again around the conservatory, the guests watching. I kept my eyes over his shoulder, steeling myself against his short breaths. The choir stood at the back of the domed hall, trilling out the first holiday songs of the year. "Merry merry merry merry Christmas," they sang, their mouths moving in unison, "merry merry merry merry . . ."

"At least smile," Charles whispered into my neck as we took another turn around the floor. "Please?"

"I'm sorry, I didn't realize my unhappiness was bothering you. Is this better?" I raised my chin, widening my eyes as I smiled directly at him. Amelda Wentworth, an older woman with a round, waxy face, stared quizzically as we passed her table.

"You know that's not what I meant," Charles said. We turned quickly, so Amelda didn't see. "It's just . . . people notice. They talk."

"So let them notice," I said, though in truth I was too exhausted to really argue. Most nights I awoke before dawn. Strange shadows would move in, surrounding me, and I'd call for Caleb, forgetting he was gone.

The song droned on. Charles spun me again around the floor. "You know what I meant," he said. "You could at least try."

Try. That's what he was always asking: that I try to make a life for myself inside the City, that I try to move on from Caleb's death. Couldn't I try to get out of the tower every day, to walk for a few hours in the sun? Couldn't I try to put all that had happened behind me, behind *us*? "If you want me to smile," I said, "then we probably shouldn't have this conversation—not here."

We started toward the far tables, covered with bloodred cloth, the wreaths set up as centerpieces. The City had transformed in the past few days. Lights went up on the main road, coiling around the lamp poles and trees. Fake plastic firs had been assembled outside the Palace, their thin branches bald in places. Everywhere I turned there was some stupid, grinning snowman or a gaudy bow with gold trim. My new maid had dressed me in a red velvet gown, as if I were part of the décor.

It was two days after Thanksgiving, a holiday I'd heard of before but never experienced. The King had sat at the long table, going on about how thankful he was for his new son-in-law, Charles Harris, the City of Sand's Head of Development. He was thankful for the continued support of the citizens of The New America. He held his glass in the air, his shadowed eyes fixed on mine, insisting that he was most thankful for our reunion. I couldn't believe him, not after all that had transpired. He was always watching, waiting for me to show any signs of betrayal.

"I don't understand why you went through with it," Charles whispered. "What's the point of all this?"

"What choice do I have?" I said, looking away, hoping to end the conversation. Sometimes I wondered if he would put it together, the regular interviews I did with Reginald, who sat at my father's table, working as his Head of Press, but was secretly Moss, leader of the rebel movement. I refused to sleep in the same bed as Charles, waiting until he left for the suite's sitting area every night.

I held his hand only in public, but as soon as we were alone, I put as much distance between us as possible. Didn't he realize that these past months, his very marriage, were all for some other purpose?

The song ended, the music giving way to scattered claps. The Palace staff circled the tables with plates of iced red cake and steaming coffee. Charles kept my hand in his as he led me back to the long banquet table where the King sat. My father was dressed for the part, his tuxedo jacket open, revealing a crimson cummerbund. A rose was pinned to his lapel, the petals wilted at the edges. Moss sat two seats down, a strange look on his face. He stood, greeting me. "Princess Genevieve," he said, offering me his hand. "May I have this dance?"

"I suppose you want to pry another quote from me," I said, giving him a tense smile. "Come then; just don't step on my toes this time." I rested my hand in Moss's, starting back onto the floor.

Moss waited until we were in the center of the room, the nearest couple two yards away. Finally he spoke. "You're getting better at this," he said with a laugh. "Then again, I guess you've learned from the master." He looked different today, nearly unrecognizable. It took me a moment to realize what it was—he was smiling.

"It's true," I whispered, glancing at the inside of his sleeve, where his cufflink was threaded through his shirt. I half expected to see the small packet of poison nestled against his wrist. Ricin, he had called it. Moss had been waiting months for the substance, which was to be supplied by a rebel in the Outlands. "Your contact came through?"

Moss glanced at the King's table. My aunt Rose was speaking animatedly to the Head of Finance, gesturing with her hands as my father looked on. "Better," he said. "The first of the camps was liberated. The revolt has begun. I got word from the Trail this afternoon."

It was the news we'd been waiting months to hear. Now that the boys in the labor camps were free, the rebels on the Trail would bring them into the fight. There was speculation that an army was forming in the east, composed of supporters from the colonies. A siege on the City couldn't be more than a few weeks off. "Good news, then. You haven't heard from your contact, though," I said.

"They promised it for tomorrow," he said. "I'll have to find some way to get it to you."

"So it's happening." Though I had agreed to poison my father—I was the only one who had unguarded access to him—I couldn't quite comprehend what it meant to actually go through with it. He was responsible for so many deaths, Caleb's included. It should've been an easy choice; I should've wanted it more. But now that it was close, a hollow feeling spread out in the bottom of my stomach. He was my father, my blood, the only other person who'd loved my mother. Had there been some truth to what he'd said, even now, even in the wake of Caleb's death? Was it possible he did love me?

We took a slow lap around the outside of the ballroom floor, trying to keep our steps light. My eyes lingered for a moment on the King as he laughed at something Charles said. "It'll be finished in a few days," Moss whispered, his voice barely audible over the music. I knew what *it* meant. Fighting along the City walls. Revolts in the Outlands. More death. I could still see the faint cloud of smoke that had appeared when Caleb was shot, could still smell the stink of blood on the concrete floor of the airplane hangar. We'd been caught while escaping the City, just minutes before descending into the tunnels the rebels had dug.

Moss said they'd taken Caleb into custody after he was wounded. The prison doctor recorded the death at eleven thirty-three that morning. I found myself watching the clock at that hour, waiting for it to stop for the minute on those numbers, the second hand quietly circling. He'd left so much space in my life. The expansive, hollow feeling seemed impossible to fill with anything else. In the past weeks I felt it in everything I did. It was in the shifting current of my thoughts, the nights now spent alone, the sheets beside me cold. *This is where he used to be*, I'd think. *How can I possibly live with all this empty space?*

"The soldiers won't let the City be taken," I said, blinking back a sudden rush of tears. My gaze settled on my father, who had pushed his chair back from the table and stood, walking across the ballroom. "It doesn't matter if he's dead or not."

Moss shook his head slightly, signaling that someone was within earshot. I glanced over my shoulder. Clara was dancing with the Head of Finance just a few feet away. "You're right, the Palace does come alive this time of year," Moss said loudly. "Well put, Princess." He stepped away from me as the song ended, releasing my hand and taking a quick bow.

As we walked off the dance floor, a few people in the crowd applauded. It took me a moment to locate my father. He was standing by the back exit, his head tilted as he spoke to a soldier.

Moss followed after me, and within a few steps the soldier's face came into view. I hadn't seen him in more than a month, but his cheeks were still thin, his hair still cropped close to his skull. His skin was a deep reddish brown from the sun. The Lieutenant stared at me as I took my seat at the table. He lowered his voice, but before the next song started I could hear him saying something about the labor camps. He was here to bring news of the revolt.

The King's head was cocked so his ear was level with the Lieutenant's mouth. I didn't dare look at Moss. Instead I kept my eyes on the mirrored wall opposite me. From where I was sitting I could see my father's reflection in the glass. There was a nervousness in his expression I'd never seen before. He held his chin in his hand, his cheeks drained of all color.

Another song began, the conservatory filling with the sound of the choir. "To the Princess," Charles said, holding up a thin flute of cider. I clinked my glass against his, thinking only of Moss's words.

Within the week, my father would be dead.

WELCOME TO THE NEW AMERICA

Don't miss a single page of the forbidden love
and extraordinary adventure in the Eve trilogy.

Visit TheEveTrilogy.com to follow Eve's journey.